MEREDITH SPES

TEA AND ANTIPATHY

DAMIEN MURPHY PET SITTING AND MURDER
INVESTIGATIONS
BOOK 1

MEREDITH SPIES

ACKNOWLEDGMENTS

Editing: Cate Ryan
Cover and Promotional Art: Samantha Santana

TRIGGER AND CONTENT WARNINGS

Please exercise care when reading if any of the following are triggers for you:

Death by violence, descriptions of murder, mentions of dead bodies, alcoholism, alcohol abuse, sex shaming (mild), harm to animals (brief mention, and the dog lives!), depression, and mention of stalking.

CONTENTS

Maybe driving to Augusta for bubble tea had been a bad idea. If I'd just gone to the little tea shop in Lester Cove and subsumed my craving into a regular tea rather than insisting on jasmine tea with salted cream top and extra popping pearls, Bonnie wouldn't be a smoking heap on the side of the road, I wouldn't be out three hundred bucks for the after-hours tow, and I'd be on time and *dressed* for the gala instead of schlepping my sweaty self to town in the hopes I wouldn't be standing up *the* Renee Rhodes and making my craptacular day even worse.

I could practically hear my agent Rory sighing and muttering about harebrained choices. Joke's on you, Rory. Taking the part of Mimic Morton in *Mimicry 2: The Mimicking* was harebrained. This is just… stressful.

Chewing on my straw, I put my back to the Lester Cove sign and held up my camera, squinting at the screen. I was mussed, but not *bad*. Just a little shiny. My cheeks were pinker than I'd like, which made me look like a teenager and not a man in his twenties. And my hair was flat, the product I'd put in that morning before I left Two Moons Bed and Breakfast no match for hours of sweat, dust, heat, and me raking my fingers through trying not to scream. My retro-chic ironic t-shirt—off-white with a big red crustacean and the words *I Got Crabs in Maine* between its claws—was visible in the shot under my open green velvet tuxedo jacket, making the entire scene look casual and pretty devil-may-care. It'd do, I decided and thumbed the record button and smiled. "Hey, folks! I'm finally here and super looking forward to the gala tonight! This is hella exciting—some of you know how much I love theater, and getting to take part in this festival with Renee Rhodes is a *dream*! I'll keep you updated this weekend!" I winked, blew a kiss, and shut off the app, still smiling until I was sure everything was closed. It wasn't the Get Ready With Me that I wanted to film for my socials, but it was better than nothing.

A low rumble and whoosh of gravel was my only warning as a car passed close enough to send me sprawling, the front corner of the bumper catching my leg, the momentum knocking me forward.

For a moment, all I could think was, *Well, I guess that settles that. I don't need to worry about being late after all.*

A soft-cheeked face appeared above me, plum-colored lips pressed into a thin line as their owner peered down, salt and pepper hair a riot of loose curls escaping from a headband and making a curtain over us. "Oh my god, are you alright? I'm so sorry! Can you feel your legs? Oh my god!"

I struggled to sit up, a moment of panic hitting me when I couldn't get a good breath of air before I realized my bag had become tangled around my upper body in the tumble. "I'm okay," I gasped, tugging at the strap. "Just…"

"Here, let me!" The woman started figuring out the twists and turns of my bag with its complicated faux leather strap, muttering at it until she finally got it untangled and in my lap. "Lord, I thought we'd have to cut you loose for a second! Me, I like my bags with those detachable straps. I can never decide between those long straps or a little handbag, so I figure, why not both in one?"

"A lady's gotta have options," I muttered, scrubbing my hands against my thankfully pre-distressed jeans. The tumble didn't do much damage to them, just grunged me up a bit, but it looked like it'd wipe off for the most part.

"Now, the important stuff: did you hit your head?" she demanded, reaching to prod at the back of my skull.

"No! No, I'm fine. Just dusty. And sore. And hot. And thirsty."

She rocked back to sit on her heels and offered me a kind, slightly harried smile. "Well, that doesn't sound okay at all, really. I'm so sorry I clipped you. I was trying to get back to the shop to do a final check since Belinda closed tonight. She's a good worker for the most part, but she does like to give away scones and such, and well, I understand some people might bat their eyes pretty and you want to give them a little something, but scones cost money." She blinked, fingers fluttering as if she couldn't decide to cover her mouth or press them to her heart. "Oh, listen to me go on! You're at death's door and I'm just pouring all this out! Let me help you into town, at least, and then I can see if Doctor Smithers has space in his schedule to see you."

"I insist," she added when I opened my mouth to protest. "I'm assuming you're heading into town?"

"Um, yes. I'm supposed to be taking part in the Summer Theater Festival."

"Oh, well that's exciting!" She offered me a hand up, which I gratefully accepted. "Are you staying at Two Moons Bed and Breakfast? Oh, what am I saying? Of course, you are! Unless…" She glanced towards the town as if expecting the entire populace to be waiting at the border to eavesdrop as she lowered her voice to just above a whisper. "Unless you're staying with Renee?"

"Ah, no. I'm at Two Moons. Ms. Rhodes suggested it, though."

"I'll bet," she muttered. "Renee is very helpful like that. Well. Come on, let me at least give you a ride and grovel abjectly!" She waved to her car, where a tiny little doggie face popped up in the rear window, all button nose and caramel-chocolate fur.

"Oh, you're not allergic, are you?" she asked, hands fluttering to her throat in dismay. "Oh! Well, maybe I can call someone. Ollie, he's a good kid, works at the pet store, he could come pick you up or—"

"I'm not allergic," I assured her. "I've been around dogs on shoots and some people back home have those little purse dogs, you know?"

"Purse dogs?" She laughed. "Oh my lord, is that what my Tony is?"

Her cackle made me grin; she was so delighted at the notion.

"Well, he does seem tiny…"

She wiped her damp eyes with the side of her hand, smearing her mascara just a little. "Well, if you're not allergic, is it you're afraid?"

"No… I really don't mind dogs one way or another," I admitted. "Never had one myself—I've never been home long enough to feel okay with having a pet, really."

She made a sad noise at that. "Well, while you're in town, you'll have to come play with my Tony. He's an absolute *doll*."

I smiled thinly at that—a playdate with a random dog seemed weirdly Hollywood, to be honest, one of those Goop-approved mental health activities or something. And from what I knew about those tiny dogs, they could be absolute terrors.

"So how about that ride?" she pressed, reaching for the passenger side door. "I promise Tony will snooze the whole way—car rides knock him right out!"

I hesitated. Even at twenty-five years old, the whole *stranger danger* thing was well ingrained thanks to my parents' common sense and also years of having to be on guard for people who thought taking advantage of a kid was an okay thing to do. But damn it, I was tired. And sore. And still had to hear from wherever they ended up towing Bonnie to find out what I could do next. So, ignoring my mother's disapproving voice in my ear and every set teacher I had from age eleven to seventeen, I nodded. "I'd love a ride. Thank you."

MARGIE WITTE TALKED a mile a minute and I kind of loved it. She didn't even blink when I introduced myself, the name Damien Murphy not ringing a single bell for her.

"Well, just because I'm not familiar with your work doesn't mean you're gonna fly under the radar in this town," Margie proclaimed, turning down yet another quaint little street that looked like something out of a 1950s TV show but with Wi-Fi and better environmental laws. "If Renee invited you to be part of the festival, I bet you'll be beating fans off with a stick in no time!"

"Oh, I'm not here for that," I said, offering a thin and uneasy chuckle. Because I wouldn't *mind* people knowing who I was. It'd be one hell of an ego boost after this past year. "Ms. Rhodes invited me to help judge the plays and take part in some panel discussions, not sign autographs." Did that sound snobby? I'd heard my friend Max King say that in response to a pap cornering him at his sister's wedding—*I'm not here to sign autographs*
—and I'd low-key been waiting for a chance to say it myself ever since.

Margie cackled, coughing for breath before shaking her head as she slowed for the curve in the road. "Oh, Renee wouldn't have invited you to take part in her event if she thought you weren't famous enough to pull an audience!"

Part of me knew I should be at least a little offended at the idea of being used for my fanbase (cough) rather than my talent, but… "Really?" The ping of hope in my voice made me cringe, but Margie just smiled.

She reached over and patted my hand, giving me one of those motherly finger squeezes as she assured me, "I've known Renee a long time. She knows what she's doing."

I nodded. "Well. I hope this evening goes better than the afternoon." "I'm guessing car trouble? No offense, but you don't look like someone who likes to go on long roadside walks." She chuckled.

"And you'd be absolutely right. Unless the roadside is a sidewalk in LA or New York."

"Oh, big cities are so much fun! I did my time, though. Learned the hard way they're just not for me. Did you get towed? I didn't see anything broken down back there."

"I called the first number that popped up when I searched. They sent someone but said since it was after-hours I'd have to call tomorrow and talk to someone. They're local, though, so at least there's that."

"Bitty and Ron's place?" At my blank look, she clicked her tongue and sighed. "Sorry, I forget sometimes not everyone is local. Live in a small town for decades and it becomes your whole world. Did you call O'Neill Auto and Nails?"

"I just called the first one that popped up when I searched *tow services near me*. Wait, what's the *and Nails*?"

"Oh, Bitty was dying to run her own auto shop ever since, let me think… Sophomore year of high school, I think it was. She's just a few years older than my late Johnathan's boy, Ben, and Ben's thirty this year, so…"

She rambled on for a bit, telling me about Bitty and Ron O'Neill's combination auto repair place and beauty salon (Ron had a knack for acrylics, apparently) as she navigated to the Palais Theater.

"Oh my god," I breathed as she pulled to a stop in the grand circle drive. "This is *not* what I was expecting!"

Margie cackled, giving my arm a little slap. "Thought it'd be some boring black box thing, huh? Sitting in a strip mall somewhere?"

I barely managed to hold back my nod. "I got to town this morning and hadn't had a chance to swing by the theater yet and… *wow*. This is *gorgeous*." Definitely not the pokey small town theater I'd imagined, by a long shot. Listless concern about having this festival in some church basement or high school auditorium was out the window, replaced by an itching desire to get on the stage that was behind those glossy black and gold doors.

"You should see the inside," she murmured, setting her parking brake as we both stared at the front of the Art Nouveau building. The parking lot was already full, and a few people were lingering by the open double doors, golden light spilling out into the growing twilight, a mix of fancy dress and —thankfully for my ego—more casual wear evident from what I could see through the open doors. "Now, it's been lovely meeting you Damien Murphy, but you're running late, and I'd best get back to the shop to make sure that girl's locked up for the night—I love kids but I do hate leaving my shop in their hands." She sighed.

I nodded, scrambling to get out of the car with a rush of excitement and anxiety warring in my chest. "Oh, shit. I mean, shoot! I should give you some gas money or—"

"Oh, hon, don't even worry about it! This is right on my way to the shop—Witte's Teas. We're on Buttermilk—that's the main drag. Right between Bull's China and Paws for Pets. Stop by and have a cup and I'll call us even!"

"Of course! I'll—"

She was already speeding off, disappearing into the darkening evening and leaving me to face my first official event in months, all on my own.

Renee Rhodes was everything. She was the raspy-voiced, designer dud-wearing, theatrical queen I'd hoped she'd be in person.

It was like Liza Minnelli and Tyne Daly had somehow managed to have a baby, then Tim Curry got involved somehow with Kander and Ebb doing the score and—

I stepped into the theater lobby, which was all done up for the reception with swags of silver and gold lame bunting and huge (fake) flower arrangements in glossy black Art Deco style vases. I barely had time to take it in before Renee Rhodes, in all her elegant glory, came sweeping down on me from behind the buffet table, calling out in her kitschy Mid-Atlantic tones, "I was so worried you'd changed your mind! You're late!"

Swept into a swirl of vintage Halston jersey, a heavy-handed application of Fracas with a soupcon of Bombay Sapphire cutting through it all, I couldn't answer for fear of asphyxiating on either a mouthful of fabric or the fumes. She released me after a tight embrace and a waxy-lipped cheek kiss which I dutifully returned (sans waxy lips—my gloss was very light, thank you, and not at all sticky), she did that old person thing where they hold you at arm's length and give you a *look*.

"I, ah, had car trouble outside of town. Something went kaflooey with the engine, I think. Or maybe the oil pan? I just know there was a lot of smoke."

Ms. Rhodes *tsked*, looping her arm over my shoulder and giving me a tiny shake. "That's why I went electric," she pronounced. "It's the only *responsible* way to get around these days, especially in a place like Lester Cove. No public transit, unless you count the ferry," she added in a throaty stage whisper heard by pretty much everyone around us. "Now, come along, let me introduce you to the charming playwrights who've submitted their work for us to judge this weekend!" I had no choice but to follow her flowing jersey knit clad back towards the long refreshment table where she topped up her drink before gesturing towards the bottles in mute offer. I nodded, reaching for a wine glass before she stilled my hand and redirected it toward the stronger stuff.

"You're gonna need it," she muttered. "Have you read the packet of plays yet? It's a lot."

"I had the chance to look at some of the entries on the way here," I said, wincing at the sharp taste of the gin rickey she'd directed me towards. "They're really engaging and—"

Ms. Rhodes snorted into her very full martini glass (the vermouth had been a mere whisper of an afterthought whisked away as soon as it entered her mind, apparently). "Most of them are amateurish, downright juvenile, which isn't surprising considering how Charlie treated the contest like some final exam for his students. The ones that aren't high school efforts are so drab I wanted to scream, darling." Something in my expression made her pause, offering me a small, not at all apologetic smile. "Forgive me. After years of being simply *immersed* in the craft, I find it's hard to shake the inherent snobbery. I appreciate their enthusiasm, but they don't understand theater," she said, this time keeping her voice low enough for just us two. The gala was more crowded than I'd anticipated for such a small town, the press of bodies dressed in everything from smart-casual wear to what looked like prom get-ups on some of the younger attendees forcing us to the side of the room, near a door discretely marked *Box Office Management*. "They *crave* it, though. So many of them, especially the older generations, go all the way to the city for shows."

"New York," I murmured, not quite a question but laced with a bit of disbelief. New York was at least a half day's drive from Lester Cove, quite a way to go for a play.

"Of course. I certainly don't mean *Bangor*," she tittered. "It's a lovely city in its own right, but the theater scene there is nothing like the city." She exhaled gustily, pushing one of her brassy curls back from her eyes and glancing about, finding her angles before taking another sip of her gin, making sure she was displayed to her best advantage like a true professional. "Nothing is, really."

"Renee!" A man giving young Kevin Kline vibes but when he was in *In and Out,* not *A Fish Called Wanda,* strode across the lobby towards us.

Dressed in a wine-red three-piece suit, he stood out among the browns, navies, and blacks peppering the crowd, though he didn't seem bothered by the looks. In fact, he gave a few familiar nods and a quick smile or two on his way over before stopping short of Ms. Rhodes and folding his arms. "It's been three months! I've been patient but—"

"Charlie! You absolute *doll*!" She leaned in and gave him a smacking kiss on each cheek. Charlie blushed and, somewhat awkwardly, returned the gesture, not quite meeting her skin but giving a little *mwah* sound.

A for effort, really.

"Damien, this is my dear old friend, Charlie Arnold. Well, *old*," she tittered. "He's a few years my junior, but shhhh, don't let on. Everyone thinks I'm at *least* ten years younger than I really am!"

I nodded, smiling. No one thought that, I was certain, but cultivating a certain mystique was so old Hollywood of her. "I'll never tell."

Charlie Arnold shifted a bit uncomfortably, tilting his head in the direction of the office behind us. "Do you have a moment? We need to talk about—"

"Charlie darling, now is *not* the time," Ms. Rhodes protested, patting his arm with the very tips of her brightly painted fingernails. "We're in the midst of a gala!"

Charlie followed the direction of Ms. Rhodes' waving arm. His lips tightened and his shoulders stiffened as he turned back to face us. "That might well be, Renee, but the fact remains you made a promise, a *legally binding* promise, and—"

Ms. Rhodes' smile was fixed and bright, but distinctly unpleasant. "Charlie," she gritted out. "This is not the time. Save your speeches for your students."

"Renee," Charlie said, straightening, shedding some of the deference he'd carried over just moments before, "you've been dodging me. Every planning meeting, every casual drinks evening, you've been avoiding the subject. It's past time you dropped the charade."

"You're embarrassing me," she whispered. "We'll talk tomorrow!".

"I've given you forty-odd years of *tomorrow, Charlie* and *later, Charlie*," he snapped, "I'm tired of waiting, Renee. You owe me this much."

"And," she said, shooting me an apologetic eye roll, "we can talk tomorrow, Charlie. I assure you, you will *not* be disappointed."

She gave his arm a firm pat then and, turning her back on him with a swish of jersey and perfume, took me by the elbow and steered me away from Charlie Arnold. "I'm so sorry about that little scene." She sighed. "Charlie's a dear old friend, but he just can't accept the fact some things are just *done*."

"A lot of folks are upset about your retirement," I demurred. "You're quite the performer."

She snorted delicately, giving me a nudge. "I'm an old broad who should've retired five years before I did," she chided. "I just hung on because I wasn't ready to admit my critics were right. I'd gotten to the point where I was just playing versions of myself, you know?"

My face warmed as I nodded. "I'm familiar with the feeling."

"We all are, at some point. Some of us just a bit sooner than others." Her sympathetic murmur made my blush even worse, if at all possible. "It's not often I talk with someone who isn't trying to convince me I'm giving up too soon," I admitted.

Her brow arched, and she peered down her nose at me. It was very Bette Davis in *Faces of Eve*. "Are you giving up?"

"Maybe?" The word wavered, drawing out one beat too long. She shot me a knowing glance and waved to one of the attendees. "I mean, I don't really *know* anything else."

"Do you love it?"

There's the million-dollar question. I'd been asking it myself for a year or so now. "I think. Sometimes at least."

She smiled, her expression beautifully calm as she waved to another supporter. "It's what I love best in life, truly. The art of performance, the craft of make-believe. If I'd never fallen into acting in the first place, I'd likely be some poor old retail worker right now, grouching about what could've been if I'd only been brave enough."

"Sounds like you speak from experience."

Her smile was sour as she eyed her empty glass. "You think of me as Renee Rhodes." She said her name with all the gravitas and drama it had in my head, darting me a small, speaking glance as she spoke. "But I was a jobbing actor once, and before then just a hopeful, going to audition after audition. And before that, just Renee Trent." Her laugh was sudden, throaty and loud, making some close to us jump in surprise and others start to turn our way, curious as to what made our hostess so merry. "Back in the day, you could just show up to some auditions without even being on the call sheet. Just walk in, write your name down, and wait to be called. I got some of my first jobs because I didn't hang back. I fought for 'em." She made an underhanded stabbing motion with her empty hand as she added, "It's what I told all the chorus kids and understudies, once I started getting real name parts. Fight for it. You can't be nice about it. If you want that dream to come true, you gotta push hard."

"Ah." I took a sip of my gin rickey, feeling the warmth of the liquor burn down into my nearly empty stomach. Was she trying to say I should try harder to make my name? That I wasn't doing enough to climb out of the *oh yeah, what's his* face rut I was in with my career? I took another sip and forced a small smile, the thoughts sitting heavy for me.

"Damien." Her voice was soft, free of the *thea-tah* cadence she'd had all evening, a murmur barely loud enough to be heard over the rumble of the crowd. "Whatever you're thinking, you're likely wrong."

I chuckled, a tinge of moroseness in my voice when I replied. "Are you sure about that? I'm assuming you're at least passingly familiar with my background…"

"But I'm not familiar with your future," she said staunchly. "And you're not giving up. Know how I know?" Before I could answer, she looked around, then back at me, and smiled. "Look where you are."

I smiled tightly. "Thank you for inviting me," I began, but she waved me off.

"Now, no time for that, darling. Tonight's for festivities. Tomorrow, we're serious. Where's my baby? Oh, here we are!" Ms. Rhodes suddenly cried, throwing her hands wide and sloshing the last of her martini on my vintage jacket, which I was pretty sure had once been a costume piece on a sitcom back in the day.

Damn it. I dabbed at it with a cocktail napkin embossed with the theater's name and a funny squiggle I realized after a moment was meant to be Ms. Rhodes's signature.

Or autograph, as the case may be.

Ms. Rhodes continued cooing and the general rumble of apprehension and some excitement in the assemblage drew my attention away from my sodden jacket (sure, I got it at a resale shop but a resale shop in Los Angeles, right off Rodeo! I checked out in line behind two Oscar winners and a Hearst!). "Here's my best beloved," Ms. Rhodes trilled, bending dangerously low considering the neckline of her gown, and holding her arms wide.

A sturdy beast that was either a small pony or a large dog came loping out from beneath one of the buffet tables, tail whipping back and forth as it headed our way. A bright pink diamante collar shone against the liver-colored fur, a heart-shaped gold tag the size of a silver dollar jangling at the dog's throat. Most everyone cleared a path, some nervously, as the hellhound trotted towards Ms. Rhodes, pink tongue lolling wide and—ew—

moist as the dog's path took it towards the other buffet table to snag some treats from the nearest tray. The creature was so big, it didn't even have to stretch to reach the tabletop, just lop out with that tongue and snaffle the nearest pig-in-a-blanket for its troubles. The teenage girl behind the table made a face and snagged the tray, promptly dumping it in the trash as the beast resumed its path toward Ms. Rhodes, trotting the last few steps. Swear to Cher, its footsteps sent tremors through the floor! Or maybe that was my knees knocking because *who has a dog that big?*

"Are you sure that's not a bear?" I demanded, recoiling as the dog grinned up at Ms. Rhodes. It sat at Ms. Rhode's feet and accepted the lavish head scritches and compliments she doled out before dropping onto its side, yawning, and setting to work cleaning itself. A few partygoers cooed over it, familiar with the demon dog, but most gave it a wide berth.

Ms. Rhodes lifted the dog's massive paws and set them on her shoulders, doing a little dance with the creature as it panted, grinning a loose canine grin and thumping that heavy tail side to side, kneecapping the younger man who'd been trying to talk with Ms. Rhodes earlier. He glared at the dog, doing a little hop-step to the side, avoiding another whack with the dog's weaponized tail. Ms. Rhodes laughed, looking up at her audience before giving the hellhound a smacking kiss on its shiny black snoot and letting it stand on all fours. Which it only did for a moment before flopping over on its side and rolling onto its back, twisting on the carpet with some happy huffs.

"Ladies, gentlemen, neither, and undecided," Ms. Rhodes projected, eliciting some chuckles from the crowd. "Your presence this evening is so meaningful to me. To *us*," she waved one hand grandly, "the burgeoning theater community here in Lester Cove. This festival might be small this year, but in coming years it will certainly grow to include theater luminaries both local and national." She turned a wide, toothy smile to me. "I'm beyond thrilled to have you as our guest this year, Damien Murphy. He brings over a decade of experience to our little festival, and a youthful perspective on the ever-changing art of performance!"

There was a smattering of applause and I smiled, acknowledging Ms. Rhodes with a nod and my raised glass.

She turned back to her admirers. "I cannot begin to thank all of you enough for supporting this festival and the gala! Theater is such an important part of our history—not just here in Maine, but as *humans*." She dabbed delicately at her (very dry) eyes before adding, "I won't take up all your time with my meanderings, but I encourage you to stop by the sign-up table by the door, and if you haven't already, put your name down for some of the workshops that still have spaces available this weekend. Support your local theater! Embrace the ancient art of performance!"

More applause and Ms. Rhodes swept into the crowd to begin her rounds, everyone resuming their chatter in little groups and knots.

A willowy teenager with her hair in a severe updo and dramatic eye makeup was edging closer, trying to look nonchalant with an older woman who bore a strong resemblance in tow. As soon as Jerome was out of my immediate orbit, she swept in, smile wide and bright, the older lady looking somewhere between awkward and suspicious. When the girl spoke, it was all in one breathless rush and a pitch that made Ms. Rhodes's dog twitch. "Hi, I'm Belinda! I'm super excited to be here; this is my first gala, and is it okay if I take a selfie with you? Oh my god, you must get that all the time! But is it okay?"

"Belinda." Her mother sighed. "Breathe."

Belinda's cheeks turned pink, and she held out her phone awkwardly. "Sorry, that's my mom, and she's cool, but, you know, moms. She drove me so that was pretty cool of her, you know? My boyfriend said he'd drive me, but he had a late class and oh my god these shoes are *not* made for walking too far and I had to bring a bunch of stuff anyway because I volunteered in the theater club to bring flowers, and anyway. Um. So, is it okay?"

I nodded, my own face feeling a bit warm. No one had asked me for a selfie in LA since *Leaving Iowa* got canceled and I stopped getting mistaken for Luke Bourne, star of that long-running show. Despite my fairly active socials, the incidents of me getting recognized were pretty low unless I was in very specific situations, like with my BFF Max King. And in that case, it was more him being recognized with *a friend*, played by Damien Murphy.

"I'd love to. Come here." Belinda did a little hop and scooted up beside me. Her mother took her phone and shot a few pictures of us smiling like it was the best day of our lives, flashing peace signs, and one of me pretending to ask Belinda for *her* autograph. "Tag me if you post 'em, okay?"

Belinda nodded fervently. Tucking her camera back into the tiny, beaded handbag dangling from her shoulder, she asked, "So, are you here to judge the plays? The website said the plays would be judged by real professionals."

"Well, not just that. I'm also giving a few workshops, and I'm also excited to hear Ms. Rhodes talk about her time on Broadway."

"Oh my god—I mean gosh, sorry Mom, I meant gosh!—that is so, so cool. I saw you on that Friendly Channel show, the one about the animal shelter that puts on a talent show, and the kids get signed to a major record label but the guy from the label was really trying to steal the dogs… What was that called?"

A hot mess. "Ah, that was *Reigning Cats and Dogs*. He was trying to steal the dog that had belonged to the King of Lorainia…" I trailed off, reverting to my practiced, studio-approved speech about movies that sucked. "It was a lot of fun to make, and I'm glad you enjoyed it."

"I loved it. Totally adorbs. Oh, and I googled you because I didn't know what you'd been in lately, and I found an article that said you did a play in

San Francisco and got good reviews, and does that mean you're making the move to theater now? That's so bold!"

I smiled, a little charmed by Belinda's breathless excitement. "Are you signed up for the improv workshop?" The keystone of the festival was Renee's expected performance of a medley of hits from the musicals she'd been in plus some monologues selected from her extensive time on the Great White Way, followed by a Q&A, and an improv session with select audience members.

"Oh, no! I could never! I'm not an actor like you," she rushed, cheeks a deep pink. "I'm a playwright. Or, I'm hoping to be! If my one-act is in the top five, Ms. Rhodes's friend in New York is going to look at it. Mr. Grady. Do you know him?" I shook my head, but she bulldozed onward." She squealed, doing a little dance. "Can you *imagine*? I mean, I know it's like a one-in-a-million shot, but… ugh, you know? My *words* may be getting seen by an *actual Broadway producer?*"

A producer? Ms. Rhodes hadn't mentioned that being a possibility for the winners. Just that the plays would be produced during the theater's regular season as special one-night events. Belinda was so excited, though, so on the verge of bursting into a fountain of sparkles, that I decided to leave that be for now. Instead, I focused on the rest of her word-waterfall. "It's hard, putting yourself out there like that. People will say it's all pretend, or that it's *just acting* or *just writing,* but it's really a huge part of yourself you're letting people see."

She nodded, eyes wide. "So true. Is that how you feel still, when you act? Or do you get used to it?"

"Oh, I definitely still feel it," I fibbed. In truth, I hadn't felt like I was doing anything but going through the motions for several years now. How much of myself could I really bring to a tertiary role in *Lucky O'Leary: Leprechaun PI,* after all? (Though the residuals were nice, and I could expect a nice boost to my checking account every spring thanks to St Patrick's Day re-runs).

That seemed to mollify her, and also open the gates for a few other people to ask me about my time in Hollywood, about roles, about what I was going to do next. Thankfully, no one seemed to catch on. Not only did I have no idea, I was pretty much a has-been on metaphorical life support at the moment. The party seemed to ebb and flow as the night went on, people arriving in waves and departing in trickles. Finally, things started to slow down and thin out near ten, with everyone but Ms. Rhode and I leaving by eleven. "That was lovely," I told her as soon as the doors were closed behind the last person and the muffled sounds of the cleanup crew in the wings got started. "I'm excited for tomorrow!"

She smiled, patting me on my arm again and giving me a slight shake. "You're gonna be great, darling. I invited you for a reason, you know. Not just because I needed a warm body." She winked at my startled, guilty expression. "We're a lot more alike than you think."

"Hardly! I don't have near the career you do," I added—that last mule was possibly a bad idea. I could feel my gears slipping and that last vestige of filter ready to dissolve. "I'm just a jobbing TV and movie actor trying to get by."

She huffed softly and shook her head, her dyed-red curls bouncing with the movement. "Darling, if I might be crass," she husked in that raspy voice she was so famous for, "you have to reach out and grab your opportunities by the short and curlies!" At my sputtering, startled laugh, she looped her arm around my back and gave me a sort of sideways hug as she led me to the doors with Muffin at our heels. I kept a weather eye on that dog—I was pretty sure it could fit my entire head in its mouth if I wasn't careful. "Muffin's a sweetheart," Ms. Rhodes chuckled, noticing my wariness. "A total creampuff!"

"If you say so."

She clicked her tongue, shaking her head in amusement as she waved Muffin past to get settled. "We're more alike than you think. We're the ones who make the magic. We're the ones who really make it all work. Without our work, our talent, our skills? They'd be nowhere."

Her words made my stomach give a funny lurch. "Well," I said slowly, "without them, we wouldn't have anyone to enjoy our talent and skills."

She chuckled, rummaging in her cleavage to produce a bedazzled vape pen. "There's always an audience, darling. The trick is making sure they're on your side."

TWO

D *ay one of my reset... So far so good, I think?* The chill air of the coastal evening had a slight scruff of moisture to it, making me speed my steps just in case that meant rain. I was only a mile from the B&B, an easy walk from the theater, and, in my romantically inclined mind, a perfect opportunity to decant my feelings about the entire thing. This was meant to be the start of my grand renewal. Or reset. Or start over. Whatever. A chance to get out of the Hollywood rut, step away from my LA life, and really figure out what to do next. And *Renee Rhodes was part of it all!* That alone had me doing a little skip-hop thing as I passed under the sole streetlight. She'd been everything I'd imagined. Well. Almost. She was a bit more acidic than I'd pictured, a skoche more acerbic, but it was *charming*.

I mean, all those years in the industry and it had to give her a bit of a tough hide, right? And she'd doled out those words of wisdom and compliments! My knee-jerk reaction was to return the flattery, to brush her off with a turn of phrase and a well-practiced tell me more. That always made people feel good and, in turn, meant I didn't have to be as on as might otherwise be expected. Besides, you found out so much about other people and goings-on if you just gave them free rein and nodded and smiled every once in a while.

We're more alike than you think.

"Not really," I sighed, tripping a little on the uneven shoulder. "A thirty-year stage career, hundreds of plays, and a one-woman show off-Broadway. I've got fifteen years of second and third-string forgettable roles, no marketable skills, and a tendency to get carded when I buy my box wine at the corner store."

The crush and thrum of a car speeding up behind me reached my ears just in time for me to slope sideways, off the road, and into the shallow ditch beside it, stumbling. My knee, still sore from earlier, buckled and I went down. The lack of streetlights and the moon hiding behind clouds meant it was too dark for me to see the make and model clearly (okay, the mules might've been partially responsible too) but the car was definitely white.

Like about a million other cars in the world, even in Lester Cove.

I fumbled for my phone with the notion of calling the police to report a reckless driver, coming up empty with a sickening lurch.

"Damn it!" I turned to stare back up the road the way I'd come. The faint lights of the theater were visible through the thick stand of rhododendrons at the curve, someone's landscaping run wild in this older part of town. I could just go back and get it tomorrow. Who's gonna call me tonight?

Though I do still have Max listed with his real name and not his ridiculous safety name. And I've got those pictures from Kim K's pool party on there from last year…

Damn it.

THE LIGHTS WERE STILL on when I got back, the small parking lot empty save for a closed dumpster in the corner of the lot and Renee Rhodes' electric car.

I trudged past the little bright red car and sighed to see the front door propped open with one of the smooth gray rocks that seemed to make up about ninety percent of the Maine coastline. "Ms. Rhodes?" I called, slipping in and leaving the door ajar. The lobby smelled like lemon cleaner and a dusty vacuum someone needed to empty, the faintest trace of Fracas and those tiny crab cakes lingering beneath it all. But it was dead silent save for the ticking of the relatively new HVAC unit overhead. "Ms. Rhodes, it's just me, Damien! I think I dropped my phone here."

A soft sound came from the theater itself, past the bright green Art Deco doors leading to the seating area. I moved closer, squinting in the gap between the doors. The footlights were on, but otherwise, the place was dark.

Probably haunted, I decided. It was over a century old, and it was a well-known fact that old theaters were haunted.

I mean, a million ghost-hunting shows couldn't be wrong.

Don't be a scaredy cat. It's just Ms. Rhodes. Hell, you saw her car sitting out there! She's probably just… vibing or making sure everything is ready for tomorrow.

The silence was expectant. Heavy. A thousand jump scares danced through my head as I hurried to the restroom to check under the sink, the bang of the door behind me making my skeleton want to flee without the rest of me. As I hurried back into the lobby, a waft of perfume—something cheap and too sweet with hints of alcohol—tickled my nose, making me sneeze twice, loud in the empty space.

The *not-alone* vibe was strong in the lobby, spinning up thoughts of ghosts and serial killers, lurking in dark corners and waiting to turn me into a movie of the week where I'll be played by some straight, middle-aged actor in a bad wig who'll get an Emmy for their brave portrayal of a gay man cut down in his prime.

Bitter? Me? Never!

I took one more slow lap around the room, forcing myself to look under things in the dark, a tiny part of me expecting to see claws and red eyes, drooling mouths and god knows what else waiting for me.

Stephen King was from Maine, after all. There had to be a reason he set so many stories in the state, and I was betting it was because the place was a hive of monsters and ghosts after dark.

I didn't find any killer clowns from outer space or number one fans with a mallet, but I *did* find my phone, hiding under one of the buffet tables. "How'd you get there?" I muttered, crawling underneath to grab it. A flat black rectangle on a flat black floor. I'd been lucky to notice it at all before giving up and fleeing into the night. I mean, walking sedately back to the inn and not running in terror at some imagined horror in the darkened theater.

I might not have run, but I definitely speed walked my way toward the doors, bringing up my rideshare apps one by one.

Nearest driver an hour away.

So that was a big ol' nope.

But my socials were a big *yes*—one hundred notifications in the past hour since Belinda had posted those pics and tagged me, plus a slew of comments on the few I'd posted with Renee Rhodes and one of me making a *wow* face at the bar set up. Max had left a comment—*Call me, you lush!*
—which had spawned dozens of replies from *his* fans asking if he was at the gala and *oh my god let's go to Maine*!

Par for the course when your bestie is Max King.

Opening my camera app, I turned on the record option and swept a quick glimpse of the lobby before turning the lens on myself. "Hey, folks! This is where I'll be this weekend, the Palais Theater in Lester Cove, Maine! I'm *kinda* not supposed to be here right now"—pause for laugh
—"but I won't tell if you won't!" My phone's battery symbol flashed red, so I hit stop and quickly uploaded the video to the 'Gram before shoving

my phone in my pocket. The theater was dead quiet, the silence weighted like the place was holding its breath.

I glanced around again, wondering if it'd be a bad idea to just sleep in the lobby. The idea of walking back down the dark road, past the closed storefronts and sleeping houses, made my skin crawl, but curling up under a table and waking up to the sight of a dozen or more people staring at me was somehow worse. "Ms. Rhodes, I'm heading out!"

Silence.

I padded back to the doors and gently nudged them open. The footlights made the stage stand in stark relief to the seating area, deep shadows curving around the edges where the light didn't reach. "Ms. Rhodes? Hello?"

I checked my phone and decided to risk the last bit of battery, turning the flashlight on and making my way down the sloping aisle toward the stage. "Hello?"

Something shifted in the shadows, fabric moving over wood. "I'm not a fan of jump scares," I called out.

Nothing.

Maybe she fell. She did have a lot to drink, and who knows if she pregamed…

A sudden flurry of movement sent me scrambling back, tumbling down the shallow steps at stage right, landing on my ass as a flying, dark shape came bulleting out of the dark. Hot, damp breath bathed my face and the high-pitched whine of the damned pierced my eardrums.

Okay, it was Muffin, but Muffin was a big dog. A big, very upset dog whining and pawing at me, eyes wild with what I could only assume was panic. "Easy," I murmured, trying to scoot back. I wasn't exactly a dog person. Or a cat person. Or any kind of pet person. I'd never had the chance to become one, between working long hours and sometimes being out of town for weeks at a time on shoots. I barely kept my pet rock alive. I liked to joke, but it was kind of true.

Peter the Pebble was missing a googly eye, and I had no idea where it went.

Muffin danced on huge paws, darting towards me, then towards the steps, whining and growling, tail tucked between his legs. Even I knew that meant he was afraid.

And I probably should be. The creature was huge and if something could scare that beast, I didn't know if I wanted to see for myself what it was.

Still, the poor thing was in distress.

"Come here," I called softly. "Come here, boy. Pst, pst, pst, pst, pst!" The look the dog gave me was almost incredulous. "That only works on cats, huh? What if I have a treat, huh? Want a treat? Hold on!" I hurried back to the foyer, hoping there'd be some leftovers from the buffet I'd somehow overlooked, but the tables were definitely still gone, and no one had left a conveniently placed bag of cold cuts sitting in the middle of the floor. I tried the office, and the door was open, a very large designer bag sitting on the desk, and I knew I'd found Ms. Rhodes' things. A leather leash embossed with the name of the same designer as the purse was coiled on the desk chair, and a mylar baggie of dog treats boasting to be organic, free-range, whole foods for 'num nums' peeked out of the top of her bag.

"Jesus," I muttered, picking the bag up between two fingers. They probably cost more than my daily fancy coffee addiction, judging by the packaging. Carrying the baggy into the foyer, I gave it a noisy shake. "Muffin! Hey, Muffin! C'mere! I have treats! Er, num nums!"

Of course, the dog gave zero cares. "Muffin, come on. Let's go find Ms. Rhodes. C'mon, doggy." I made kissy noises as I headed back into the dark theater, shaking the treats as I walked. Muffin sat on the stage, doing this weird little dance with his front paws like he wanted to run to me but was being held in place at the same time.

And there was still no sign of Ms. Rhodes. Maybe we'd somehow missed one another in the darkened theater. Maybe she was in the ladies' room after all, or on her phone in the balcony section? *Or maybe her martinis kicked in and she's taking a nap up there.* I hoped it was the last option because things were feeling very not great as I took another few steps into the darkness. "Ms. Rhodes?" I called again. The dog uttered a soft whimper and tugged on my jacket sleeve, catching the nubby fabric in his teeth and pulling. "Hey! Easy, buddy! This thing is older than both of us combined! What's going on here?"

My phone's battery warning flashed more urgently, but the light was on for the moment. I gave in and started after the dog when it darted away, deeper into the shadows at the back of the stage. "Ms. Rhodes, I'm on the stage. Where are you?"

Then Muffin stopped in front of me, dropping to his belly and nosing at something in the dark, outright crying now. Cautiously, I swung my light to see what was so interesting and upsetting, and damn near dropped it as a tangle of red hair, nearly black with blood, caught the light.

"Ms. Rhodes," I whispered, unable to force my voice to go any louder. "Ms. Rhodes? Are you okay?"

The dog threw back his head and howled.

And honestly, I didn't blame him. I sank down to the floor and buried my face against my knees until I heard someone call out for me to make myself known.

"Step into the light and hold your hands where we can see them," a man's voice came from the open theatre doors. "This is Lester Cove PD! Identify yourself!"

"You first!"

"I just said…" There as a loud sigh and a bright flashlight beam found me on the stage where I'd risen to my shaking legs and held my hands out to my sides. "I'm Lieutenant Heath Nichols. Did you make the call?"

I nodded. "I've got a huge dog with me here."

Lieutenant Nichols was a bit older than me, but not by much. He looked almost too young to be the one in charge of the crime scene with his uniform slightly wrinkled and hair in disarray, as if he'd just tumbled out of bed. "And you said you found her here. You didn't touch her?"

I shook my head, unable to look away from the sheet-covered lump on the stage. "I touched her bag, though. It was in the box office manager's office." Showing Nichols the bag of dog treats in my hand, I added, "Muffin's leash is back there, too. Someone should get it if it's not evidence."

All the lights were on now, and a small cluster of uniformed people were moving around the theater. It had taken over an hour for the EMTs to arrive, the nearest hospital being several towns over and slammed with an accident between a tourist boat and some fishermen. Lester Cover had a grand total of ten cops—five being part-time, and only four were in town that weekend since the other six were all related and in Orono at a cousin's wedding.

The remainder of the police force had taken a look at Ms. Rhodes, the pool of drying blood, the distressed dog, and the panicking man (played by Damien Murphy) and promptly decided to call in the MCU—the state's Major Crimes Unit.

The MCU investigator rolled his eyes, waving one of the local cops over. "Did you get that list of attendees this evening?"

Lieutenant Nichols shook his head. "No one kept any real records, apparently. It was an open reception. Everyone in town could come and go as they liked."

"Hm. Anyone else here from out of town for this?" the statie asked, directing the question my way.

"I have no idea. I'm—I was—supposed to be presenting some workshops and helping judge the one-act play contest. Ms. Rhodes invited me out for this. I don't think she had anyone else coming out, but some locals were participating in the contest, and I think she mentioned one of the theater professors from the university was giving a playwriting workshop for beginners…" The intense buzzing in my head made it hard to finish a thought, much less a word. When I realized the cops were still staring at me, I unstuck my tongue from the roof of my suddenly very dry mouth and shook my head. "I came back to get my phone and… Oh!"

The statie straightened, darting a glance at the local cop. "Remember something, Mr. Murphy?"

"A car! I nearly got hit again today! Or… yesterday? What time is it now?"

"Half-past twelve," one of the EMTs offered. They were carefully moving Ms. Rhodes onto a gurney. I looked away; the puddle of blood much larger than I thought. The stained sandbag that had been atop her was rolled to one side, soaked with red drying to brown. The stage was stained, and Muffin—I shuddered—had blood on his front paws and muzzle where he'd tried to nose Ms. Rhodes back to life as I panic-dialed 911.

"I was walking back to Two Moons," I murmured. "And a car… White, I think. A white car zoomed past and nearly hit me. I realized my phone was missing after that. But the car! Do you think you can track down who was driving? They had to be the last ones to see her alive. Maybe even the one who—" I jerked my head at Ms. Rhodes being rolled past, exit stage right.

The statie sighed. "Get the plate number?"

"Oh. No. But it was a white four-door!"

"Who here drives a white four-door?" the statie called. About a third of the people raised their hands. "Look." He sighed, closing up his notepad and handing me a business card. "This is the number for victim services. We share resources with a few counties so there might be a wait to get hold of 'em, but I suggest you talk to someone about what you saw here. And stick around a few days, understand?"

I nodded, numb. "I'm a suspect." The idea was laughable, but I'd been in enough cop shows as the victim of the week or the young, two-episode- arc rookie who learns an important lesson or ends up being that aforementioned vic of the week himself to know the fact I'd been the one to find her meant I was, if not number one, at least high on the list. "Damn it, my fingerprints might be on her bag in the office! I took the dog treats out of it." Rory would flip his toupee if I ended up in a murder scandal. *Think of the notoriety, kid! Look at what it did for Broderick!*

Lieutenant Nichols smiled kindly as he handed me a card for the local department. "If it helps, I don't think you did it." He pointed to my shoes, bright green classic high tops I'd paid a ridiculous amount for in a resale shop in North Hollywood. "No blood."

Unwillingly, my gaze returned to the puddle. "Who's cleaning that up?"

Lieutenant Nichols and the MCU investigator both shrugged. "I'll see if Miranda can get out here this weekend. She used to do cleanup for the department in Bangor before she retired. I think she still has some bottles of that stuff they used," Nichols said. He gave the MCU investigator a nod and me a tight, sympathetic smile before heading back to his little cluster of local officers to compare notes or whatever it was they were doing.

The MCU—Jones, I finally noticed, the small tag bearing his name hidden beneath the flap of his jacket which *finally* fell back enough to show the silver bar—sighed and looked around once more, his gaze falling on the dog. "Keep an eye on that one," he said to no one in particular. "Animals can take this almost as hard as humans. Sometimes worse, really."

I nodded again, trailing after the officers as Muffin clung close to my side. When we got outside, I realized one tiny problem I'd forgotten in all the chaos.

I was still without a car.

And my body was *not* going to hang together for a walk this time of night.

Morning.

Whichever.

"Can I get a ride?" I cried. "Hey!"

Jones shrugged again. "I'm heading back to Augusta."

Nichols sighed, and, shooting a glare at Jones, motioned for me to get in the car. "I'll drop you off, but if he pees in my car, you're cleaning it out."

"Wait, let me grab Muffin's leash!" I called, turning back towards the theater.

He sighed, thumping his hand against the roof of his car as he fixed me with an exasperated glare. "It's evidence. So is her bag. In fact, I should take those treats, too."

I held them out. "How will you get Muffin to follow you without treats?"

"That," he said, approaching with an evidence bag and a smirk, "is officially not my problem."

We rode in silence back to Two Moons—save for Muffin's snuffles and snores in the back seat. "I suppose I can take him to a shelter or something," I muttered as Nichols pulled to a stop in front of the inn.

"Ah, no," Nichols admitted. "We don't have any shelters in the area. The nearest one is over in Shell Point, but they're almost always running full, especially in the summer. We might find a foster or something, but this time of night? Or morning, I suppose." He tipped his chin at the dashboard clock. It was just past two a.m. "It'd be damn near impossible, honestly."

I gave Muffin's ears a cautious scritch. He heaved a heavy sigh and pressed his chin harder into my shoulder from behind. "So, what's going to happen to him?"

"The fact is, there's no one in town to take him. And if Renee Rhodes had any family or friends who could come get him, we have no idea of knowing until we're able to get hold of someone who knows her well." He gave me a pointed look. "He seems to like you well enough."

Wait, what… "I can't take him," I protested. "I'm staying at a hotel!"

"The Moon sisters won't mind. They love animals." Nichols reached up, looping his arm under the dog's massive head and giving him a sort of wraparound ear scritch.

Muffin sighed and leaned into it, probably as tired as me, if not more so.

Fidgeting with the seatbelt, making it click and pop, I muttered, "What are they going to do about… about…"

Nichols dropped his hand and shot me a sympathetic if slightly harassed, look.

"They'll take her to the morgue in Augusta."

I nodded, my fidgeting increasing to a steady *click pop click pop click* with no break between. "I'm not sure what to do next."

"Next," Nichols said, laying his hand atop mine to stop the noise, "you take Muffin and go inside. Get some sleep. I'll stop by tomorrow with one of the MCU folks if they have any questions."

"About the festival—"

"That's out of my wheelhouse. I'd track down one of the other presenters or even Charlie Arnold. He was helping Renee, last I heard, get the thing going." Nichols leaned back and motioned for me to open the door. "My shift ends in barely an hour, and I'd like to get my paperwork done, so if you don't mind…"

"Right. Of course."

He sat at the curb until Muffin and I disappeared into the inn.

"What on earth—"

Carmel Moon, the younger and friendlier of the two Moon sisters, was coming out of the private quarters area, tucked back behind the narrow wooden staircase. She clutched her long pink bathrobe closed near her throat, eyes bleary as she stared at me and the giant dog beside me. "Ah," I sighed. "Um. Muffin is Renee Rhodes' dog and—"

"I know Muffin." She sniffed, growing more awake by the moment. "What happened to Renee? Sienna," she called over for her sister, holding up a finger before I could answer. "Put the cats away and come out here! I think something happened to Renee Rhodes!"

Sienna stumbled out of their quarters, shoving her long hair out of her face as she glowered at first me, then Muffin. "Well, hell." She sighed. "She's dead, isn't she?"

Carmel made a startled sound, hand flying to her mouth. "Sienna! Don't even joke about that!"

"She's not wrong," I murmured. "There was… there was an incident at the theater. Um, is it okay if Muffin stays tonight at least? I need to call Charlie Arnold and see if he can take him. Or track down a shelter or—"

"Come on," Carmel said, snapping into hostess mode. "Let's get you some tea and sit down a minute."

"Oh, thank you, but tea will keep me up and—"

"And it's chamomile," Carmel interrupted brusquely. "Come into the kitchen. I'll find something for Muffin to eat and you have your tea, tell us what happened, and then off to bed. You look like death warmed over."

Carmel's hissed *Sienna, no* was met with an eye roll. "He knows what I mean. C'mon through."

THREE

H ot, stinky breath in my face was not my preferred way to wake up. The dog was big enough to bring our faces even with one another while I was in bed, and he was sitting on the floor staring at me from mere inches away. "Do you mind?" I muttered, rolling to my other side. My head throbbed, memories of what happened mixed with the slight hangover and created a headache that beat in time with my pulse.

Do not recommend, zero stars. Ugh.

Muffin gave a soft *wuff* and pawed at the bed.

If my bladder was unhappy, his must be too.

Damn it.

Jesus. Last night... It came crashing back in a heavy wave. Renee Rhodes was dead. I'd been the one to find her, that pool of blood still fresh and her body still warm.

I peeked at the time. It was just past eight, and I wondered if that was too early to call Charlie Arnold and not only let him know about Ms. Rhodes but see also if he could take Muffin. He'd apparently been friends
—or at least close acquaintances—with Ms. Rhodes, and he'd likely be better able to take care of her dog than I was.

I mean, he wasn't staying in a hotel with no set plans to settle down, so that was like two points in his favor, at least.

Hell, who knew about Ms. Rhodes already? If small towns were anything like I'd been led to believe, the news would be everywhere by now. I glanced at the clock and amended my estimate. It was just before eight in the morning, so maybe give the grapevine another few hours to spread the word.

A pang of sadness stuck in my heart like a thorn. Renee Rhodes was *dead*. I hadn't known her well—some might say not at all, not really—but she was dead, and I'd been the last person to talk to her.

Maybe.

That thought dragged me up short.

Had I been?

Muffin huffed another annoyed sound, and I groaned, forcing myself out of bed and to the small bathroom across the hall. I returned a few minutes later, slightly more awake and with minty fresh breath, to toss my Dopp kit back onto the bed. "You could do with a bit of freshening yourself," I said. "Whatever you ate for dinner is not doing your breath any favors."

Muffin sniffed, loping his way to the door and giving me an expectant look.

"Alright, alright. Just a sec. Not all of us are ready to go at the drop of a hat. Some of us need work before we're presentable."

Years of experience meant I had my casual morning routine down to fifteen minutes on no-shower mornings and forty-five on shower ones. Exfoliation is not to be rushed, after all. By the time I got my hair looking unstudied but neat, my lips buffed and moisturized, and a dab of mascara to get rid of that startled rabbit look my pale lashes tended to create, Muffin was about at the end of his patience, dancing in place as I grabbed my atomizer and added a spritz of Thierry Mugler Angel above my navel—a trick taught to me by a costar who played my mom in the short-lived series *Hand to Todd* where I played pint size precocious terror Todd's babysitter's boyfriend, Newton. Cheryl swore it was the best way to have a signature scent that didn't overwhelm but rather *suggested.* Armor firmly in place, I looked down at Muffin and frowned. "No leash," I muttered. "Promise not to bite me if I hold on to your collar?"

I didn't know dogs could roll their eyes like that.

Grabbing my phone from the nightstand, the message alert showed I had over one hundred notifications waiting for me, most replies to my Insta posts the night before, but a fresh handful from people who'd heard about Renee Rhodes already. The only ones I gave a damn about were the ones from my BFF4ever Max King. My agent, Rory Flick, had also sent scads of messages, but a quick glance told me they all boiled down to one thing: *Call me! Immediately! This is huge!* He'd sent a load of links to articles already percolating through the gossip ecosystem.

Muffin made a disgruntled noise, his baleful glare reminding me he wasn't potty trained like that dog one of those models Max dated had—little dude could not only use the facilities but flush and splash his paws in a special bowl of water after.

Somehow, I doubted Muffin would be amenable to that sort of training.

"C'mon, dog breath. Let's get you outside before I have to pay an extra cleaning fee."

Muffin tippy-tapped down the steps, surprisingly light on his feet for a dog the size of a small pony, and practically leapt out the front door as I followed at a more leisurely pace, frowning at my phone's litany of notifications.

"Broadway 'Star' Dead!" Hm. That use of quotes was kind of bitchy.

Renee Rhodes, star of Purple Sunset Over Lake Walton, A Million Miles to Brooklyn, and A Girl's Guide to Murder and Housekeeping, found dead by former child star Lew Murphy. Wow. Just… wow. Lew? Seriously? Not even a simple Damian instead of Damien? Just went for the entirely wrong name there…

I held my breath and took a peek at a few of the notifications. Okay. My socials were disgusting, and now I wished I hadn't fired my PA last year because, *yikes,* those follower lists needed some serious culling.

I skimmed a few comments on one of the articles, just to see if everyone was as gross as my commenters.

Oh, no! I remember seeing her in the touring company of Glass Menagerie! How tragic!

An angel has gotten her wings! RIP RENEE!

I can't believe this!

Wow—I thought she died like five years ago…

Max's messages at least had a shade of humanity about them.

MAX

Are you okay? I just heard.

Do you need me to send someone to pick you up? Need to get out of there?

Shit, it's like 6 a.m. there. Text me when you get this. I'm between locales and might not have service for a bit.

His last text had been just an hour before. It made me feel all kinds of warm and fuzzy that he cared—Max and I had been friends since we were first cast on a crappy Friendly Channel movie together: *Zombies-R-Us.* We were two of the kids in the toy store army that fought back against the toxic sludge zombies using nothing but the toys (cough, cough product placement deals, cough) on hand at the mall where we'd been trapped.

Max became a breakout star from that abomination.

Hey. I'm okay. Shaken. Does that sound dramatic? Shaken, stunned, sad. Lots of S words.

No need to send help, but thank you. Love you, dork. I'll call later and tell you about it.

On the private line, that is.

Speaking of private lines…

It took me a minute to rummage out the info packet Ms. Rhodes had sent me a few weeks ago. Tucked in the very back was a list of contact numbers. The theater, her cell number, and one for Charlie Arnold. Figuring a text was *not* the way to break this news, I steeled my spine and dialed his number, listening to the tinny ringing for a moment until it switched over to a generic voicemail. The automated voice told me his mailbox was full, which was just… dandy, really. Awesome.

Muffin returned from a discreet part of the front yard to do his business as I shut my phone, and I had a moment of panic when I realized I didn't have any poop bags for his rather shocking leavings. Carmel Moon, the younger and friendlier of the two Moon sisters, had me covered, though. She was waiting on the porch when I came rushing back towards the house, holding out a plastic grocery sack with a smirk. "Thanks," I panted. "I didn't think…"

"I figured." She chuckled. "Muffin can come inside with me while you clean up. We'll rustle him up some breakfast while you…" She tipped her head to the Jurassic-sized mess.

And that was where I found Muffin when I got done cleaning up and scrubbing my hands so hard they were pink with the effort. My manicure was still holding strong, but it wouldn't hurt for me to find a place in town that could do my nails without it being a whole *thing* if I was going to be here longer than my planned week, though. An appointment at that O'Neill Auto and Nails might be in my near future, I decided. Two birds with one stone—check on Bonnie and get some new color, providing the nails side of the place was actually any good and not just a gimmick. I followed the smell of coffee to the kitchen, where Muffin waited patiently beside Carmel as she sliced fruit at the table and Sienna methodically tapped open a soft- boiled egg at the counter.

"Morning," I murmured. Sienna shot me a placid but disinterested look. Carmel, however, dropped her paring knife and hustled over to give me a surprise hug. "Oh, hi?"

"How are you, hon?" Carmel asked. "Can I get you anything? Another cup of that calming tea? I've got the herbs out back, and I can just go snip a few bits." She mimed snipping with one hand. "Lavender does wonders for the nerves."

"I'm okay." My smile was small and wobbly, but it seemed to do the trick after Sienna gave me a careful, squint-eyed assessment.

"If you say so. I'd best finish up with breakfast. I'll rustle up some sausage for Muffin, too."

"An accident," Sienna murmured, busying herself with cutting her toast into neat strips. "You didn't say last night how it happened."

"I have no idea. She was just… there." I swallowed down the details with my coffee, uncertain if I should share them with anyone just yet. The cops hadn't told me to keep it under wraps, but still, it felt invasive somehow. Her death was gruesome, but more than that, death was such a private, personal thing, really. And I'd been the first one to see her in that intimate moment.

Maybe.

I mean, it was very possible whoever was in the white car was just a late leaver from the reception, someone who had stopped to chat with a friend maybe or find their own phone. Maybe they left before Ms. Rhodes died. Or maybe she was already dead up there in the shadows, but White Car had no idea. The theater itself had been closed off to the reception-goers, so no one really had a reason to go in there.

Except, apparently, Renee Rhodes and her dog.

Sienna broke a piece of ham from her breakfast and offered it to Muffin. "There's a shop on Buttermilk where Renee got Muffin's food. Ran into her there a few times when I'd go get Gertrude Stein's treats for her skin condition. They can tell you what kind to get him."

"I'm sorry, Gertrude Stein?"

"Our cat," Sienna said, poking at the remains of her scrambled eggs with a scowl. "The other one is named Alice B. Toklas."

I pressed my lips together into a tight line to keep from laughing, settling for a muttered *mmm* and nod. Carmel, when I glanced up, was smiling, not even bothering to hide it. "Anyway," she continued, "you'll need at least a small bag of food for him unless you can get it from her house. And his bowls and toys and—"

"Doesn't she have someone who can take care of him?" I demanded, perhaps a little panicked. "I can't keep him here! Besides, I literally just met him last night!"

Sienna snorted. "He's a dog, not a potential hookup. He doesn't care how long you've known him, just that his person isn't here."

Carmel dabbed at her lips with her napkin before giving me a kind smile. "Renee took Muffin everywhere. Virtually everyone in town's either met him or knows him on sight. He looks a little scary due to his size, but he's a marshmallow. Aren't you Muffin I know you were hoping Charlie would take him, but… well he lives in one of those pokey little shoebox apartments on the edge of town. Barely enough room for him and two fleas, much less Muffin. Muffin turned wide, liquid brown eyes up to her and exhaled slow and heavy through his nose.

Same, Muffin. Same.

Sienna didn't bother with polite things like wiping bacon grease from her mouth or swallowing most of her food as she muttered, "Lot of good having that dog did her, though. Marie Nichols at the post office said he was just whining at her side. Not even barking or anything."

"Marie Nichols? Any relation to Lieutenant Nichols?" I asked, picking at the fluffy scrambled eggs on my plate. My appetite, usually birdlike thanks to years of practice, was dialed all the way down to nonexistent at the moment.

Maybe it was those pastries and booze last night. I was being haunted by carbs.

"They're brother and sister," Sienna said, finally swallowing her mouthful. "Said Heath—that's Lieutenant Nichols—told her that Muffin was just distraught. No one heard him bark or nothing. Did you?"

The sharpness of her question made me draw back, startled. "Uh, no. I mean, when I came back in for my phone, I thought I heard someone in the theater, but I didn't see anyone. And when I found her, Muffin was already near frantic."

Muffin sank to his belly, resting his head between his paws and sighing as if to underscore my statement.

Carmel sighed, standing to clear her plate and mug. "Well, you're welcome to keep him here with you, Damien. We don't mind a bit. So long as you make sure he's fed, watered, and gets his exercise."

"He ruins the carpet, it goes on your bill," Sienna said, rising to follow her sister back into the kitchen. "I'll let the other arrivals know there's a dog on site, so they don't freak out," she added. "And keep him away from Gertrude Stein and Alice B. Toklas!"

"Uh, I think they died a while back so—"

"The cats," Sienna growled. "They don't care much for dogs."

Carmel gave her sister an affectionate, exasperated shove on the shoulder as she reached for the bowl of fruit salad in the middle of the table. "We've got some guests coming Saturday for the festival, so I'll make sure to give them a *friendly* head's up." She saluted us with the bowl, taking it back into the kitchen.

"More people for the festival?" I asked, dread and disappointment warring with sadness in my gut. Then, a horrible thought: "Oh, no! Who's going to contact everyone? It's supposed to start tomorrow!"

Carmel stuck her head out of the kitchen, that small, kind smile back in place. "Isn't the saying the show must go on?"

"I think we can make an exception in this case," I retorted.

"Well, word will get around fast enough. If Marie Nichols has anything to say about it—and I'm sure she does—most of the town will know by now. And hon, I'm sure you were the only out-of-town guest this year."

My face warmed at that. Did it mean I was the only one desperate enough to accept her invitation? Or maybe I was the only one she thought she could rook into taking part?

Or maybe you're the one who thought it'd be a great start to a new chapter and there's nothing shameful about it.

Ugh, why was my mom's voice in my head so loud? I should call her. It always got quieter after a dose of the real thing.

AFTER BREAKFAST, Sienna gave me a length of nylon rope and showed me how to make a temporary harness for Muffin before giving me directions to the pet store on Buttermilk. It was a nice walk, just a bit over a mile with the cool morning air in my face, blowing off the cove and scented with salt and green, growing things. You'd never guess the afternoon would be uncomfortably hot, I thought, smiling and nodding at a few curious glances as I made my way down Lester Road toward the center of town.

My first stop was O'Neill's. "Mr. Murphy, I presume," Bitty smiled as I entered. "We haven't officially met, but I'm the one you talked to about the tow truck yesterday. Glad to see you're doing alright."

"It's been a hell of a twenty-four hours," I admitted. "I don't suppose you've got good news on Bonnie?"

She shook her head sympathetically. "I haven't had much of a chance to take a look yet. I should be able to later today but, I gotta say, from what I was able to see earlier…"

The quiet head shake was telling. "Well." I sighed. "Let me know when you, then."

Bitty's frown was a punch right in my gut. I tried to cheer myself up by ducking into the nail place next door to make an appointment to get a manicure the day after tomorrow, but the fact I was likely about to be out a car—Bonnie!—was making my stomach ache.

"Come on," I muttered to Muffin as we stepped out onto the pavement. "Time to get you some food, huh?"

The one good thing about a tiny town was how walkable it was. LA was the direct opposite of walkable. Cars were king there and public transit was a joke. If you wanted to walk anywhere in the city, you'd better be prepared for a hot, stinking, sometimes dangerous hike. Lester Cove, though… It was like walking through a Lifetime Movie set or something, but with less Christmas, and no one was learning a Very Special Lesson about family or reuniting with their high school sweetheart on the town square.

The day was still young, though, so I was holding out hope.

The walk from O'Neill's to the pet shop was an easy one and fairly direct—the main drag was one long, wide road with a gentle curve and a slight slope down towards the shore. Maple trees shaded most of the walk between O'Neill's and the first shop of the town center, leaves broad and green and cool in the summer sun. A faint whiff of salt water and something smoky and coffee teased me along the walk, Muffin loping by my side.

Maybe he wasn't so bad. At least he hadn't tried to eat my entire head yet. Or drooled all over my shoes with that floppy tongue of his.

Paws for Pets was tucked between Bull's China Shop and Witte's Teas. The pet shop, like most of the shops along the road, had a sandwich board sign out front. *Paws for Pets Summer Special: Buy two toys, get one free!* A cartoony dog and cat peered out from the corners of the sign, each holding a toy in their mouth.

Muffin couldn't read, but he definitely knew where we were, making a beeline for the shop door and giving it a shove with his mighty head before I could reach for the handle.

The teenager behind the counter at Paws for Pets knew Muffin and came around the counter to give him scritches and condolences. "You poor thing," he crooned, flopping Muffin's ears gently back and forth. "You're gonna miss your mama, huh?"

"Uh, you mean Ms. Rhodes?"

The kid looked up at me, smiling faintly. "Well, yeah. She loved this guy. Treated him like her own baby. Right, Muffin?"

Muffin wuffed and started to wander off, tugging on the rope harness. The kid scowled at that. "That's not good for him. Where's his regular stuff?"

"In an evidence bag somewhere."

The kid's eyes flew wide. "Oh! You're the guy! The one who…" He made some hand gesture that I assumed meant *found her body.*

"Yeah," I said slowly.

Wide-eyed, he leaned in and whispered, "Is it true the killer wrote a message in her blood?"

"What? No! No, no, no! It…" Would I be lying if I said it was an accident? I shook myself mentally and said, "I didn't see anything other than poor Ms. Rhodes on the ground. The police are investigating," I added.

The kid shook his head, looking a smidge disappointed as he moved past me towards the dog food aisle and grabbed a huge bag of something called Wheat Free Organic Chunks.

Swear to whoever's listening, that's the name of about half the menu items in LA.

"Well, it's a shame. I was kind of looking forward to the one-act plaything. My girlfriend strong-armed me into being in her play," he admitted, the tips of his ears glowing red with either embarrassment or pride. Maybe both.

"Is her name Belinda, by any chance?"

"That's my girl!" He grinned. "She's got this wild idea about moving to the city to be a playwright or something. Ms. Rhodes was always telling her to follow her dreams and that malarkey."

"You didn't think she could do it?" I asked, a pang of sympathy for Belinda giving an edge to my words. Hell, I didn't even know the girl, but I *did* know what it was like to dream big and have impossible-sounding goals.

Wait. I might not be the best example of success in that regard.

The kid—Ollie, per his nametag—shrugged. "Nah, she's mad talented, you know? But I'm kind of more down to earth than Belinda. She's the creative one. I'm the one who's busting my ass with two jobs to pay for community college so I can get my EMT cert." He shrugged again. "That gonna be all?"

"Uh," I glanced at Muffin, who was sniffing a rack of mass-market dog treats with great interest. "Do you have those organic num num treat things?"

Ollie's brows crept up. "Those… what now?"

"The bag just said num nums on it." I sighed. "I didn't notice the brand name. Mylar pouch, looks costy?"

He shook his head. "Never heard of something like that here. Ms. Rhodes always gets him these." He reached over the counter and grabbed a pouch of something that looked like beef jerky and had a strong, meaty smell even through the sealed package. Muffin seemed to know what was up because he stopped window shopping and bolted to the counter, rising on his hind legs to beg. Ollie snorted. "You greedy gut," he chided. "Has he had breakfast yet?"

"Sienna Moon fed him some table scraps."

Ollie *tsked*. "That's not good for dogs, man. Get him home and give him some real food before he gets the runs from eating Sienna's cooking."

I nodded, scowling. Muffin's intestinal upset was something I hadn't considered and the idea of being responsible for the cleanup was… I'll go with daunting.

"You going to get a harness?"

"Uh, sorry?" Usually when I got asked that, it was in very different situations and involved quite a few glasses of wine first, so it took me a moment to parse.

Ollie shook his head. "Even if the cops let you have it back, you should get another one, anyway. She used this fussy little skinny thing that Muffin could've broken through whenever he wanted." Muffin did a little happy dance when Ollie reached down and flopped his ears back and forth, giving him scritches. "You're a big strong boy, aren't you? Yeah, you are. A handsome Cane Corso like you shouldn't be prancing around with diamantes. No, they shouldn't."

Dog people are so weird. Then again, my BFF Max had his pet sitter hold the phone up so he could talk to his weird naked cat when he was out on location shoots, so… "Then why use it?"

"Aesthetic," he drawled. "It was diamond studded, like his collar. Meant for show rather than function. Here." He reached over to a rack of leashes and harnesses, selecting a harness that looked sturdy and utilitarian, adding a thick lead in matching material. They were plain black, made out of some woven synthetic material, and not even a little *aesthetic*. Maybe it was my imagination, but I thought Muffin looked a little disappointed. "As long as you're keeping an eye on him, might as well make sure you have the right equipment. He was used to Ms. Renee, but you?" He shook his head. "He'll probably try to break away when he sees a seagull or something."

He rang me up to an eye-watering sum that I paid numbly. The dog needed to eat, after all, and it looked like I was pet sitting until I figured out where to send him. Maybe Ms. Rhodes had relatives back in New York. Failing that, maybe there was a pet rescue that accepted hellhound-sized dogs nearby.

I was halfway out the door before the rest of what the clerk said sank in. "Wait, you said she used a little skinny harness? She didn't have a different one she'd use sometimes? Like, thick leather?"

Ollie snorted. "God no. Ms. Rhodes had an *image*." He laughed. "Muffin's harness and leash match his collar."

"Are you sure?"

"Dude, I'm the one who sold it to her. She was in here at least once a week to restock on treats or get him a new toy. I'd have noticed if she was using something actually meant for that size dog."

I nodded as he called out to the kids to hold on to their dog, moving around the counter to go help them pick out whatever it was.

I let Muffin tug me out the door, a dozen uncomfortable things perking in my thoughts as he followed the smell of baked goods just a few doors down.

"Seriously?" I asked him. He flashed me a sloppy doggy grin that made me wonder if he really missed Ms. Rhodes at all. "Drowning your grief in baked goods isn't healthy, you know."

"Who are you talking to?"

The low, sharp voice startled me into a yelp. I looked up—and up—to meet the narrowed blue-eyed gaze of one of the prettiest men I'd ever seen in my life. Like if both Mr. Darcys had been combined into one person but with a low-key Boston accent. And, I realized, he was the same man I'd seen speaking with Renee at the gala, who had been not very happy to see Muffin in attendance. Up close, he was so much better looking, which likely meant he was going to be no good for me. History had proved that any Mr. Darcy type I fancied ended up being a Wickham. He was staring at me expectantly, and I remembered he'd actually asked me a question. *Damn those dreamy eyes. Stop it, Damien.* "Uh, the dog?"

"And is he talking back to you?"

Oh, this is how we're gonna be? I squared my shoulders and lifted my chin, fixing one of my best, frostiest, smiles on my glossy lips. "Yes, and you're interrupting. I'm sorry, Muffin, what were you saying?"

"Good lord," he muttered.

The man, not Muffin.

"Excuse us," I said, tilting my chin up and casting him the haughtiest look I could manage while wrestling a bag of dog food the size of a small child and a dog the size of an older, slightly easier to manage child with the tendency to lick things.

"Wait," he began, but I shook my head.

"Nope. Too late. Go have an imaginary conversation in the shower like the rest of us because I'm done here."

The man's phone rang as he opened his mouth to reply, so I seized the opportunity to make a break for it. Muffin helped, throwing his paws against the door as I leaned against the handle, holding Muffin's leash and the cumbersome bag of food on one side while trying to push the door open with the other. It gave under our combined efforts and we swanned on in, ignoring the sputtered protest of the man behind me. "Ms. Margie," I said as she emerged from the kitchen area with a startled sound. "I was hoping to grab a to-go cup of tea from your shop before I took this one back to the   inn.”

“Oh Damien, you are having the worst visit to our little town, aren’t you?” Margie sighed, giving me a tentative, swift hug. Muffin’s tail stilled as Margie reached to pet him. “I usually don’t allow pets in here, but I can make an exception for this boy, can’t I?” He didn’t growl, but he definitely got that *I’m gonna mess you up* posture that was a precursor to Very Bad Things. Margie drew her hand back and gave me a tight little smile as she bustled back around the counter, one eye on Muffin who had adopted a very guard dog kind of posture—tail stiff, legs braced, back straight, ears pricked forward.

I was glad to have the new harness because that bit of rope Carmel had given me would *not* have held him if Muffin decided to make Margie regret not allowing dogs in her shop.

“Maybe he smells my Tony on me. Ten years old this month, spoiled rotten,” she added in a stage whisper as if Tony could hear or would care if he could. “He’s always up in my arms when I’m home, and I swear he’d ride in one of those baby carrier things if I found one that had little holes for his feet. My Johnathan gave him to me just a few months before he passed and, well, I like to think it’s his way of making sure I don’t get lonesome.”

“I’m so sorry.”

“About the dog or my husband.” She laughed. “Oh, don’t make that face. Johnathan and I loved one another very much, and he’d have thought it was hilarious. Now,” she said, leaning on the counter and motioning me closer, glancing warily at Muffin, “I heard about Renee,” she added, shaking her head sadly. “I’m sure that must have been a shock.”

“I can’t believe it. It feels surreal, like this is some messed up dream.”

“You poor thing.” She sighed. “I can’t imagine. Renee was so vibrant, so *much*. Just thinking of the world without her in it is…” She shook her head, waving invisible somethings away from her face. "It's going to be a huge change, her being gone."

"How long did you know her? I mean, if you don't mind me asking!"

"Oh, well, that's a hell of a thing, really. We'd known one another back when we were barely more than girls, in New York of all places. My father worked in a few of the theaters there and, well, Renee and her shoot star." She made a fluttering, whooshing motion with her hands and whistled. "Our paths crossed a few times. She was always so *driven*."

"I'm so sorry," I murmured, feeling a pang of sympathy for Margie. "Losing a friend you've known for so long, that's difficult."

"Oh." Cheeks pink, she leaned in and whispered, "We weren't really good friends. I don't want to speak ill of the dead, of course, but we'd drifted apart ages ago. Her moving to Lester Cove was such a shock. When I saw her walking down Buttermilk Road while my Johnathan and I were taking Ben—that's Johnathan's boy—to get ice cream, well, I about screamed!" Margie's smile was distant, distracted. Whatever she was seeing was long gone but had all of her attention. "She was just a picture, you know? Bright green pantsuit, gold belt like some prize fighter. She had one of those little flip phones—this was so long ago now!—and was just parading down Buttermilk."

Margie blinked, her focus swimming back towards me. "Oh, listen to me rattle on. The poor woman's dead, and no amount of reminiscing will change the fact. What about you? What are you going to do now? I know you were here for her festival…"

"There's the million-dollar question." I sighed. "Lieutenant Nichols dropped me back at the inn and said I should be available for questions for the next few days, but I don't know. I didn't see anything when I went back for my phone, so I'm not sure what I could tell them other than what I already did."

Margie stared at me for a long moment, her lips crimped into a frown. "Well, I hope they're not blaming you for this! I thought it was an accident." She paused, offered me a small smile, and said, "That's been the rumor, anyway. Just a horrible accident. Unless… Do you know different?"

Word moves fast in small towns. At least all those episodes of *Welcome to Smithville* I did get that right. "I haven't heard," I hedged, setting the bag of food down and taking a seat at one of the twee little tables. The door behind me swung open, the bell ringing jauntily, so I took that as my cue to change subjects. "What kind of teas do you have?"

Margie hesitated again, glancing past me, but then smiled and launched into a litany of the available teas and tisanes. I settled on something called Ben's Brew, a black tea cut with lemon peel and candied ginger. "So, I was thinking," she said as the kettle started to boil, "if they're not *officially* saying it was an accident, maybe they think someone, ah, helped Renee along."

I thought of the white car. Of the sound behind the door. Of the weird feeling I'd gotten. But I shrugged, forcing casual nonchalance. "Or it just means they're doing their jobs," I said blandly.

Margie harrumphed, turning to get the kettle to pour over the tea strainer for my cup.

"I was going to head back to the theater after I drop Muffin and his giant ass bag of food off at the inn, see if I can find anything of Muffin's while I figure out what to do with him." I didn't care what Ollie had said about Muffin's leash being some pink jeweled number—I definitely saw that brown leather lead at the theater, and I wanted to make sure Muffin had all of his things whenever I found someone to shove him off on—I mean, someone to take care of him.

"A leash?" She paused, mid-prep, and frowned.

I nodded. "It was in the office where Ms. Rhodes had left her things. Her purse, some dog treats, a leash… I'm hoping there are some bowls or toys or something of Muffin's she'd brought along because I just spent a packet on his food and would rather just use what he already has."

Margie resumed making the tea, frowning and quiet as she added leaves to the strainer and poured over the hot water into the to-go cup. "It's so strange that they haven't made an official statement yet," she said after a moment or two. "I wonder if they've got someone in mind for this." Shoot me a sympathetic, curious glance, she added, "They *did* ask you to stick around, after all."

"They're just doing their jobs," I sighed, shaking my head. "Investigations are never as quick as they are on TV."

"*Or* it means they're hiding something."

"It's been less than twelve hours!"

Margie shook her head. "Renee's death is just so unexpected. Do you think maybe…"

"No."

Both of us turned at the sharp word. The man from outside loomed behind me, scowling. "Margie, no. Don't start this. You're always trying to stir the hornet's nest in this town and it's old. It's *been* old since I was a kid."

"Benjamin," she said stiffly, pushing my to-go cup across the counter to me. "I didn't know you were coming by the shop today. I thought you were working from the house."

"I didn't want you to dodge me," he groused. "I was looking over the books for the shop earlier, comparing them to previous years—"

"Ben," Margie chirped, her face suddenly lighting up as she pushed me towards Mr. Darcy the Third. "This is Damien Murphy! He's an actor! From Hollywood! And he found Renee last night. Damien, this is my stepson, Ben!"

I stared, slightly startled, and, without thinking, held up my cup of Ben's Brew. "You're delicious," I blurted.

Ben drew back, brows furrowing. "Excuse me?"

At my knee, Muffin growled, ears flipped back. He pressed close to my leg, paws doing a little march like he couldn't decide who to go for first. "Muffin," I chided, really wishing I could bolt myself. "Don't eat the nice people!"

Margie had paled and hurried back behind the counter, but Ben was just glaring. "Really?" he demanded of Muffin. "I've known you for years and this is how you treat me?"

"Maybe he smells Margie's dog on you," I offered, repeating her suggestion of just a few minutes before.

Ben made a face at that. "You think that's the reason?"

"Damien's about to head back to the inn to drop off his stuff, then head over to the theater," Margie interrupted. "Why don't you give him a ride? It's getting warm out there and that's not a very safe walk."

I rubbed my thigh, where she'd clipped me the day before. "Tell me about it."

Margie had the good grace to flush, ducking away as Ben turned his gaze to me and the giant bag of dog food. And the giant dog. "You need a ride."

It wasn't a question or even confirmation of Margie's suggestion. It was a flat statement of fact. "Oh, it's fine. Walking's good for me." I patted my flat belly and added, "Helps me keep my boyish figure."

Ben swept a gaze from head to toe. Warmth flooded my face and throat, that damn blush of mine, the one I was unable to hide even with makeup, rearing its ugly head. He met my gaze and shrugged. "I'm heading that way, gotta pass the theater to get to the house, and the inn isn't far out of the way. That bag's too heavy for you to carry that far, anyway. I can give you a ride so long as you keep Muffin in check."

"Oh, I couldn't—"

He didn't respond. Instead, he pulled his keys from his trouser pocket and nodded at the door. "I'm going now, so if you're ready…"

I nodded, tugging Muffin's leash to follow Mr. Darcy's evil twin.

FOUR

The drive back to the B&B was short and quiet, hardly enough time for me to get settled in the seat. When Ben pulled his BMW to a stop in front of the inn, he drummed his fingers on the wheel as I unbuckled, clearly wanting to say something. "Go on," I muttered. "Whatever it is, just spit it out and you can get on with your day. You're late already, if I recall correctly."

"I know you're one of those creative sorts," he began.

"Like Margie?"

"Hardly. I mean actually creative. Professionally. And I'm sure you're used to drama and intrigue in your life back in California. But in Lester Cove, an accident is an accident, and you need to remember that."

I barely held back a laugh. "Seriously? Have you been practicing that in your head this entire time or just since we left the theater?"

"Damien—"

"I don't know what you think about me, but I can guess," I cut him off. "And that's fine. That's your thing. But I need you to understand something: I'm not flaking out on Renee Rhodes, even though she died. If the festival goes on, that means I'll be up at the theater. I'll be around town. And yeah, people are going to ask me questions, and I bet you anything I'll answer them. So, if you want to think that's getting mixed up in something, fine.

But you need to put your lawyer hat on here, Ben, and realize I'm *already involved*. I found her body. I'm the last one to see her alive. I'm the one the cops told to stay in town!"

"That's not what I was going to say. I—"

"Thanks for the ride," I interrupted, opening the door, "but maybe you need to remember you're not the end all be all in Lester Cove. Or anywhere else for that matter." He winced when I slammed his fancy car door.

I didn't look back as I traipsed up the walk. He sat there at the curb, though, until I shut the front door behind me.

The foyer was dim and quiet, the cool air a relief on my warmed face. Muffin flopped down on the smooth wood floor, panting, and sighed. "Mood," I muttered. "Come on, let's find you some water. I bet it's almost lunchtime for you, huh?"

"Damien." Carmel stepped out of the sitting room at the far end of the foyer, an odd smile on her face as she motioned for me to join her.

"Hey, I was just going to find Muffin some water and then maybe head back to that pet store and get him a bowl or something to tide him over, so I don't have to use your bowls."

"Why don't you let me get Muffin sorted and you come see your guest."

"My… what now?"

"Someone's here to see you." The smile was distinctly fixed as she took me by the elbow and pointed me toward the sitting room. "Have fun," she murmured, giving me a shoulder nudge as she passed. "We'll be in the kitchen."

My first thought was *Rory Flick, you jerk.* My agent had been sending me texts and voice mails nonstop since I left LA earlier in the week, ranging from *Hey just checking in* to not-so-thinly veiled threats about lawsuits and possible name-smearing if I didn't get back to him.

I had seriously considered blocking his number just that morning until I could get my head on straight again, or as close to it as I could manage.

After the barrage of texts about Renee Rhodes' death, info about proposed interviews with outlets ranging from bottom-of-the-barrel tabloid trash to almost respectable entertainment websites, I'd turned off his message alert tone, but now I wished I'd just given in to my impulse and cut off contact entirely. Especially since he'd apparently decided to track me down.

Maybe.

I mean, maybe it was Max coming to see me. Maybe he managed to find some sort of supersonic airplane and make it here from Switzerland or Sweden or wherever in record time.

Here's to hoping.

Taking a deep breath, I channeled Reggie Markham, a character I'd played in the three *Running Wild* movies. Sure, he'd been the main character's younger brother (despite the fact I was actually five years older than the guy playing the Wild Markham), but he'd been a badass in his own right and took no guff from anyone. I could do this—I just had to be someone else for a few minutes, so I didn't fold under Rory's haranguing.

Throwing the door open, I strode into the study. "Alright, I don't have long. What's the problem?"

"Um."

The soft, startled sound shot my facade all to heck. "Oh! Belinda! I'm sorry! I thought…" I slumped into the loveseat across from where she sat, perched in the wingback chair by the cold hearth. "I thought you were someone else," I finished weakly.

Her smile was watery and small. Wearing all black, her eyes red- rimmed and swollen, it was obvious she'd thrown herself fully into the role of Mourner Number One. "Only sometimes."

I bit back my initial urge to roll my eyes and maybe cringe a little. I'd been that theater kid. Hell, I think I still was, if left to my own devices. And feelings were big and hit hard, especially when you're a kid. Instead, I offered her a smile and asked if she wanted a drink or something to eat—I knew Carmel and probably Sienna were lurking about, and I could likely get something if Belinda wanted.

"No, I need to get back home. Mom's already annoyed I missed work this morning."

"You work for Margie Witte, right?"

A complicated expression crossed Belinda's face, but she nodded. "Only part-time. I also help at the front desk over at Bitty's. She's my mom's cousin's wife and is cool with me working around school hours."

"That's a lot of jobs for a… sixteen-year-old?" I guessed.

Belinda laughed, but it was watery. "Eighteen. I'm graduating in June."

"Then off to college?" I asked, remembering what Ollie had mentioned at the pet store.

"Maybe." She shuffled the papers she'd been clutching like a life ring and bit her lip for a moment before saying in a rush, "The thing is Ms. Rhodes promised me she'd have her friend look at my play, and now she's dead, and I don't know if I should, like, send it to him or what. And also, I was kind of relying on her for a letter of recommendation for this program in Boston, and the deadline is Wednesday, and she said she wrote the letter, but I don't *know,* and I need to send it like *tomorrow* to make sure it's there in time and—"

"Whoa, whoa, whoa, hold on a sec!"

Belinda gulped air, her face pale and cheeks pink as she tried her best to look calm despite the tremor in her hands and her wide, uncertain gaze.

"Why are you here, Belinda?" I asked gently. I was fairly certain I already knew and turning her down was going to likely trigger a waterfall of tears.

"I'm overwhelmed," she admitted, sniffing delicately. "Between work and the play and, well…"

I nodded.

"I need help, and I was hoping—"

"Belinda, wait. Look, I appreciate that you think I have any sort of clout with this program in Boston, but I'm really more of a screen actor, and I'm not in any position to speak on your skills as a playwright."

She blinked, her lips parting. I braced for pleading—my star hadn't reached very high, but that didn't mean squat to climbers in LA. People like that grabbed onto the next rung, no matter how low it was. "Um, I'm sorry," she said, brows furrowed in confusion, "do you think I'm asking *you* for a letter of recommendation?"

"Ah… yes?"

"Oh. Awkward." She shuffled those papers again, her cheeks red, before holding out a few sheets to me. "I wanted to ask if you'd handle Ms. Rhodes' memorial service. It's kinda short notice but…" She shrugged, looking a little abashed, and a lot hopeful. "You're the only other person in town who could give her a good eulogy, you know. I mean, other than Charlie Arnold."

Delicately, I interjected, "Ms. Rhodes and Mr. Arnold were much closer than she and I were. Maybe he'd be a better option."

Belinda shook her head so hard, her ponytail narrowly missed hitting her in the face. "He was so mad at her when he left, otherwise I'd ask him to do it. I mean, it's bad enough I had to go to him for the letter this morning. He knows he's my second choice," she added, those red cheeks going almost nuclear.

"Oh, he's an actor too?" I asked, gingerly accepting the papers with the full knowledge that I'd just agreed to do the damn eulogy.

"He's the theater teacher at Lester Cove Consolidated."

"Oh!"

She made a face at my surprise. "What'd you think he did?" she giggled. "Just hung out at the Sleepy Pelican all day? He's super awesome as the Stage Manager character when we do *Our Town* every spring for the Rural Theater Festival in Horse Bay!"

"This state sure loves its theater festivals," I muttered, and Belinda grinned.

"We're a hidden gem of theatrical talent," she pronounced, and I knew without her telling me that she was quoting Renee Rhodes. A tinny alarm sounded, and she startled, grabbing her phone. "Oh, shoot! I'm gonna be late if I don't get out of here! Bitty will be so pissed if I'm late again! Thank you so much for doing this, Mr. Murphy!"

Belinda breezed out leaving the stack of notes and half-written, tearfully purple-prosed snippets for a eulogy. I was glad when, less than ten minutes later, Carmel stuck her head in the door to let me know Ben Witte was waiting in the foyer to take me to meet Charlie Arnold at the theater.

"What? Why?" I asked, trailing after Carmel to find Ben frowning at his phone in the dimly lit entryway.

"Charlie said you guys needed to work on the plans for this weekend and asked if I'd come get you. His car's at O'Neill's to get the shocks replaced," Ben said, rapid-fire, barely looking up from his phone to shoot me a distinctly harassed look. "I've got an hour or so between calls with the office, so I've got time."

Carmel gave me a little nudge, a small smile on her lips. "Go on then, Damien. Go with Ben."

I narrowed my eyes at her. "Seriously?"

"I'm sure Ben wouldn't have offered to drive you if he didn't want to," she said in such a sticky-sweet tone that Ben shot her a glare over the top of his phone.

"Carmel," he muttered warningly. She snickered and waved us off, disappearing back into the private quarters she shared with Sienna. Deprived of his original target, Ben turned that acid glare on me. "Come on. I don't have all day."

MS. RHODES' little red electric car still sat in its spot front and center in the parking lot, but the place seemed empty.

"I'd have thought the cops would be back," I murmured as he set the parking brake, both of us staring up at the front of the building. "What if it's locked?"

"Chances are it will be. Even if there hadn't been a death, it's Thursday, and no one is on site."

"There will be tomorrow," I murmured. "Unless someone notifies the rest of the festival attendees. Hell, I hope Charlie knows what he's doing."

Ben sighed and shut off the engine. "We'll find out."

I followed the direction of his finger, pointing to a sadly familiar car pulling up in front of the theater. Margie had driven Charlie and wasn't bothering with the parking spaces, just paralleling it right at the foot of the walkway. "This is turning into a group project," I muttered.

"And those always go so well." Ben got out of the car and didn't look back, shutting the door behind him and striding towards the theater.

"Oh my god," I muttered, scrambling out of the car.

Margie waved, standing in front of her car with Charlie, who looked marginally better than just a few hours before. His color was closer to human now, less like wet cardboard, but his expression was still hollow. "Hello, boys," Margie called as we drew closer.

"I asked Margie to come along," Charlie muttered, looking a wee bit abashed.

"Moral support," Margie said staunchly, tipping her chin up at Ben's moue of distaste. "Besides, there's safety in numbers."

Ben made an annoyed sound somewhere between a cluck and a growl. Like a really angry goose or one of those RPG monsters Max kept trying to get me to memorize back when we were starring on *Wizard's Run*—like *Logan's Run* if it was set in Medieval Times and instead of a jousting show people used actual magic.

It never made it past the first season. Tragic.

"It was an accident," Charlie said. "Who would want to kill Renee? She was an absolute—" He paused, closing his eyes against a wave of emotion. "She was just a light in the world."

Margie patted his arm, making soothing little sounds as she did so. "I'm sorry, hon. Just with so much uncertainty, I won't rest easy until I know for sure this case has been closed and Renee's demise was truly accidental."

Charlie's jaw worked on some words he was desperate to spit out, but instead, he turned a watery smile my way and gestured up at the theater doors. "Come on, let's see what we can salvage for this weekend, hm? For Renee."

"Damn it," Ben muttered, and we all looked his way. He had the grace to look a bit embarrassed at his outburst but waved his phone in explanation. "Work. I need to take this. Damien, I'll wait in the car for you."

"You don't have to—"

He was already walking off. Charlie chuckled fondly. "Ben's always been stubborn as a mule."

Margie sniffed. "It wouldn't hurt him to unbend a bit sometimes."

I wisely bit my tongue—letting my thoughts dwell on Ben Witte even in the abstract would *not* go well. Between the current situation and my moratorium on dating for the foreseeable future, it was best to just to nod, smile, and let it go.

Except he'd now apparently appointed himself chauffeur for my day.

Get it together Damien.

"After you, Charlie. Let's see what we can do for Ms. Rhodes' festival."

The main doors were locked—a fact which annoyed and saddened Charlie all over again. "I gave Renee my spare key." He sighed. "She lost hers last week."

"There are only two keys to the theater?"

Margie blinked up at me. "Well, there used to be three, but I think Lew Higginbotham accidentally took his with him when he and his girlfriend moved to Vermont a few years back."

Charlie nodded. "He offered to mail it, but I think he forgot and, well, getting Lew on the phone means just blocking out that whole afternoon because that man can *talk*."

Small towns… yikes. "Well, I think first things first, we figure out how to get inside, then we see about getting more keys made."

"Oh, we can't. They're the sort that has *Do Not Duplicate* on 'em," Charlie said with great solemnity.

"Then let's get the locks changed," I said through a very stiff smile. "I'll pay."

Margie *tsk*ed. "Now, Damien, don't you throw your money around like that. The theater club has a fund, from what I recall, and they can pay from that."

Charlie nodded, but I held up a hand to stave off further argument. "Let's just get inside first, okay? Is there a window or something? Maybe I can wiggle through if we can get it open."

"I can do you one better," Margie said with a hint of hesitancy. "My Johnathan loved volunteering here during the theater group's seasons and, well. Come here." She turned and hurried around the side of the building, sticking close to the tidy landscaping. At a dull gray door tucked around the corner, out of sight of the parking lot, she stopped and did a little Vanna flourish. "Ta-da. The side entrance. They use this to get into and out of the offices and the backstage storage area without having to go through the main doors all the time."

Charlie made a displeased face. "They were supposed to have that new electronic lock already set in here," he complained. "The theater club paid good money for that back in May."

"Well, it's a good thing it hasn't happened yet," Margie chided gently. "Still the same old door. This door's never locked," she said, giving it a yank. It stuck for a moment, then wheezed as she pulled it open, the bottom scraping in the accumulated sand and dirt on the walkway. "It's been like that since before Johnathan passed away."

"Seriously? That's not safe!"

Charlie gave a mirthless, annoyed chuckle. "It's Lester Cove, not Chicago or Boston, or even New York. There's nothing in here that anyone wants to steal. Worst that happens is the teenagers who slip in and smoke pot on the stage." He gave me a sweeping arm motion, urging me to go inside.

The door had opened onto a narrow corridor full of coiled cables, painted wood panels propped against the wall, things that looked like boxes of fabric and small props. At one end, a red light glowed high near the ceiling while at the other, thin brownish light streamed in through a high, narrow window.

"Left," Charlie murmured close to my ear. "It leads to the stage left steps and down into the audience seating."

We picked our way down the corridor using weak light from the windows, Charlie close behind me and Margie bringing up the rear. We were passing behind where Ms. Rhodes had been found less than twelve hours before and that knowledge not only pricked at my heart with sadness but made my skin crawl. Just ten feet away, Ms. Rhodes had bled out her life on the dirty stage floor, alone in the dark. Had she called for help? Had she known she was dying?

Well, no, I reminded myself, she hadn't been alone—she'd had her dog with her, for all the good that'd done. Muffin hadn't been able to stop the sandbag from falling on her, staunch the blood, or call 911.

Behind me, a solid thump sounded, making me jump. "What was that?"

Charlie patted my back with a small chuckle. "The door. It's on one of those spring arm things and takes forever to close unless someone helps."

"I think that's what I heard last night, the door closing," I murmured. Charlie looked confused while Margie just looked wide-eyed and more than a little nervous. "Last night, when I came back for my phone, I heard something, and I thought maybe that was Ms. Rhodes in the theater. It was that door, I'm sure of it."

Charlie swallowed audibly, the small clicking sound somehow remarkably loud in the narrow space. "Maybe Renee was coming back in for something," he whispered. "Didn't want to come in the front doors."

"Her car's parked out front though," I remembered. "Why would she be coming in this door?"

Margie tittered nervously. "Same reason we are, I'm sure. She was locked out. If she'd lost that silly key already, probably locked herself out and forgot she had Charlie's!"

Charlie nodded slowly. "Sounds like her." He sighed. "Damn it, Renee…"

We pushed along, Charlie directing me through the dimly lit corridor and into the office area, which had been part of the original building and included front box office manager's room where I'd seen Ms. Rhodes' things just last night. "This used to get me all turned around," Charlie admitted, opening a wooden door at the end of the skinny corridor and letting us into the manager's office. "When they built the place, these were the dressing rooms back here." He gestured to the doors opening off the corridor. "And the actors could just hurry down this side route and get backstage for their cues without being seen."

Margie huffed a small laugh. "Johnny used to sneak me back here to— Well. We were newlyweds," she said, clearing her throat. "So, she left her purse?"

I smirked, feeling my cheeks pink as I stepped into the office ahead of Margie and Charlie. "I'm sure the cops took it all last night. But I'm hoping maybe there's some of Muffin's stuff in here they missed."

A quick search showed me all the cops had left was dust and a small storage closet full of broken typewriters with receipts from the 80s on the back, and some old costumes in need of repair or burning—people need to face the truth that synthetic fibers will *never* not stink of B.O. after a while.

Margie started fussing over the mess left behind, informing us she was constitutionally incapable of leaving a space cluttered. Charlie motioned for me to follow him out into the foyer. "The thing is, even if I wanted to, it's too late to put the brakes on this thing, Damien. We just need to steer into the skid, so to speak. And try to do Renee proud."

"What were you thinking?"

"Honestly, I haven't been able to really think clearly on it. Ever have a rotten tooth? How it aches and throbs but sometimes stops for a minute, and you think hey maybe that wasn't so bad, maybe it's not a bad tooth and I just needed to pop my jaw or something? It's like that."

"I haven't lost someone close," I admitted after a moment of heavy, dragging silence. "A few coworkers, some crew members I knew alright. But I can't imagine how painful this is for you, and I wish I had better words, but I'm an actor, not a writer."

His smile was small and wry. "I'm both, and I still don't have good words for it." He walked into the center of the foyer and seemed to settle into some new presentation of himself, shoulders pulling back and chin lifting. I recognized the maneuver—I'd become a master at it myself over the years. Some people call it acting, I call it lying to myself. And it was what Charlie was doing, putting on a show and pretending he was okay, that this was all going to be okay. But the glint of unshed tears in his eyes, the way he clenched his fists at his side, told me it was a lie.

He sniffed, nodding towards the tables still set up from the gala. "I'm thinking we can just leave the sign-in and such as-is. Belinda and some of the kids from my high school classes have volunteered to run that, so we don't need to do any fancy footwork there."

Nodding, I moved to join him, and for the next hour or so, we sorted out a fragile plan for how to move forward with the weekend. Charlie had a relatively recent version of the email list of attendees, so he'd send out word about Ms. Rhodes' demise and the changed plans. I'd spend time that afternoon hitting my socials and generally just getting the word out otherwise, and also speed reading the rest of those one-acts now that I was the only judge.

No pressure, right?

"What about the playwright Ms. Rhodes was going to send the winners off to? Callum Grady?"

"Callum… Where the hell did you hear that from?" he demanded, irritation making him loud. "Callum's been retired for ages. Who told you that?"

"Er, one of the attendees last night. She's got a play in the competition and said Ms. Rhodes had told her…" I trailed off. "Um, is that a no, then?"

"That's a hell no. Callum Grady's been retired for over a decade now. Finally burned out, packed up his shit, and moved to Aruba with his boyfriends." He frowned. "Maybe it was Barbados? Which one is the one that has the funny roofs?"

"Barbados."

"There ya go. Barbados. Had a going away party and everything. Renee and I went together…" He trailed off and gave a mighty sniff. "Well. He ain't reading anyone's plays, that's for damn sure."

"Then why would Ms. Rhodes have told Belinda he'd be reading the winning one-act?"

Charlie's expression was arrested, then slowly slid into disappointment and disgust. "Goddamnit, Renee," he muttered.

"Belinda seems to think this O'Grady's involved," I pressed, brow furrowing in a way I knew would greatly upset the aesthetician I saw back home. *Wrinkles, Damien! Your face is your fortune!*

"Renee," Charlie began, then paused as he stared up at the ceiling for a long, quiet moment. "Renee loved being the main character," he breathed. "The louder the applause, the more roses on the stage, the happier she was." He huffed. "Was. That doesn't feel right to say at all."

I watched his back as he turned, wandered towards the open doors of the auditorium, and just stood there staring into the dimness. "I know this means a lot to you, doing this for her," I said carefully, "but there's still time. We can make the announcement right now, get the word out…"

"No," he barked, still turned away. "No. This is the last thing Renee did. I want to make sure it goes off as smoothly as possible for her." He took a few steps into the auditorium, then paused. "Is this… is this where she was?" he rasped.

"Mr. Arnold. Charlie…"

"No, no, I know it is. It has to be." He glanced back, giving me a sad, thin smile. "You're staying all the way back there. You don't wanna go in there because that's where… that's where you found her." He sniffed again, wet and broken, before waving me off. "Damn it, I need some air. Gimme a minute." He strode past me, popping the front doors open from the inside and stepping out into the balmy afternoon.

Margie popped out of the office at the sound of the doors, brows raised askance. "Outside," I said, and she nodded, hurrying after Charlie.

Alone in the echoing space, I took another look through the office, not surprised to see no sign of food or water bowls for Muffin. Margie and Charlie hadn't returned, so I slipped through the auditorium doors to take a look at the stage. Someone had already been there to clean it, I noticed. The smell of bleach and some other chemical I couldn't place was strong. There was no sign of the sandbag, and the dark stain was virtually unnoticeable unless you knew where to look.

Unfortunately, I did.

"Ms. Rhodes, I know you can't hear me right now," I murmured, then paused. "Wait, can you? Gotta admit, I'm not sure about a lot of stuff, including the afterlife. And if there is one and you're there, I really hope you're not spending your time watching us do this because, gotta say, boring AF. I'd be spending my time hanging out with Burt Reynolds or something. Anyway. So. You can't hear me, but if you can, I'm sorry this happened. And I wish I'd come back sooner. Maybe I could've helped."

I waited, not sure for what, and finally, when the quiet and emptiness got to be too heavy, too intimate, I hustled myself back to the foyer.

The main doors were open, and in the doorway, frowning at his phone, stood Ben.

"Your face is going to stick like that if the wind changes," I called.

He glanced up. "I'll take that under advisement. Are you done?"

I nodded. "There's nothing."

"Damien, are you coming?"

I jerked my chin up and matched Ben's glare. "I thought you'd already gone."

"Do you really think it's a good idea to leave you in here alone? Especially if you think there's a murderer on the loose?"

"I never said that!"

He rolled his eyes again. I had the feeling the man got plenty of practice, finding other people to be so unbearable and all. "You didn't have to. I've known Margie long enough to know the look of someone thinking about making other people's business theirs."

"Hey!" I jogged after him, regretting my vintage Vans slip-ons. Zero arch support and they were *not* meant for a speed above *leisurely stroll*.

"This *is* my business since I was the one who found her, and now I'm the one the cops want to stick around in case they have questions!"

Ben stopped halfway down the walk. "Were you planning on running off, then?"

"Good lord, what are you, a lawyer?"

His smile was sharp and smug. "Yes. Yes, I am."

Well, hell.

Ben strode towards his shiny black car, leaving me to follow at a less swift pace.

It was because I was so focused on expressing my displeasure through my walk that I almost missed the tow truck, Ben's heavy hand on my shoulder stopping me from striding out into the path of the oncoming vehicle, a lime green beast emblazoned with *O'Neill's Auto and Nails.* .

Ms. Rhodes' fancy little electric car was on the flatbed.

Ben stopped next to me, both of us watching the driver get the car secured for several moments. "Are you towing that to O'Neill's?" Ben called.

The driver gave him the thumbs up. "Storing it till someone can come take it off our hands or the estate gets sorted."

"The cops are done?" I asked.

The driver shrugged. "With the car at any rate. Lieutenant Nichols called us in this morning so…" He shrugged again. "One of you'ns family?"

"Uh, no. I'm just here for the festival," I said.

Charlie made a soft, disconsolate sound and turned away, walking unsteadily towards Margie's car.

Margie muttered something about keeping an eye on him and hurried after, leaving just Ben and me with the tow driver.

He grunted, pushing some lever on the flatbed and nodding in satisfaction at the thunking sound it made. "Well. Looks like that's off, huh?" He disappeared around the side of the truck and a moment later came the sound of the cab door closing.

Ben tugged me back a few feet as the tow truck started up and began to move. We watched it pull out with Ms. Rhode's other pride and joy in the back, disappearing through the arbored gate and onto Lester Road.

After an awkward few moments, Ben jingled his car keys and gave me a nudge toward his car. "Look, Margie is a very… creative person sometimes. And she lives for drama. Don't let her convince you this was anything other than an accident."

Pique poked me right in the chest as I shot him a glare. "How do you know? It could be—"

"Damien, they wouldn't have the car towed to O'Neill's if it was a suspected murder. They'd send it for processing at an official site over in August or Bangor."

He had a point, and I hated it. Still, I let him goad me back into the car, my desire to walk all but gone now. Something about seeing the car towed off, knowing Ms. Rhodes would never be back for it, that she'd never be back for Muffin, just made everything feel heavier. More real.

Maybe this trip wasn't the start over boost I'd been hoping for. Maybe it was just a big ol' sign that it was time for me to stop.

FIVE

My funk held strong even after I returned from the theater and trudged up to my room, Muffin—fat and sassy from an afternoon of sneaky treats slipped under the table courtesy of the Moon sisters—trotted after me, amber eyes glowing in the poorly lit corridor. "C'mon, spooky," I muttered, letting him lope ahead of me into the room. He turned his nose up at the fancy treats again—I lived in hope he'd decide they were the bee's knees and eschew the ones that stank of old leather and 7-Eleven hotdogs—and curled up in front of the cold hearth, heaving a contented sigh before falling into a snoring snooze. I flopped onto the bed and rifled through the papers Belinda had left, Carmel or Sienna—my money was on Carmel—dropping them off in my room while I was gone. I rifled through the handful of papers she'd left me and found them mostly useless—a hastily written eulogy by Belinda that was more purple than not, a printout of Ms. Rhodes' acting credits dating back to the late seventies, and her earliest roles in some off-off-off-Broadway productions that sounded awful, even by the standards of the era (though I must admit *Sex and Cheese on Long Island: A Musical* sounded like a nice way to pass a Sunday afternoon). The last page was a list of names, the only ones I recognized being mine, the Moon sisters, Ben Witte, Belinda Gleaves, and now Charlie Arnold. "Great," I muttered.

I huffed another sigh and flipped back to the front of the packet. Belinda's rough outline wasn't bad, but it desperately needed fleshing out, which meant off to Broadway Database I went, once I was able to unfog my head and maybe shake off some of this ick feeling that had settled over me. A walk sounded like it was in order.

Muffin raised his head, attentive beastie that he was, and gave a soft *wuff* of curiosity as I sat up. "Walk?" I suggested.

He hopped up and headed for the door, tail wagging dangerously fast.

Before I reached the stairs, the whisper-shouting voices of the Moon sisters stopped me in my tracks.

"Damn it, Carmel. I know you've got a soft spot for him, but you need to tell that man to calm the hell down. He's gonna get himself hurt."

Me? Were they talking about me?

"Charlie's hurting, Sienna," Carmel snapped. "He needs a friend right now!"

"See what happened to his last *friend*?"

"Sienna!"

Okay, definitely not me, but what the hell?

"He's insisting on seeing this festival through." Carmel sighed after a tense silence. "I told him why that's a bad idea but—"

"But," Sienna said with a sniff, sounding closer now, "he's never not going to bend over backwards for Renee Rhodes."

"Sienna, please," Carmel groaned. "I know you and her didn't get along, but try to see it from his point of view! They were best friends for years before he moved here for work. Now she's dead just when they were starting to get back in one another's good graces. He's rattled."

"Addled more like," Sienna grumbled. "I can't tell you what to do—don't give me that look, Carmel Anne!—but I can tell you to be careful. You're my baby sister, damn it. Charlie's not right in the head. Between the drinking and the mooning after Renee, he's never been as good a friend to you as you've been to him."

I edged back towards the stairs as it sounded like they were near the kitchen door now and would be able to see me if they opened it even a little bit.

Carmel made a frustrated sound, followed by Sienna's heavy sigh of resignation. "I'm going to change clothes and stop by to see him," Carmel said flatly. "I'd hope someone cared enough about me if I lost my best friend to at least check on me without the expectation of getting something out of me in return."

The kitchen door slammed open, and Carmel strode past. I don't think she even noticed I was there as she stormed towards the quarters she shared with Sienna.

Speak of the devil. Sienna stepped out of the kitchen and caught my eye. "Belinda asked you to do the eulogy, yeah?"

"Yeah," I agreed, only a little whiplashed from the sudden change in tone. "I barely knew Ms. Rhodes, but Belinda handed off some research." I shrugged. "It's the least I could do, really. She brought me all the way out here, she busted her back to get the festival started…" Trailing off, I watched Sienna glare at the bags of flour and nuts she'd brought from the pantry. "Am I missing something here?"

Sienna uttered a mirthless *ha*, nodding her head in the direction Carmel had departed. "Yeah. Loads."

She started measuring the flour into a huge metal bowl, back firmly to me.

I'd been dismissed.

The appeal of getting out of the inn and shaking off the weird heavy feeling of *something's not right here* increased tenfold. Muffin was only too happy to be of assistance, shaking off his middle of the floor nap and loping to the front door with an expectant glance over his shoulder at me.

"Yeah… yeah, good idea. Let me grab your leash. And figure out when I became the sort of person who has full-on conversations with dogs."

LESTER COVE WAS a charming little town, from what I'd seen, and with everything going pear-shaped in the past twenty-four hours, I decided it wasn't a bad idea to take a nice long walk, get some air, and see some more of the town, if only to get my mind off things. Securing the harness and lead to Muffin once more, we headed out towards the main street area of Lester Cove, just about a mile from the B&B. The street Two Moons was on—Lester Court—was a quaint little square that had once been carriage houses and servants' housing back when the town was first coming up in the eighteenth century, but time and necessity had turned it into a neat little neighborhood of small old homes centered around a postage stamp sized park with a statue of Generic White Guy in the middle (allegedly Amias Lester, the original landowner and town founder, but it looked like every other Our Founding Father statue between here and Philadelphia). Turning right would take me to a narrow old nameless lane that led down to the shore and the lighthouse path, but going left would put me on Buttermilk Road, the adorably named main street in town. I told this all to Muffin as we walked, but he didn't seem to care very much at all.

"For a guy who just lost his best friend and caregiver, you're sure taking things in stride," I informed him.

He did not deign to give me a reply.

It was all fairly decent walk from the B&B to the main drag, a long portion of Buttermilk Road where old-fashioned storefronts and standalone shops mixed with some newer places, like O'Neill Auto Repair and Nails at the very top of the street. Deciding to start my tour of downtown there, I gave Muffin a gentle nudge towards the far end of Buttermilk Road, where it curved down towards the New Yacht Club, according to the sign posted at the entrance to the street. *New Yacht Club: 2 Miles. The Sleepy Pelican: 1.5 Miles. Lester Cove Museum and Gift Shop: 1 Mile,* and so on, all held up by a cheerful painted crab wearing a tricorn hat.

There was just a lot going on there, aesthetically.

A few knots of tourists lingered outside some of the little shops, and there was a line at the tiny museum which surprised me—I guess the history of Lester Cove, Maine was a draw for a certain segment of the population. *Max would love this place,* I thought, glancing at the group waiting to get into the old house turned museum. *History, seafood, and cheesy t-shirts all in a one-block radius.*

Speaking of Max, I realized he hadn't gotten back to me, so I shot a quick text off.

ME

> Hey. Proof of life bestie. You never texted me back this morning.

My phone buzzed urgently in my hip pocket just as soon as I tucked it away, a familiar cadence I'd picked out for Max ages ago. With a sigh of something like relief, I answered before the pattern was even done. "I cannot believe you didn't call me," Max whined by way of greeting. "I had to find out about this from *Starpalooza*!"

"The hell? The tabs have this already?" I guided Muffin towards a bench tucked into one of the many little pocket parks that dotted Buttermilk Road, old gardens or empty lots that once had houses and were now conveniently located sitting areas full of local plants and the occasional demanding seagull. Muffin gave me sad eyes when I didn't automatically produce a handful of those smelly treats and instead pulled a chew toy from my jacket pocket. He accepted grudgingly, though the fervor with which he attacked it a moment later told me bygones were bygones over the treats.

"It's vulture o'clock," Max intoned in a creepy voice. "It hit the end-of-day news cycle, apparently. Well, early here, end of day there."

Checking my phone, I noticed it was just past four in Maine, which made it… I frowned, my brain not sufficiently caffeinated enough to do math. "What time is it where you are?"

"Just past 10 p.m. in Stockholm. Want me to get you a little straw goat from the gift shop at the hotel? It's apparently a thing here."

"Yes, please. And what are you doing in Stockholm?" Last I'd heard, he'd been in Zurich.

"Working, lazy bones. What're you doing in Maine? Oh, wait, I forgot —you're getting involved in a murder."

The way he said murder, like Brian Blessed giving it his all, made me snort. "Hardly. I mean, I did find her but—"

"That's what was in *Starpalooza*! And I quote, former child star found with body of Broadway actress."

"Oh my god." That was enough to get me to abandon my search through Renee Rhodes' wiki abandoned in favor of some not-so-low-key freakout.

Also, who knew she had a Wiki? Not me. It'd been updated by *MrReneeRhodesFan* less than a week before, adding some little-known bit parts from her teen years as an up-and-coming actress, and her only two commercials, one for some brand of hairspray in the early eighties and another for a time-share in Boca that was apparently a very local and limited run situation since a footnote indicated the time-share had been seized by the feds for some tax reason or other.

"Rory's called me three times this morning, trying to get in touch with you. You should ignore your messages by the bye. Except for the ones I left."

Max hated my agent, Rory, with the burning intensity of a thousand desert suns. He'd tried to get me to move over to Kathleen Biggs, his agent, for years, but I'd resisted out of some sense of loyalty to Rory. Rory had been the one to get me my first parts, and he'd stuck with me even when my career trajectory was more of a slightly wavy line rather than a meteoric rise. Or any kind of rise, really. Rory was a prick, self-aggrandizing, over-charging, and had the tendency to push for sensationalism when it came to promotion, but the chances of me finding an agent willing to work with me at this point in my career? Okay, they were better than I told myself, I was sure, but making that leap was terrifying.

Max was fond of reminding me I could do *so much better,* and that Kathleen had contacts in theater and with some of the big streaming services, but… Well, I was scared, okay? With Rory, I knew what I was getting. And I owed him, as he was fond of reminding me. Without him, my first movie would've been my last.

Some people worked out and developed muscles, I over thought and developed guilt complexes.

"He must be loving that lede," I grumbled, scooting lower on the bench, stretching out my legs and startling Muffin into a soft *wuff* of confusion before he seemed to remember where he was and who I was. Or wasn't, as the case may be. He flopped his head back down and cushioned on the fancy chew bone I'd spent too much money on at the pet store and heaved a beleaguered sigh before ignoring me again.

"No PR is bad PR," Max muttered in a near-perfect imitation of Rory's smoky voice. "And did I just hear a dog? Or are you back to bear hunting again?"

"Shut up," I grumbled. "That was one summer, and it did not work out."

"I don't know. That one guy you picked up at Boy Bar seemed attached."

"Jerkface. He was a stalker. I had to get a restraining order and everything." It had been my first big foray into the queer dating scene and, looking back, had been a very bad idea. Not because I'm not into bears (sometimes I am) or I have something against the bar scene, but because I picked the most see-and-be-seen bar in WeHo, crawling with *I'm a waiter while waiting for my callback* climbers. Exhibit A: The burly bear who was not allowed within fifty feet of me or my place of work but seemed to think I was his ticket to stardom.

I'd made strict no bars, no apps, no blind dates rule after that experience.

Max muttered for me to hold on and for a moment, the phone muffled as he had a brief conversation with someone on his end. "Hey," he sighed. "I need to go in a minute. My scene's been moved up. Twyla's got *food poisoning* again."

"Seriously? I thought she had that sober companion to stop that from happening."

"Twyla fired her last month," Max sighed. "The director's about had it. Our filming schedule's all goofy right now while he tries to arrange shooting around her bouts of *food poisoning* and *jet lag*."

I winced. "Can't her agent do anything about it?"

Max sighed. "Maybe. I don't really know. Twyla's old-school, and her PR is all about keeping her retro Hollywood vibe. They're trying to get her through to the *Foxy Ladies* reunion movie next year and after that…"

He trailed off and I could only sigh along with him. It was a sad fact of life our field attracted, or maybe created, people with problems like Twyla's. Not always alcohol, but you couldn't swing a PA in Hollywood— or Broadway, for that matter—without hitting someone doing the steps, or needing the steps, or in some form of recovery or other.

"Seriously, though, you doing okay?" Max asked. "I saw that headline and nearly broke my neck getting back to my trailer. Did you really find her?"

I gave him a quick rundown about my past twenty-four hours, including my brief encounter with Mr. Darcy's Evil Twin.

"Dude, sounds like Mr. Darcy, period. The guy was a dick in all iterations of the story."

"Why am I even friends with you?" I complained, and Max laughed. "He was misunderstood." I sniffed. "Awkward."

"Mmmhmm. And this Ben guy. Is he misunderstood and awkward?"

"Oh, shut up. He's just a schmuck."

"If you say so," he teased. "Sorry you got stuck with the eulogy, though. I mean, it's bad enough to stumble on her body and have a third-rate tab accuse you of murder. but—"

"It was an accident," I said staunchly. "A horrible accident."

I could practically *hear* the arch of his brow. "That's what the authorities said?"

I fidgeted. "They haven't *not* said it wasn't an accident."

"That is the most tangled sentence I've heard since the time we went to see the am-dram production of *Rosencrantz and Guildenstern are Dead*."

"Wow," I drawled. "That was a deep cut."

"I'm an actor, not a writer. I'm not so good with the words and analogies and junk unless someone writes it out for me beforehand."

That reminded me… "Hey, want to know something weird?"

"Always."

"One of the people who entered the one-act contest for the festival mentioned Ms. Rhodes was going to send the winners' plays on to Callum Grady. He—"

"Retired," Max cut in. "My friend Paul—he's an absolute maven of industry gossip for New York, especially Broadway—I remember he told me about it, and it stuck out so much because it was the same day he finally got the guts up to ask me out."

"Why would Ms. Rhodes tell people that, though? Do you think maybe she misspoke?"

"I think," he said carefully, "you are a very big-hearted person and prone to believe the best in people."

"But why would she lie?" It came out as a whine but couldn't be helped —the idea of her lying, especially about something so important to the entrants, was just bizarre.

"Was that in the contest info? I can't imagine it being out there and no one catching it until now. No offense."

"It—" I paused, frowning. "I don't think so," I admitted. "Only one person mentioned it to me. And she sounded like a Renee Rhodes super fan. Or maybe she's just a fan of being a fan?"

"Huh?"

"You know the kind. They envision themselves as the in-crowd sort. Knowing all sorts of insider info, being close to the stars…"

"Ugh. Yeah… Remember that girl in the 80s, the one who was in that horror franchise? She had that number one fan who…" He trailed off.

A chill raced down my neck and spread through my ribs. "Sarah Jackson," I murmured. "Star of the *Hollow Hills* movies. She was murdered by a waitress she'd befriended at her favorite restaurant."

"Polly Newsom," Max said, barely above a whisper. "She'd told people Sarah had gotten her in with her agent, if I recall correctly."

"And when Sarah confronted her about it, Polly killed her." It had been one of those stories that, over the years, had faded to the back of the public mind but was whispered as a cautionary tale to most young actors, warning us not to believe offers of friendship, not to get too close to those not in the industry. A boogeyman story born of tragedy. Poor Sarah Jackson had been shot outside of her trailer on set, Polly gaining access to her because a security guard believed her when she claimed to be Sarah's stand-in, running late to the set. Polly went to prison still swearing Sarah had made her promises, no matter how many times her claims were disproven.

Belinda couldn't be another Polly, could she?

"So, Renee Rhodes didn't get shot, did she?" Max asked in a rush. "I mean, you know I won't tell anyone if—"

"I know. And no, it was a sandbag."

Max made a startled, choking sound. "A *what*?"

"You know, the kind used in the old-school rigging systems in the days before safety was a thing? It fell on her."

I didn't say what I knew we were both thinking: *Maybe.*

Max was quiet. I could almost see him rubbing his temples like he did when I effed up royal. "Damien, be careful, okay?"

"Of course. Wouldn't want to give Rory an excuse to come down here and see me in person, would I?"

We said our goodbyes and, a moment later, Max sent me a text with Paul's contact info.

Muffin huffed his annoyance at me, so I decided that was enough of our sitting. "Come on, Muffin. Let's get our steps in."

<hr>

"SO APPARENTLY, at least two other people think her death is sus," I informed Muffin as we walked down the cobblestone sidewalk. He was a fairly good sounding board, as far as these things went. He didn't mind me rambling all my ideas out, and I didn't mind his fondness for landscaping. I was glad I'd stuck to my green Vans and hadn't opted for my three seasons old Gucci loafers, no matter how cute they'd look with my skinny jeans and the t-shirt I'd splurged on at the Linda Linda's show last summer. "Polly Newsom," I muttered to Muffin. "Poor Sarah. She was younger than me."

Obsessed fans were a fact of life in the industry, some actors taking it as a weird, horrifying compliment when they got unhinged letters and boxes of, ahem, personal items sent from fans who didn't understand we're real people and not some fictional character they've dreamed up. But most of us were scared of the possibility. Of fans like Polly Newsom deciding we'd wronged them somehow and taking it upon themselves to get some sort of revenge.

Don't forget even non-famous people get murdered too… I winced at that thought. It was true, though. I'd been so focused on the fan angle that the notion Renee Rhodes could've been killed for other, personal reasons hadn't crossed my mind yet.

A jilted lover? A business partner? Someone she wronged? Or maybe, I thought as we drew to a halt for Muffin to investigate one of the planters that dotted the street, someone who wronged **her** and wanted to shut her up before she called them out publicly?

Sandbags don't just fall for no reason.

We walked a bit further, passing Witte's Teas on the opposite side of the street. Ben Witte was just going in, his tall, black-clad form a dark shadow against the brightly painted storefront. I don't know if he felt me looking or if it was just bad luck, but he looked up at me as we drew even. His glare was sharp enough to cut me at fifty paces, but I hadn't spent my life around divas and cutthroat agents for nothing. I could issue a cut direct that'd make an Austen heroine swoon. Wishing I had my green faux fur swing coat on for the drama of it all, I tossed my head and strode down the cobbles, Muffin trotting along apace.

Until I tripped over one of those damned charming stones and went knees-first into a puddle of runoff from Lester Cove Organic Produce-N-More's rain gutters.

"Oh no!" A woman with a basket of overpriced melon rushed over from one of the old-fashioned displays by the shop's doors. "Are you alright?"

"Tell me something," I said through a tight smile. "Is there a man in front of the tea shop?"

She glanced up. "Yes."

"Is he good looking?"

"Uh…"

"Tall, dark-haired, looks like butter wouldn't melt in his mouth?"

"Um, no. It's just Charlie Arnold. He's alright I suppose." She cocked her head, frowning. "Maybe a bit too old for my personal taste, but not bad all in all." Her eyes widened slightly. "He's heading over."

"Crud. Thanks."

She nodded, scuttling back to perusing the outdoor display of produce while Muffin ignored me entirely in favor of the very interesting tree doing its best in one of those street planter things.

Charlie Arnold reached my side before I managed to get to my feet. "Are you alright? That was one hell of a spill, son."

"I'm fine, all good here." Except my smart-casual rose-pink skinny jeans were now mud-stained and had a tear in one knee. And I'd drawn the attention of everyone in the grocery store as well as a few people on the sidewalk.

Oh my god, please don't let this be the moment I suddenly have wide recognition.

Charlie helped me up and sorted out Muffin, who'd managed to tangle his leash around a leg of the wooden display case of rainbow chard. "You being a good boy, little man?" Charlie asked. For a horrified moment, I thought he was talking to me, but Muffin's yip and prance routine relieved me of shoving my foot all the way down my throat. "He's always been such a good pup." Charlie sighed, looking up to meet my gaze. "Let me buy you a coffee or some tea. You look like you could use a cup!"

"Oh, I was just out running some errands," I muttered. "I was actually going to stop by the tea shop later."

Charlie's expression grew sharp. "Ah?"

Damn it. That slipped. "Oh, since I'm giving a eulogy, I figured talk to people who knew her best. In fact, I was thinking maybe you'd like to give it?" We were halfway across the road, and he stopped, turning his face up to the sky and shaking his head mirthlessly. "Charlie, you okay?"

"You'd better do it, son. I knew her for… well, a lifetime, but me giving the eulogy? I don't think I can."

Someone honked, so we moved again, Muffin leading the way into the tea shop.

Inside, it looked empty, but the sound of barely restrained voices seeped through the strains of sixties pop music playing on the speakers. "She's chatting with Ben," Charlie said, shrugging. "She'll be a minute. Those two are oil and vinegar. Always have been."

"You sound like you've known both Margie and Ms. Rhodes a while," I noted. Muffin circled at my feet and flumped down as if the weight of the world was on his shoulders. Charlie reached down absently to give him a scritch before replying.

"Lester Cove is a small town," he said. "It's not exactly a tourist hot spot these days. People would rather go to the Vineyard or Provincetown if you swing that way." The look he gave me blatantly said he knew I did. "This little town used to be different, though. It drew people in from New York, Boston, hell even Toronto. We'd get a few folks from the flyovers and out west, but Lester Cove was more of a see-and-be-seen place for people out here." He shrugged again, looking a little sheepish but proud at the same time. "One of those post-Gilded Age weekend retreats for the robber baron's sons and daughters, then later on the movers and shakers whose money was too old for LA but not old enough for Manhattan."

"I noticed there's a yacht club," I offered. "That sounds pretty rich people activity to me."

He snorted softly. "Lester Cove has a big regatta mid-autumn, before Halloween but after school's back in. The old yacht club at the far end of the cove was one of those see-and-be-seen places back in the day. The new yacht club though…" He trailed off. "Well, Renee would have been the first to tell you that it was too *common*, not exclusive enough; it'd lost its purpose."

"Its purpose being exclusivity?" The more I heard about Renee Rhodes, the sicker I felt. It was one thing to be charmingly eccentric, but she was starting to sound mean.

Charlie spread his hands. *Just so* the gesture said.

"The whole reason Renee moved here in the first place was because she wanted to be the one to bring Lester Cove back to its former glory—her words, not mine."

He smiled sadly, both of us pretending not to hear Margie's sharply barked, *"Get the hell out of my kitchen, you ungrateful child!"*

"Was she succeeding?"

"Maybe. I'm not sure." He laced his fingers together on the tabletop. I didn't miss the tremor that ran through them as he straightened his spine and pinned me with a watery, uncertain stare. "The thing is… Renee made a lot of promises she couldn't keep. She'd always been like that. And I think… No, I know she made promises to some folks that were going to come back and hurt her deeply."

"Mr. Arnold," I began, but he shook his head.

"Charlie. Please."

"Alright. Charlie. Why are you telling me this?"

Charlie blinked, lowering his chin and turning his face away from me quickly. His shoulders shook, and it took him a long moment to compose himself while the girl group singing overhead went on about being asked to dance, about how that boy looked so nice, so they took a chance. When Charlie faced me again, his eyes were red and wet, his color virtually nonexistent and the school dance had changed to a calendar girl. "I'm going about this so wrong." He sighed. "None of it feels real. You were the one who… who…"

"Found her," I murmured. "Yes."

"I heard someone say she'd been stabbed."

The flat, hurried way he said the words told me they hurt him, they haunted him. That he was visualizing Ms. Rhodes' demise even now. "No," I murmured. "She wasn't stabbed. Who told you that?"

His quick glance towards the kitchen answered that question for me. Ben or Margie had either started the gossip or let it filter back to Charlie.

"How…" he began, but I shook my head, cutting him off.

"I don't think it'd do you any good to know the details," I said.

He looked like he wanted to fight about it for a moment but slowly, he sank back into the padded back of the booth and nodded.

"Charlie, I wanted to ask you something. About the one-act contest."

The kitchen door swung open, and Ben Witte strode out, lips pressed into a thin line and color high as he rounded the counter and headed for the door, stopping only when he noticed us sitting in the booth. "Damien," he muttered stiffly. "Mr. Arnold."

"Ben," Charlie acknowledged. "How long you in town for?"

Ben glanced at me before answering. "Depends. When's Renee's memorial?"

Charlie's remaining color leached out of his face, and his chin wobbled.

"Wow, way to be compassionate, Ben," I snapped. "The man's grieving!"

If it'd been possible for Charlie to make himself smaller, he'd have winked out of sight at that moment. His hitched breath was louder than Elvis's insistence he was evil as could be.

"Ben," Margie barked. "I thought you were leaving."

Ben shot me a slightly confused look but nodded, heading for the door once more, only to stop and look back at me and Charlie. "I know this is an awful time for you, Charlie. And I'm sorry to have been part of it."

What the hell?

Charlie didn't so much nod as wobble his head slightly.

Margie jabbed her finger at the door and Ben gave her an angry wave, leaving in a clatter of bells as the ones over the door jangled angrily. "I'm so sorry," Margie murmured, hurrying to our booth. "I didn't hear you guys come in. Ben just surprised me and…" She trailed off, fluttering a hand by her throat. "Well. He'll be heading back to Boston on Monday, thank the heavens."

Charlie's sniff this time was less grief and more distaste. "He and Renee always did butt heads, but she respected him. And I'd like to think he did her, too."

"Ben's your stepson," I said, pointing to Margie before swinging my attention to Charlie. "Did you teach him in high school, Charlie?"

"He never took theater or drama classes," Charlie shrugged. "He was in one play, from what I can recall—it's been over a decade, understand. He somehow managed to crash the entire set during opening night."

I'm sure my gaping maw was just *so* attractive as I stared at Charlie. "The… *how*? I mean, I've bumped into things on set before, but I've never managed to take down an entire set. I think the worst I did was some props on a kitchen table once." If I recalled correctly, that was also why Menton Greely refused to work with me anymore. He insisted on all 'his' actors having 'natural, fluid grace' and I was 'a lumbering jackass' at age thirteen.

Hollywood, folks.

Charlie huffed softly. "I have no idea how he managed it. I remember being in the balcony, headset on, and then," he made a hand motion that looked like something dropping, then hitting and splattering on the table. "All the sandbags came down, the backdrop fell, and Delly Dutton broke two toes in the ensuing stampede off stage."

"Sandbags," I repeated, seizing on the phrase like Muffin with that chewy rope Carmel gave her that morning. "He caused them to fall?"

Margie had gone still, lips parted as she white-knuckled her mug.

"Boom," Charlie agreed, making the hand motion again. "Narrowly missed hitting Jessie Minette. The only good thing to come of it was the school board let us fundraise for a better rigging system, and we replaced the whole shebang with something electric the next year after Jessie's parents threatened to sue over their daughter's life being endangered."

Margie shook her head slowly. "I remember that. Johnathan and I'd just gotten married that past summer. Ben was so angry. I'd hoped being involved in something like theater would've helped him express his feelings better. And, well, pardon my observation, but he's not a bad looking young man. He'd have been fantastic on stage."

Charlie's eye roll was subtle, but I still caught it. "Ben had no interest in theater. Or drama. Now band… He did love his music." Charlie sighed, wilting in on himself again. "Renee would've been so good with kids like him," he murmured, eyes filling with tears. "I can't believe someone would have done this to her!"

Catching Margie's wide-eyed gaze, I shrugged diffidently. "He's heard rumors about her cause of death, but they're wrong. I… I saw her. And I can assure you she wasn't stabbed."

"How then?" Margie whispered. "Damien, if someone's out there killing townsfolk, we deserve to know!"

I didn't know how disclosing Ms. Rhodes' cause of death would do anything to alleviate Margie's concerns and I said as much, adding "Lieutenant Nichols seems convinced it was an accident, and I haven't had one single call or visit from the authorities either here or at the state level."

"Oh, that Heath Nichols," she muttered, brushing her hands on her smock apron distractedly. "I'd always hoped he and Ben would kiss and make up, but I suppose not everyone can be as lucky as me and Johnathan were."

Charlie pushed away from the table and hurried towards the bathroom at the back of the store, Margie sputtering in surprise. "Ben and Lieutenant

Nichols?" I asked, unable to focus on anything else for the moment. "They dated?"

"Oh, for a year or two, yup," Margie said, staring after Charlie. "Ben insists it was just a youthful fling, but Heath…" She glanced at me, offering a small, tired smile. "Well, Heath took it hard. Ben was so heartless about the breakup."

Yikes. "Is he usually cold? I mean, he seems kind of brusque, but is that like an all the time thing or…"

Margie sighed and leaned back in her seat, fixing me with a hard look. "Damien, I know Ben's not hard on the eyes, and he's got that whole Rochester thing going on—"

"Darcy," I mumbled, and she snorted softly.

"Well, Byronic hero, how about that?" She chuckled. "He's good on paper, but I've known that boy since he was barely thirteen, and he's not easy to be around. Always angry, curt, and, well, frankly, I don't think he has much empathy. I wouldn't say it's a diagnosable thing but that boy… Well, I don't like to talk ill of the dead, but I think maybe he takes more after his mother than Johnathan liked to believe." She lowered her voice and whispered, "The late Jenny Witte was a little unstable." She tapped her temple. "It's why they divorced. Frankly, Johnathan was worried for *years* that Ben might have taken after her."

Charlie emerged from the bathroom and headed for the table. "Sorry," he muttered. "It's still new, so…"

We murmured sympathetically as Charlie resettled at the table and Margie fussed over his tea, taking it away to bring him a fresh, hot cup. When she returned, Charlie shook his head, giving her a pleading look as he asked, "Why would someone want to hurt Renee? I can't believe it was just an accident, not after everything."

"Did Renee say something to make you think she was in danger? Should we talk to Heath about it?"

Margie's sharp gaze grew even more intense somehow, making me shift uncomfortably on the squeaky bench seat. Charlie drew a shuddering breath, and when he spoke, his voice was tight and thin. "Renee and I had our differences, but we were working them out. We were supposed to talk this weekend about it and…" He couldn't finish.

Margie clucked over him, scurrying to the kitchen and coming back with a brookie on a tiny white plate and a cup of something that smelled of lavender and oranges. "Now," she said in a soothing, maternal sort of way, "why do you think someone… harmed… Renee?"

Charlie picked at the crisp edges of his brookie for a moment or two before mustering his answer. "When she finally got around to returning my calls last week, she mentioned she was avoiding someone. She'd had some sort of an argument and she was worried they were going to get revenge. That was her exact wording: get revenge."

"For what?"

Charlie jerked back, startled and having apparently forgotten I was there.

"Why was someone seeking revenge against her?"

Margie fussed some more, adding some sugar to Charlie's tea and urging him to drink it, not letting him answer for a minute or two. When he finally gently but firmly shook her off, he *was* calmer, so maybe I couldn't be too annoyed with her for her ministrations. She did know Charlie after all, and maybe she knew how to handle his upset. "Renee is… Was. She was a bold person," Charlie murmured. "She wasn't afraid to go for what she wanted, and she would be the first to tell someone if what they were doing was either doomed to failure or destined for success."

"According to her, anyway," Margie muttered. "Renee was a very big personality. You know the sort, Damien, I'm sure. *Gotta go out there and grab life by the throat*!" She made a choking gesture between us. "Get what you want, all that jazz."

"Oh yeah, for sure. The industry is full of 'em. I imagine it's the same for stage as well as film."

Margie nodded, satisfied. "Not everyone appreciated her particular brand of candor."

Charlie sighed and started to stand. "She was scared of someone," he said, "and now she's dead. Lieutenant Nichols is being a lazy ass, and I'm going to tell him to his face."

"Sit down, Charlie," Margie chided. "Don't go off half-cocked. I know you're upset and, well, frankly, it *does* look strange, her dying like this, but trying to rile up Lieutenant Nichols is only going to make him double down. Isn't that right, Damien?"

"Er, I suppose," I allowed. The sandbag shouldn't have been there. The system had been replaced years ago. There'd been a similar accident when Ben was in school. Someone was mad at Renee, and Ben seemed dismissive of her death. He had been at the gala and seemed annoyed with her…

"And," Margie continued, giving me a very pointed look, "we'll help you find out who killed her, won't we, Damien?"

I nodded slowly. Renee Rhodes was dead and, for all intents and purposes, alone. No family to speak of, no close friends, a sparkling career that was already far enough in the past to ensure she would only be a headline in one or two niche publications and forgotten by next week… She'd struggled her way up to sustainable success, something I'd yet to do. *We're alike*, she'd said at the gala, practically her last words to me.

Muffin chose that moment to wake up from his nap and snuffle gently at all of our feet, sighing when he didn't find who he was looking for. "Yes, yes we will," I blurted. "In fact, we'll start now. Come on, Muffin, let's go."

"Where are you headed?" Margie demanded.

"To talk to Lieutenant Nichols! I have questions about that sandbag!"

"Sandbag?" Charlie gasped. "What do you mean?"

"Renee Rhodes was killed by a falling sandbag," I said. *In for a penny…* "If there's no sandbag rig at the theater, how the hell did that happen?"

Margie had gone pale and wide-eyed. Charlie was still as the grave. "A sandbag," he muttered. "She was killed by…"

"Charlie," I began, but Margie sprang into motion, waving me off.

"Go. I'll take care of him! You talk to Heath and get this ball rolling!"

SIX

"**D**amien Murphy." Lieutenant Nichols said my name with a sort of lilt and a small smile that made me think I'd amused him somehow. He was the only one in the department, from the looks of things. The other three desks in the bullpen were empty, and the front desk had an *Out to Lunch— Back at One!* sign on it.

It was half past.

It'd taken me nearly an hour to find the little police department—a cottage-sized building hidden between the Town Hall and Lester Cove History Museum and Gift Shop. I'd debated leaving Muffin with the Moon sisters, but I'd already trespassed on their hospitality enough, beyond just being a guest of their inn. They'd been so accommodating of Muffin's presence that asking them to watch him for a bit so I could talk to the cops felt icky. And the idea of doubling back was just… a lot. I wanted to get this over with.

Also, I wasn't sure how to explain needing to talk to the cops. I think Ben Witte might've killed Renee Rhodes, and Belinda's kinda sus, too. Mind watching the dog for me, byeeeeee!

And really, I wasn't sure how to even drop that bombshell on Nichols either. He was staring at me expectantly, a small smile on his lips as he reclined in his desk chair, legs out and ankles crossed in an attitude of relaxation. "Lieutenant Nichols," I began.

"Heath."

"No, Damien."

"No, *Heath.*" He chuckled, pointing to himself. "Call me Heath. I'm on lunch break, so no need for formality."

Oh, no. He got to his feet and closed the distance between us, stopping just out of arm's reach. Muffin, the traitor, wagged his tail and did a little prancey dance I was starting to recognize as his expression of happiness. He'd done it for a few people, for bacon, for, well, a muffin, and for the gross-smelling beef jerky treats from Paws for Pets.

Not so much on the food, though. That he'd just sort of sulked at before slowly munching on the kibble and shooting me baleful glares.

"So, Damien, what brings you by the office?"

"Uh, Renee Rhodes' murder?"

"Are you asking or telling?"

"Both."

He leaned back against the desk, giving me an assessing and amused look. "Both? How's that work out? Is that an acting exercise I've never heard of?"

"Seriously?"

Nichols' smile grew just a little wider. "See, I knew you're an actor, but gotta be honest and say I hadn't seen much of your stuff. So, I did a little digging and found an old YouTube video of you looking like you had to be about ten or so, doing some improv exercise with what's his face, that actor who used to do the gross-out comedies but got all into Shakespeare?"

Damn it. Rory had promised me that video had been scrubbed *years* ago after Nelson Twick—the actor in question—posted it on his podcast's website and encouraged his audience to critique my performance.

The jerk was just mad I'd called him out about getting handsy with Max's then-girlfriend.

I sniffed, tugging Muffin closer, away from his perusal of Nichols' work boots. "And somehow came up with acting exercises as a conversation opener?"

He chuckled again. "Maybe I just wanted to start with a subject you were comfortable with."

"It's definitely not that. No, I came here to tell you—"

"Come to lunch with me."

When I stared at him like a startled fish, he took that as an opening and continued, "I'm supposed to be on lunch right now, but Cherry had to run get her kiddo from daycare, so when she gets back, I'm grabbing a bite. Come with me."

"Er, why?"

His smile shrank just a tiny bit. "Maybe I want to get to know you better."

"Am I a suspect?"

There went the rest of his smile. "Seriously? I suggest lunch and getting to know one another, and you assume it's me trying to feel you out as a suspect?"

"I feel like I'm missing about thirty percent of the conversation here," I muttered. "Are you asking me on a date?"

His ears were red and his jaw set. "Just out to lunch. That's it." Darting a glance at the desk, he suddenly busied himself with shuffling some papers that didn't need reorganizing. "Not a date. Just… getting to know you."

Nichols wasn't hard on the eyes, all square-jawed and sandy blond guy-next-door cuteness, like the opposite end of the spectrum from Broody Ben with his closet goth vibes and snappish attitude. *How the hell did those two last a month, much less a year or two?*

Nichols stilled his hands, deliberately folding his arms so he wouldn't fidget. "Well?"

Damn it. "Can I take a raincheck? I. um… I have some errands to run to get this whole eulogy and memorial service dealt with and prep for the festival, such as it is now. But I was about to head back to the inn to start my research. I was thinking…"

He raised an eyebrow expectantly. "Thinking what?"

"Thinking I should learn some more about Ms. Rhodes."

"Well, I'd like to learn some more about *you*," he said, shuffling his feet against the desk. "But I'm not gonna push. How long you in town for again?"

"I thought you weren't going to push."

Muffin wuffed in agreement.

"This isn't pushing. This is information gathering. You're acting skittish, showing up here at the department unrequested, mentioning murder, and now you don't want to tell me how long you're around. Maybe I'm putting two and two together to get five, but what I'm picking up on is some mighty suspicious behavior."

"Yet you still wanted to ask me out."

His smile was slow and easy, the very antithesis of Ben Witte's permascowl. "I like to live dangerously," he chuckled. "Now, if you're not gonna let me take you to lunch today, why don't get to the point of your visit."

"I—well, not just me, but a few of us—think Renee Rhodes' death wasn't an accident."

"Huh." He held up a finger and moved around behind his desk, rummaging in a file folder to present me with a thin packet of papers. "That's not what the Major Crimes Unit thinks. See, they did a whole investigation and determined it was just a tragic accident. And I'm supposed to ask you to sign off on the statement you gave to affirm it, and once that's done, this investigation is closed."

"Oh. Oh!"

"Yeah." He chuckled. "Oh. As much as I get being bored in a small town, gotta break it to ya that this is just an accident. Nothing dramatic here."

"But the sandbag—"

"I know what you're gonna say. There was no rigging."

I could only nod silently.

"It was an old one. The fabric was rotting, apparently, and the rope holding it was shredded. It must've been left up on the catwalk after the old rigging was taken down. It was just a case of horrible timing."

"No," I murmured. "That's… No."

Nichols' smile twisted into one of annoyance and resignation. "I know this is a slow little town sometimes, but you people need to find something else to focus on. Her death was an accident. The state wasn't interested in pursuing the investigation, I frankly don't have the resources here to do it, and like I told your little group this morning—"

"What little group?"

He hesitated. "From the festival. Belinda Gleaves, Ollie Hamm, some of the kids from the high school theater club?"

"I didn't send anyone over here, if that's what you're implying. Wait! Charlie Arnold? Did he come by?" Charlie seemed to imply he hadn't spoken with Nichols yet, but maybe I'd misunderstood.

Or maybe he'd lied.

He'd seemed truly grief-stricken, so the idea of him being involved in Ms. Rhodes' death just didn't gel for me, but stranger things had happened. I mean, I'd gotten the role of Hamlet in *Sixty Second Shakespeare* last year in San Francisco, so anything was possible.

Nichols pushed away from the desk, that smile well and truly gone now. "Charlie Arnold? Seriously? That man always had more sense than not, even when I was in high school. What's he on about then?"

"He… and some other people… think Renee Rhodes' death was intentional. That someone who had a problem with her killed her. Charlie mentioned she was afraid recently, that someone had threatened her over some slight." Muffin tugged hard on the leash, slipped from my grasp, and ducked under the front desk. "Muffin! No!"

Nichols beat me to it, grabbing Muffin's harness and wrestling him back out from under the desk. "That's evidence, mutt," he grumbled. "Stay out!"

I took the leash back and wrapped it twice around my wrist. Maybe if he had to drag me, Muffin would think twice. Then again, he was the size of a small pony. I'd looked up Cane Corsos after Ollie had mentioned his breed and they were *strong,* apparently.

I added a third wrap and hoped for the best.

"Did Charlie give any other reason, or was it just that someone was mad at Renee, and she was feeling called out?"

"He only said that. He was really broken up about her death and—"

"Of course he was," Nichols muttered. "They were married for a few years, and I don't think he ever got over her asking for a divorce."

My jaw dropped so fast I got a cramp. "They *what*?"

"I thought you knew Ms. Rhodes well?" he mocked, cocking one hip to get comfy on that desk.

I was starting to see why Ben broke up with him.

"Not really. And her being married to a high school drama teacher was never in any of her online bios! Tell me more!"

He raised his eyes heavenward, silently asking for strength by the looks of things. "I shouldn't have said anything to start with. Mom always said I had a waggin' tongue."

"Oh, come on!" I pleaded, bouncing a little and giving him the ol' puppy dog eyed innocent look I'd perfected from years of being the sidekick/innocent bestie/expositional yet nameless character there to just remind the audience of what's going on by asking the protagonist *wow what happened?* "You can't just drop that bombshell and then say never mind! Don't be a tease!"

Nichols' cheeks pinked under his dark blond scruff at my pleading. "It was a long time ago, from what Charlie said. Every once in a while, I get called down to the Sleepy Pelican to go pour him back into his apartment on Oyster Road. Whenever I do, he always tells me how Renee was the prettiest, sassiest girl he'd ever met, and he just didn't love her like she deserved."

"Yikes."

"In a word."

The desk phone started ringing and Nichols motioned for me to just wait. "It's probably Cherry telling me she's running late. Hold on."

I nodded, but he'd already turned his back on me to grab the phone.

Muffin snuffled, then whimpered softly, then with a deft twist and jerk pulled free of my attempted anchorage.

Shit.

Nichols didn't notice—whoever he was talking to wasn't Cherry, I was guessing. They were reporting something, and he was talking them through what needed to happen next, getting their information. Slowly, I sidled up to the desk where Muffin was snuffling for his life.

He was sniffing at a cardboard box, pawing and whimpering as he tried to get into it. "Hey, settle down," I muttered, crouching to see what was so interesting. The box had *Ev. 1-1, RR, LC, Palais Theater* on the side, and I knew without a doubt what Muffin had found.

Peeking out from around the desk, I saw Nichols was still on the phone but now sitting behind the front desk, typing at the computer as he took the call. "Shhhh," I urged when Muffin whimpered anew. "Let's see, okay?" In the box was Ms. Rhodes' purse, a bagged and broken martini glass, some papers—also in an evidence bag—that had scrawled notes I couldn't make out, and the thick leather strap I'd taken to be Muffin's leash when I saw it at the theater. On closer inspection, it was a removable purse strap, but it was heavy brown leather and looked cheaply made, one side still unfinished and rough while the other was dyed a darker brown and had a streaky finish. The little clasps used to attach it to the correct purse were brassy, though in spots they'd started to show signs of the artificial color wearing away.

And it definitely did *not* go with Ms. Rhodes' bag, a boucle zebra pattern Kate Spade bag with a gold chain strap. Nichols' voice rose as he argued with whoever was on the other end of the line and I knew I didn't have long before he was done. Muffin was whimpering near constantly at my side now, driving me on. "Shh, shh, shhh…"

The purse was the only thing not bagged up. I gingerly poked my finger into the unfastened bag, pushing it a bit wider. Muffin's pink diamante leash sparkled back at me. *In for a penny…* I slipped it out, or tried to, cursing under my breath when I realized it was tangled in a heavy fob; keys to her electric car and several house key types dangled. No doubt, including the missing key to the theater she didn't return to Charlie. I shifted, checking on Nichols and finding him still busy on his call. Another glance under the desk showed me something else—something that made my stomach execute a slow, greasy flip. Blood-stained fabric and frayed rope.

The empty sandbag, contents gone for testing or something. *Shit…* Seeing her blood through the clear, thick plastic was unsettling, the sight of her life literally spilled out of her body now shoved in a bag under someone's desk. Muffin pawed at my arm as if telling me to hurry. Nichols sighed heavily and told whoever he was talking to that he had to go, that their concern was noted, and he'd bring it up with the board. I grabbed my phone, snapped a few pictures of the purse, the brown strap, and the bloodied rope before popping up just in time for Nichols to turn around and see me at his desk, tugging on Muffin's harness. "Sorry," I said with a breathless laugh perfected after years of playing the awkward sidekick, "Muffin must smell his person on this box."

No use trying to lie about that part—Muffin was going mad trying to paw the thing open and get to the contents himself. "Maybe I should get him home."

Nichols glanced between me, the dog, and the box, his gaze narrowing in suspicion. "That's evidence. Even though it was an accident, we need to hold on to it until her body's released."

"Oh. When's that going to be?"

"As soon as her next of kin or power of attorney signs off on it. And in this case, that'll be Charlie Arnold himself, unless he gets it in his head to demand an autopsy."

I nodded. "Of course."

Nichols peered at me thoughtfully, his stern expression softening. "Damien, you alright? I know I can come off a bit brusque, but I really do want to get to know you better."

I smiled, Sunny Smile Number Six, and nodded. "And we should. After the memorial, though? It's supposed to be on Sunday, and I'm in town till Wednesday, so…"

He nodded. "Here." He grabbed a card from the desk and wrote something on the back. "My personal cell, not my work one. Give me a call when you're ready."

"Oh! Um, thank you." Sunny Smile Number Four. Muffin started to make a soft, mournful howling sound, making us both wince. "I need to get him away from that box, sorry."

Nichols didn't try to stop me, though it felt like he was watching me with a dollop more scrutiny than necessary as I edged past him to the exit.

"Hey," Nichols called just as I opened the door.

I totally didn't snoop, I swear! What pictures? "Yeah?"

"I know Charlie Arnold's a pretty nice guy, but he's got problems, you know? Sometimes his imagination gets a little wild. And Belinda… Well. Teenagers. She was Renee Rhodes' one-woman fan club here in Maine. Renee could do no wrong in her eyes, so she's taking this pretty hard."

I nodded. "Well. I won't be seeing them today so…" At least I didn't think so. I hadn't planned on seeing Charlie earlier, so who knew what the rest of the day would hold.

Nichols made a thoughtful noise but didn't pursue that line any further. "Well. For the record, I'm free Tuesday afternoon."

"Okay?"

"For lunch?"

"Oh! Right! Tuesday! I'll, um… I'll call!"

Muffin tugged at me, so I gave Nichols a sheepish shrug and let the dog drag me onto the sidewalk. "I'm not really a dog person," I muttered to Muffin, "but you're a great wingman today."

SEVEN

I didn't run to Witte's Teas, but I might have speed walked, Muffin tugging at the lead as soon as he realized where we were going.

What can I say—the guy had a thing for scones.

Margie was behind the counter, three people in line waiting for their turn as I gave her a tiny wave and motioned towards the corner table near the window. She nodded, sending me a slightly distracted smile before returning her attention to the customer who couldn't decide between green tea blends.

Muffin huffed his way beneath the table, curling around the base and melting into a sigh when I tried to offer him one of the organic treats, turning his nose up at it even as I tried to make it seem appealing.

"Seriously?" I muttered, shoving the treat back into the mylar bag and tossing the bag onto the table. "That was some Oscar-worthy acting there. You're telling me you didn't believe for one second these are delicious and magical?"

Did you know dogs could roll their eyes? I didn't.

The chime over the door rang in another handful of people, so I took out my phone to kill some time.

Fifty emails waiting. Yikes. I didn't even want to see how many notifications I had on my socials. Kinda wish I hadn't let my PA go last year. The topmost email was from Paul Santos, with the subject line: ***Hello Max's Friend.***

It wasn't much, just an acknowledgment that Max had let him know I'd be in touch and offering whatever help he could.

Margie had five people waiting now, so I settled in for a bit, shooting Paul off an email letting him know I was looking mostly for information about Ms. Rhodes' early life, either pre-Broadway or her earliest days on the stage, and any personal tidbits he might have in his archive. My fingers itched to add *and let me know if she ever pissed off anyone enough to get her killed,* but even I knew that would be a bad idea.

Maybe?

"What are you doing here?"

I jumped, hitting the send button at the sound of Ben's gruff tone. He towered over me, glaring down at me and Muffin, both in our little corner nook. "Waiting on my tea," I lied.

He raised a brow. "There's no table service here."

"I'm special."

Ben's eye roll was disturbingly similar to Muffin's. "Look, I know Margie's a very…" He gritted his teeth and closed his eyes for a moment. "A very well-meaning person, but—"

"But," I interrupted, flipping my phone so he could see the screen. "I'm just reading these one-acts for tomorrow. In case you missed the news, the festival is still on. Charlie Arnold wants to keep it going in memory of Ms. Rhodes, so I've got things I need to do. Bye now."

"Damien." Ben sighed. "I know you're not familiar with this sort of thing, but I can assure you that whatever drama you think you've got going on, it's *not real*. You're only going to get yourself—and probably Margie— hurt."

I hummed to myself, opening the first one-act on my list. Belinda's, coincidentally. The screen was tiny and not exactly ideal for long reads, but without rushing back to the inn to grab my tablet, I was low on options. *And why the hell won't Ben just go? Stop staring at me, weirdo!*

"Ben," Margie called, her tone distinctly strained. "If you're going to bother people, put yourself to use and get behind the counter."

"I don't have time for that, but I need to talk to you."

"Behind the counter," she said firmly. Ben threw up his hands and strode past the customers and past Margie, heading for the back of the shop.

Margie turned a thin smile to the customer at the counter. "Kids," she chuckled. "Even when they're adults."

Having every eye in the room on me wasn't an unfamiliar feeling, but under the curious, darting gazes of the customers, I felt uncomfortably exposed. Belinda's play open on my phone, I bent over the screen and focused on the words, trying to block out the attention bouncing between me and Margie.

A Knife to the Heart by Belinda Gleaves
Summary: A young girl is betrayed by her mentor, and she seeks revenge over the course of one night in 1920s New York.

I rocked back in my chair and stared.

Seriously?

It was fast-paced and frankly well-written. But it made my skin crawl with the denouement:

"Hey! You're Damien Murphy, right?"

"Oh my god!" My phone clattered from my hand, and I clutched at my chest, staring up at the statuesque redhead towering over me. "Oh my god!"

"I'm so sorry," Bitty gasped, clapping a hand over her mouth. "I thought you saw me walking over!"

"Oh, it's okay!" I breathed, heart racing. "I'm sorry, I just… reading, you know?"

She chuckled lightly and nodded. "Sorry, I just came in to get my daily dose, you know? And I saw you sitting here and thought I'd let you know your car's ready for you to come by and, well…"

I winced. "That bad, huh?"

"Well. Come by and see. This afternoon work for you?"

I nodded. "Perfect. Tomorrow's going to be brutal. It's the first day of the festival and I'm judging the one-act plays."

She hesitated, her expression cycling through a few complicated configurations. "I'd heard the festival wasn't canceled," she finally said.

"Just reduced." I sighed. "The one-act contest, a few workshops, then a memorial for Ms. Rhodes on Sunday. The public is welcome to give a few words during the service."

Bitty sniffed, but it didn't strike me as being from sadness. "Well. That will certainly be something."

The bell over the door jingled again and a cluster of tourists streamed in, chattering about the tall ships on display down the coast. Bitty pushed a smile and brushed her hair back from her face before gesturing at the counter. "I'd better get in line. Ron's holding down the fort at the desk for me till I get back, and he's got some appointments coming late today so…"

"I'm one of them." I laughed. "I'll stop by on my way."

She nodded and hurried to take her place in line, leaving me with the one-acts and a queasy feeling about Belinda's obsession with Renee Rhodes. It was easy to get lost in the plays, more than I thought it would be. Sure, most of them were obviously amateur, even first-timers, but the stories were fantastic. Everything from macabre to romantic to complex local history retold as a space opera (trust me—it worked… It was weird, but it worked). I was knee-deep in Wally Schram's play about a Depression- era shop's last day that reminded me strongly of *As I Lay Dying* when Margie was finally able to come by the table.

"Here we go," Margie caroled, dropping into the chair beside me. It'd been almost an hour since I'd arrived and her sudden influx of late in the day customers had come pouring in after me. "It's not as warm as it could be, but I'm afraid if I take the time to heat it up again, it'll be some sort of Bat Signal to the tourists that I'm taking a break, and in they'll come!"

I chuckled, accepting the cheese and onion scone from her with a happy groan of thanks. "Where'd Ben go? He came in earlier, but I didn't see him leave."

Margie's cheerful expression crumpled before she could catch herself and smooth it out into something close to dismissal. "Oh, he left by the employee entrance. He was in a snit and, well…" She ducked her face, using the sleeve of her light sweater to dab at her eyes. "Sorry, sorry. You'd think I'd be over it by now," she chuckled sadly. "Ben and I always butted heads. and it only got worse after Johnathan passed. Ben's obligated to be part of the business, but he'd rather I was gone."

A niggle of unease started to gnaw at my stomach. "Margie, did he do something to you? Like. Hurt you or something?"

"Oh! Oh no, never that! I mean, maybe he's wanted to, I'm sure, but no, he just uses his words." She sighed. "Irony, huh? Parents are always telling their kids to use their words, but you forget those are just as hurtful, too!"

I scrambled to my feet, hurrying to grab some paper napkins from the counter and bring them back to Margie so she could dab at her eyes and nose. "I'm so sorry, I shouldn't have asked," I began, but she waved me off.

"Oh, you weren't to know how he gets. He's just the opposite of his father, really," she murmured. "Now, enough of that mess. Ben's temper isn't something I want to think about at *all*. Tell me what's happening with the," she paused and glanced around as if expecting a sudden rush of customers to pop out from behind the display cases. "The you-know-what!"

I told her about the visit with Nichols, avoiding the gleam in Margie's eye when I mentioned his attempt to ask me on a date.

"Well, you know, he and Ben were a thing for a while there, back when they were in high school. Johnny and I'd always hoped they'd get back together once Ben got off his high horse about this town, but…" She sighed. "Well. Heath is a good guy. You could do worse!"

"Well, I mean," I stumbled, "I'm not in town long, so even if I was interested…"

She smiled, patting the back of my hand gently before squeezing me. It reminded me so much of my mom, my chest hurt. *Maybe the next stop needs to be home.* "Well. Moving on then. Were you able to find out anything helpful?"

I relayed what I'd found in the evidence box. "The thing is, I'm sure that didn't belong to Ms. Rhodes."

"It was with her things, though," Margie said, nose crinkling in confusion. "Who else's would it be?"

"That's the thing," I admitted. "I don't know. But it didn't go with her outfit, for one thing. She had on a black Halston, and there's no way she'd have carried a bag with a brown leather strap. She had a Kate Spade bag with her that night, one that complimented her vintage gown. And"—I sat up, warming to my theme—" even if she *did* have a different bag, she definitely wouldn't have had a cheap knockoff. It might have been intended to *look* like one of those old Dooney and Burke bag straps, but the leather was *not* quality, and the clasps were showing so much wear. The patina was flaking off and you could see the cheap metal underneath!"

Margie pursed her lips. "Well, hon, you gotta remember, even though Renee liked to look expensive, she wasn't exactly rolling in dough. Broadway actors rarely get paid so well. It's only a tiny number who are truly wealthy. Even the famous ones."

"Trust me, I know how the pay disparity works—I can name five super famous actors off the top of my head who are living on credit and one movie flop away from bankruptcy while trying to keep up the appearance of living large. But no, Ms. Rhodes is one of those people who wouldn't be caught dead—oh my god—with a knockoff. She'd go without rather than fake it."

Margie's brows beetled, and she frowned at me over that. "Hon, I think you might be getting carried away about Renee here."

"Maybe," I allowed, but I didn't think so at all. "If nothing else, it tells us there was someone else there with a purse, likely a woman."

"That's quite a leap, kiddo! Maybe it was a prop or something?"

"Why would it have been with her things in the office? It was sitting right next to those treats Muffin hates. Oh, by the bye," I pushed the mylar baggie towards her. "You said Tony likes this kind?"

She nodded, taking the bag gingerly. "He's on a special diet—he gets these skin itchies, you know—but he does like them when I allow him a little treat."

"Take 'em. Muffin won't touch the things. I think he's sulking."

She smiled sadly down at Muffin, still snoozing on the floor at my feet. "Poor thing. Who knows what he saw."

"Ugh, I wish I could Doctor Dolittle this one!"

She snort-laughed at that. "You sound like you're at your wit's end, Damien. Let me make you a cup of something soothing, hm? What're your plans for the rest of the day?"

I followed her to the counter, leaving Muffin to drowse in a sunbeam. "Ugh. Finish the plays before tomorrow, work on the eulogy, go by O'Neill's…"

"You're not half busy, are you?" She laughed. "Here, try this. Blueberry green tea with a hint of lemon."

It was delicious, and I said as much, taking another sip of the hot brew and letting the heat soothe me for a moment as Margie cleaned up behind the counter.

"Well, I suppose I should ask what's next."

"Er, I guess I'll start with O'Neill's, since I'm out."

"No, I mean the investigation," she whispered. "What next?"

I hesitated, letting the wiggling little thought I'd been toying with since the talk with Nichols take flight. "I think I need to go to Ms. Rhodes' house and look around. Charlie said someone was scaring her. Maybe there's some evidence of who it was."

Margie's eyes widened to near comic proportions. "Damien, I don't know…"

"I'm going to be careful," I said with more assurance than I felt. "And besides, I'm not a terrible actor. If I get caught, I'll just talk my way out of trouble!"

EIGHT

B itty O'Neill was behind the front desk when I stepped into O'Neill's Automotive and Nails. She flashed me a grin, brandishing her to-go cup of tea at me in a sort of salute as I stepped up to the counter. "Can't go through the day without a hit of pur-eh," she said, chuckling at her rhyme. "I hope you're feeling better. You looked kind of frazzled in the shop. No offense."

"It's been a hell of a week," I admitted.

"Well." She sighed. "I don't know if this is gonna help at all." Bitty motioned for me to wait just a second and disappeared into her office, returning with a clipboard and grease-stained papers. "The engine's shot, and I have no idea how you made it this far with the transmission being in this bad of shape. All the belts are, well, melted, and…" She glanced up, shooting me a sympathetic look. "Honestly, it could be rebuilt or replaced, but it'll cost more than the car's worth. Unless you've got some real compelling reason for keeping her, I suggest letting insurance total her out and using the money towards something new."

My poor car shouldn't have made my eyes sting like that. But Bonnie had been the first big purchase I made as soon as I had access to my own money. Sure, she hadn't been flashy or super expensive, but she'd been *mine* and represented adulthood, freedom… I sighed. "Can I see her?"

Bitty nodded. "C'mon, buddy. She's out back."

Bonnie was tucked between a beat-up Volkswagen Del Sol and a vaguely familiar pearly gray car that took a minute for me to place. "That's Margie Witte's car!"

Bitty nodded. "Her shocks are sprung." She sighed. "She said she was hauling paving stones up to the house, redoing the back patio area before the holiday party season starts. I told her these little cars aren't made for hauling heavy sh—stuff, but here we are." She patted Margie's car fondly. "Old girl's about worn out."

I hoped she meant the car and not Margie.

Tearing my attention away from Margie's car, I shuffled to Bonnie and laid my hand on the hood. "I'm sorry," I muttered. And felt like an ass, talking to my car in front of Bitty like that. She was looking away, giving me a moment apparently, so I whispered, "I know you're just a chunk of metal and rubber, but we've been through a lot together and I'm sorry it's come to this."

I did a quick check inside the glove box for anything important—about a million ketchup packets and straw wrappers stayed, but the insurance card, my car lip balm, and the hundred-dollar bill I kept for emergencies came with me. When I was done, I gave her another pat and stepped back. "Alright." I sighed. "That's it."

Bitty nodded sympathetically and looped her arm around my shoulders. "C'mon. Let's get the paperwork started for your insurance company. It'll be quick, I promise."

It was a matter of minutes to get the paperwork signed and send my poor car to her ultimate resting place. Muffin was disinterested in the entire experience, pacing back and forth as I shakily signed off my car and tried to cheer myself up by ducking into the nail place next door to make an appointment for the next day to get a manicure. I took one more glance at Bonnie before heading out, pausing at the flash of red peeking out from under a black tarp near Margie's car. "Is that…"

Bitty nodded. "Renee Rhodes' car. Once her estate decides what to do with it, it's outta here. For now, they're paying our storage fee. Not gonna lie, the thought of selling it outright to pay for that damn electric charging station she forced us to install is tempting…" With a sigh, Bitty grabbed the ringing phone and turned away. I was dismissed.

"Come on," I muttered to Muffin as we stepped out onto the pavement less than an hour after we'd arrived. "Time to get you some food, huh?"

IT DIDN'T TAKE LONG to get Muffin settled back at the inn. A bowl of food, some water, and a tour of the side yard with a plastic baggie and a strong stomach had him chilled out for the afternoon, happy to flop on the porch near Carmel as she peeled potatoes and talked on the phone to someone about a book fair in Bangor. I headed out, back down Buttermilk Road towards the cove end of town. Buttermilk took me through the little downtown area before coming to an end at a memorial park for lost seamen, names and dates going back to the sixteen hundreds when the first European colonizers settled the area, but some as recent as the nineties. Several were marked with little stars, indicating they'd been lost at sea and bodies never found. It was such a grim thing to be in the middle of an explosion of coastal wildflowers and a delicately wrought path made of blue-veined pebbles and dotted with weather-worn wooden benches. Death seemed to hide in little pockets in the town, I thought, glancing back toward the busy stretch of road behind me. Ms. Rhodes' death, this memorial, the little, tucked away patches of flowers and statues named for long-gone town founders or people who were once held in high regard by the town. Hollywood revered its dead in grim, fetishistic ways—poor Marilyn, the suicide ghost at the famous sign, the Black Dahlia, a long-ago Superman… They were all picked apart over half a century past their deaths, fame buoying them into pop culture, into prurient interest podcasts and even movies about their lives and death all with a vulture's eye view.

Would that be me one day? Would it be Ms. Rhodes? Was it the price we paid for chasing public adoration? For choosing paths that relied so heavily on a lack of privacy?

The sharp caw of a gull snapped me out of my spiraling funk. The road I wanted was a narrow and hidden little branch just off the park, a small gate opening onto a cobblestone path that looked ancient with a tiny sign fixed to it reading *please close after opening*. No one called out to ask what I was doing or why I was there as I opened (then closed) the gate, stepping onto the tree-lined street that was little more than a wide path, a bit of the oldest part of Lester Cove no one had tried to change in centuries. According to Carmel, there were only two houses on the street. The first one was near the memorial park, set back from the road and almost hidden behind tall, feathery grasses and a heavy-limbed honey locust. The front door had a nautical-themed wreath and several kid-sized bikes littering the paved path from the street to the porch.

Likely not Ms. Rhodes, then.

According to good ol' Google, the road was less than a mile long and led to the shore, near an old boardwalk for the lighthouse, which peeked over the tops of the trees that swept from the town to the beach itself. I sent up a silent thank you for the summer weather not being as onerous as LA's summer and for whoever had thought to make sure the trees proliferated here as I kept walking, eyes peeled for the next cottage.

And that's when Belinda found me.

She appeared in front of me, uttered a startled yelp, and stumbled back, almost tripping and falling on the cobbles. I grabbed her arm, and she flailed out to grab onto a fence overgrown with wildflowers and crawling berry fines at the same time. "Oh my god! I thought you were a ghost or something!" she panted. "What are you doing here?"

I looked back in the direction she'd come from and saw the faintest hint of yellow and cream peeking through what I'd taken to be a patch of woods. "Ah, just wanted to pay my respects privately," I extemporized.

Belinda's already liquid eyes spilled over. "Same," she admitted. "But I'm *so so mad* and I feel bad for being mad, you know? I mean, aren't you pissed too?"

"Er, yes, but it's more kind of a general vibe with me. What's going on, Belinda?"

"I thought she was my friend! My *mentor!*" she wailed, pawing at her lemon-yellow overalls and coming up with her phone. She unlocked it and turned it to face me. "I talked to Mr. Arnold today. He… he…" With a wet sniff, she shook her phone at me to read.

I looked at the screen, her shaking hand making it hard to read. Just a few lines from Charlie, what looked like a forwarded text.

Swear to god, that Gleaves girl is a pain in my ass. I can't get ten minutes without her begging for tips and hints and blah blah blah. She annoys me and if I didn't need to make nice with the town council, I'd be the bitch to her she needs me to be so she grows up and stops being such a sycophant.

Belinda sniffed roughly, yanking her phone back and shoving it into her chest pocket. "I can't believe it! Why would she say that? After everything!"

"Maybe it was a joke," I suggested, my mind already spinning in a dozen directions, the most uncomfortable being toward Belinda. *Maybe she's the one lying.* What was she doing there? Was she trying to cover her tracks? Did she know about this sooner? That play she wrote seemed a bit on the nose otherwise. Maybe this is the lie, trying to cover her tracks…

She shook her head, freely crying now. "I didn't believe him either, but I saw him at the tea shop after the email and I asked him again. He confirmed it! She *hated* me! Between this and lying about Callum O'Grady…"

"Charlie told you about that, too, huh?"

"Margie did. I mentioned it to her, and she said how it was impossible." Belinda dashed at her wet cheeks with the back of her hand and shook her head. "I thought she was telling stories, but Mr. Arnold confirmed it. They all knew one another back in New York, like when they were kids."

"I thought she and Margie met as teenagers," I mentioned, confused. "In theater club or something."

"Nope. Little kids. Like fifth grade. I guess they had a falling out or something," Belinda muttered. "I don't know. But they *both* told me Ms. Rhodes was lying about the playwright!"

"Belinda, listen. Maybe they were wrong, you know? Ms. Rhodes has a lot of connections from her career that I'm sure they've never met. Heck, I've known my bestie Max since we were twelve and he's got loads of people in his phone I've never even heard of, but he works with on the regular."

Belinda cast me a doubtful glare. "Why would she lie to me?" she demanded. "I thought she liked me! She let me interview her for the paper! She gave me advice about my plays and boys and…" She sniffed roughly, looking away as if suddenly embarrassed.

I winced inwardly as I lied to her, hating to see her so upset and wondering just how much was real, hating that I even wondered. "Maybe she was trying to protect the real identity of the person she was planning on sending the plays to? I know a lot of actors and producers who'll use fake names, even the names of dead famous people, to check into hotels or even place online orders. They're worried about overzealous fans."

She flailed again, waving her hands to indicate herself head to toe. "Do you think I'm an overzealous fan?"

"No, just very dedicated," I said kindly. "Belinda, what are you doing here?"

"Same as you, as I said. I was—*am*—mad, but she meant a lot to me, you know?" She shoved her hands into her overall pockets, glancing up at the house, her expression hurt. "I wanted to just say my piece. Before the service on Sunday."

"Got it," I murmured. "You need me to call someone? Did you drive down here?" I didn't see a car on the street, but it didn't mean she hadn't parked somewhere down the road, where it dipped down towards the water, out of sight just in case she didn't want to be seen.

"I walked from the tea shop after Margie closed for the day," she admitted. "It's not far. I live on Clarendon, behind Buttermilk."

"You gonna be okay?"

She shrugged, folding in on herself a bit. "I guess so. I mean. It sucks but…" She trailed off. "Want me to wait for you?"

"Nah, I'm good." Please go, please go, please go.

"Alright. See ya tomorrow, I guess? It's, um…" She sniffed, dashing at her eyes with the side of her hand. "It's the one-act day."

Another nod. "Bright and early."

"Yep."

I waited until she'd walked off a few feet, heading towards the memorial park. "Hey, you didn't go inside, did you?"

She didn't turn to face me, but she shook her head. "No. I just went to the porch. Left some flowers. Talked shit."

"Okay."

She didn't say anything else, and I waited until she'd disappeared through the park gate at the far end of the road before heading up the walk to Ms. Rhodes' house.

The porch was dirty, sand and soil piled along the edges in little drifts, footprints marring the formerly white boards. The cottage was still adorable, but very definitely starting down the road of neglect. A handful of wildflowers tied with a rubber band were on the seagrass mat. Either

Belinda had been telling the truth about that, or she'd seen the flowers and extemporized. I took a chance and felt under the doormat, then on the narrow lintel over the door before I found a grungy key that fit the front door lock. I held my breath as I unlocked the door, not sure what I was expecting on the other side. The ghost of Renee Rhodes to come swooping at me? The killer, lying in wait like a giant spider for their next victim?

I knew she had not died at home, but I fancied I smelled a whiff of death as the stuffy air inside the house hit me like a wall. My fingers itched to flip the light switch by the door, but I channeled every role I'd ever had in a police procedural, no matter how ridiculous, and forced myself to keep it together. No touching anything unless I absolutely had to. No turning on lights. No lingering.

It would be so much easier if I knew what I was looking for.

RENEE RHODES HAD A VERY maximalist aesthetic, her tiny cottage overwhelmed with textures and colors that shouldn't have worked but somehow did. It all had a very mid-century vibe but with a late seventies funky twist to it, including framed original (or what I assumed to be original) show posters lining the walls of the living room and the short corridor that led to what I presumed to be the bed and bath area. To my right, just off the entryway, was a kitchen already deep in shadows. The light of my phone showed glimpses of laminate countertops in mustard yellow and brown tile flooring that made me wince with the thought of trying to keep it clean. The table was small, barely big enough for two, and then only if you really liked one another, and not a thing lay out on the counter or in the sink.

Her house might be cluttered with decor, but it was still tidy where it counted, apparently. I took a few careful steps toward the living room, trying to decide where I'd hide something if I were Renee Rhodes.

The same place I'd hide it myself—in plain sight.

I started with her bookshelves, lightly populated as they were with popular novels, a shelf of old sci-fi, and another two shelves of nonfiction and acting-related books. An e-reader lay on one of the shelves, plugged in to charge. I wrapped my finger in my shirt sleeve and gave the screen a nudge to see it pop to life, the lock screen the cover image for some new release. The icon indicating a download was flashing, letting her know something she ordered was waiting for her to read.

That thought made me suddenly very sad. I turned away from the bookshelves and scanned the rest of the room. The TV was one of the newer plasma types, set on a sleek stand that blended in with the rest of her decor, four remotes lined up beneath the screen in size order from largest (which looked to be an old, out-of-date number) to smallest (for the streaming device no doubt attached around the back of the TV).

The first thing out of place caught my eye as I moved back toward the bookshelves.

A leather day planner lay open on the floor behind the sofa. It was open to the address section and showed its age, the pages foxed around the edges and the ink faded. The numbers all had New York area codes, except a few with Los Angeles ones. It was open to the A's and B's; some names were illegible, some just descriptions (*Artie's Dogwalker; Amazing Lover with the limp; Amazing Lover with the wife*). The pages were loose, but I couldn't tell if it was from their age, from use, or because someone had pulled something out and torn the bindings in the process. I took a picture of it where it lay open, reluctant to touch it, and rocked back to sit on my heels, looking around the room again.

"Belinda, did you lie to me?" I murmured, peering under the sofa and seeing nothing, not even an errant dust bunny. What I *did* see was the base of the days of future past coffee table, a capsule-shaped wooden situation that had doors on the side facing me, all done in dark wood with a tiny little, black-painted keyhole.

A quick tour of the living room, then the kitchen netted me a paper clip from Ms. Rhodes' junk drawer. I hurried back to the coffee table and dropped to the floor, straightening the paperclip until it was mostly unkinked. I had never lockpicked outside of a few movies and some episodes of TV shows where I'd played the delinquent best friend or the bad boy boyfriend of the week for a Very Special Episode, but I'd hoped I'd gleaned enough to make this work.

Stretching out on my belly, I wiggled the wire into the tiny hole and gave it a little twist and shove, feeling for some resistance that would tell me I'd found the latch. It took almost no effort, barely a turn to the left, and it popped open with a soft whisper.

"Hello there," I murmured, inching up onto my hands and knees to peer more closely. In the storage space were photo albums. Not the fancy kind you'd leave out to show off for company, but the more utilitarian kind, little more than binders really. Each one was labeled on the spine with a span of years. Some only had one (1978 was apparently a very busy year, picture-wise) and others had a wide span (1970-1975 was thin, especially for something containing five years' worth of photos.) Gingerly, I reached in and tugged one loose, hand wrapped in my shirt sleeve again. The pages were plastic pouches containing publicity stills, headshots, and handbills for off-off-off-off-so-far-off-it's-practically-Connecticut-Broadway productions with Renee Rhodes' name somewhere on them. Most of the ones I came across in the five-year binder had her name in tiny print with a glut of others at the bottom.

Chorus, I realized, or one of the numerous extras and understudies who may or may not ever be seen on stage for the run of the play but were just excited for their name to be in print, on an actual playbill where they should show someone—maybe that disapproving family member, that ex who said they'd never be on stage, a random passerby who gave zero damns—that they'd made it, that they were in a *real play* and were a *real actor, look, here's my name and everything!*

I didn't linger, reaching the end of that binder and reaching for 1976. This one had more professional-looking pictures tucked away in the front, and the playbills got more official-looking, the theaters bigger and productions less *my friend wrote this* and more names I'd heard of, names that'd lingered over the years. They weren't all winners, though—several were painfully seventies-sounding *(Tea with Nixon and Dinner with Goldwater: The Musical),* a few were Shakespeare in the Park type situations, but it was clear her career was ticking upwards around this time. Her name was in a larger font more often than not. In a few, her face was featured. I'd almost reached the end when I realized the page I was holding felt different from the others.

Thicker.

Something was behind the promotional still from a repertory theater production of *Hello, Dolly.*

The playbill was poorly photocopied and worn around the edges, the old printer ink smeared where someone had handled it too soon.

The picture was a basic silhouette, just a step above clip art, really. A figure in a slice of yellow, meant to be a spotlight. The figure was on its side, one arm tucked under their body and the other flung up over their head where a dark shape meant to be blood surrounded them like a halo. Beside the figure, a sandbag lay, split open and spilling dark grains of sand. The figure wore a gown, a martini glass broken at their feet.

The only thing that kept me from making a break for the bathroom was the fact I was technically (okay, literally) breaking and entering. If my arc on *Legal Beagle* taught me anything, it was criminals who did something foolish like leaving biological evidence at the scene of the crime always got caught.

And I really didn't want to see how Rory would use my jail time as a PR boost.

I slipped the playbill from its protective plastic sleeve and tucked it into my handbag. After a moment's hesitation, I flipped back to the beginning and grabbed my phone, setting it to record, and then slowly flipped page by page through the binder. It was faster than taking individual pictures, I reasoned, and spending any more time in the house than absolutely necessary made my skin crawl. The house felt… occupied. Like any moment now Renee Rhodes would swan in from the kitchen and take a seat across from me, regaling me with gossip fifty years out of date and little bits of behind the scenes info about each play I came across.

The dull thump of the heater kicking on made me yelp, which in turn made me jump, the sound of my voice making me think someone had seen me and screamed.

"Damn it, Damien," I muttered as my heart started to slow to a more reasonable speed. "Get it together."

Binder recorded, I shut off my phone again and tucked the binder back under the coffee table with the stack of old magazines and newspapers. Ms. Rhodes' house was just one or two steps from a hoarding situation, every nook and cranny stuffed with pictures, awards, papers, mail, and cards. Fairy lights hung limply from the living room ceiling in what must have been festive loops at one time, cobwebs stretched between the lengths. The carpet was matted in places, flattened into squares or circles like something had been standing there for ages.

Like furniture.

Like it had been there and moved.

Slowly, I stood, clutching my bag to my side. Had someone been here before me, looking for something? Did Ms. Rhodes have something hidden away, something someone would kill for?

And how the hell would I know when I found it? I slowly backed out of the room to stand in the wide foyer, staring at the patterns in the carpet, trying to replace everything where it had been before. The round marks looked like they belonged to the mid-century modern sofa with the tapered legs, moved from near the fireplace to the middle of the room. And the squares were from the coffee table, the recliners, and the wooden chest now moved feet from their original position. Shoved out of the way, possibly, by someone looking underneath them for something, someone who didn't bother to put anything back.

My footprints in the carpet were fluffing away, the fibers bouncing back slowly. I breathed a sigh of relief—at least that was one thing in my favor this evening. The dark of the hallway to my left both beckoned and repulsed me. Surely the playbill was enough of a clue, a hint at least that whoever had killed Ms. Rhodes had staged her body.

But why? That would be the first thing Nichols asked me. Why would someone stage her body to look like the art from an obscure play from fifty years ago?

Coincidence, he'd say. My wild imagination.

Damn it.

A soft click sounded from the dark hallway, turning my blood to ice. I couldn't move if I wanted to, the sound coming again less than a minute later. *Quick, think of an excuse. Some reason to be here! I'm a really big fan, that's it. I'm grieving her loss. We'd been in touch.*

"Hello?" someone called softly. "I know you're there."

The click came again, and this time a narrow beam of light emerged from the dark, finding me in my little corner of the foyer. And then a heavy sigh. "For god's sake. Damien!"

NINE

Apparently, the back door to Ms. Rhodes' place was quiet as a mouse because I hadn't heard Ben Witte slipping inside. Between his stealth and the rain starting to fall, I'd missed his entrance entirely and now was faced with his glower as he led me—frog-marched, really—down the short gravel drive to his fancy car.

"What the hell were you doing in there?" he asked once we were in the car and he'd turned up the heater. We were both a little wet, but he didn't seem to care much about his leather seats, not even bothering to shed his wet jacket before sitting back and getting that leather good and damp.

"Same thing as you, I imagine," I shot back, heart still racing a thousand beats per minute, hands shaking as I shoved them under my arms to hide my nervousness. "Trying to find out who killed Ms. Rhodes!"

"Good lord," he muttered, scrubbing his hands over his face and closing his eyes. "I should kill Margie myself. It'll make life so much easier."

"Uh, considering what's going on right now, do you think it's a good idea to make threats against your stepmother's life?"

"Just… stop talking," he mumbled. "Stop. For five seconds."

I raised my brow and leaned back, silently mouthing the numbers as he glared at me. "So anyway, what were you doing in there if you weren't looking for evidence? Trying to hide it?"

"*What*? For crying out loud! I represent Renee Rhodes' estate! Well, the firm I work for does. When the silent alarm in her house was tripped, the office was called since she has no next of kin or other contacts listed."

"What about Charlie Arnold?"

Ben was unimpressed by my attempt at a *gotcha* question. He slipped the car into gear and swung away from the curb, jaw tense and knuckles white.

I hummed tunelessly, turning that over in my thoughts. One, Ben Witte was in town and obviously didn't want to be. Two, Renee Rhodes was dead —murdered, in fact —and Ben Witte, a representative of her estate, was in town when it happened. Three, she was killed by a sandbag, something which Ben would know a bit about since he'd caused one to nearly harm or even kill a classmate several years ago.

"But what about the playbill?" I murmured, not realizing I was speaking aloud until after I'd done it.

"What playbill?"

"Hm? I don't know what you're talking about."

He stopped the car in the middle of the empty street. "Damien, you just said *what about the playbill*. What playbill? Were you in the house to steal some souvenirs?" he asked, tone snide and sharp. "Looking for something to sell to one of those ghoulish collectors? I have to say, Renee Rhodes was successful and has a cult following, but I don't think you're going to earn much from selling a playbill. You can find those online, order reprints if you know where to look, and—"

"Oh my god, shut up!" I fumbled for the door handle, fighting to open the door as Ben kept pressing the lock down from his side. "Seriously?" I demanded. "First, you're in a dead woman's house, then you're *holding me against my will*? Isn't there some law against that? I wish there was a lawyer around I could ask. Oh, wait!"

"Settle down, Damien! Between the two of us, I'm the one with the right to be in her house. You're the one I caught breaking and entering!"

"I used a key!" Okay, I'd called it breaking and entering in my head before, but I wasn't about to admit that now. "It's not a B&E if I use a key. Oh, hey! A rhyme!"

"Oh my god."

"You're not making yourself look less like a suspect," I pointed out. "Charlie Arnold told me about that little accident of yours back in high school."

"So that makes me a murderer, then?" His glare intensified, and I fought the urge to squirm under the sharp blue gaze. "Walk me through your reasoning here, Damien. What TV show did you get your law degree from?"

"I've never played a lawyer," I replied tartly. "Cops, victims, a paralegal once but that was only two lines—*Here you go, Diane,* and *Oh god, I can't breathe.* I've played the boyfriend of a lawyer a few times, and I had a brief stint on *Lawson Orders* as the son of a former ADA who goes to work at his parents' restaurant after he has a nervous breakdown. Lasted only a season," I added as his sharp glare became bemused and maybe a little confused as well. "I was Pete Lawson, the grandson. It would've been a great four or five season show, but the producer got caught buying coke off an undercover cop, ironically, and it all kind of went to hell at the end of season one."

Ben closed his eyes and let his head rest back against the seat. "I think I'm getting a migraine," he announced after a few heartbeats. "I never had one before, not even in law school, but I'm pretty sure this is one."

"I've got some Excedrin in my bag," I offered, opening the knock-off Prada to rummage out my tiny travel-size bottle of headache medicine. "I don't have anything to take it with, though."

"I think I'll live till I get back to the house. And it's not a secret Renee didn't have many friends in town," he added, looping back around to the original accusation. "She preferred it that way. Years of being used for her fame, for her connections, and she'd decided keeping as much to herself as possible was the best thing. And it helped create an aura of mystery, according to her, so she cultivated it. And it worked." He shrugged. "Renee was tickled by the fact that people either loved her to bits or couldn't stand her. She loved being polarizing and reveled in the persona that had cropped up around her over the years, especially since leaving New York. This little play festival she was trying to get off the ground was just a stick in the eye for the town council, and my stepmother, if I'm going to be frank here."

"What does Margie have to do with the festival? She didn't even go to the gala, and that was open to the public. And when I asked her about it after she hit me with her car and she gave me a ride, she seemed disinterested."

Ben's jaw worked mutely for a moment before he shook his head and motioned for me to buckle in. "I'm taking you back to the inn," he declared. "This day has been ridiculous. Between Margie needing a ride to that damn vet in Malm's Corner when Dr. Sommers is just *fine* and only two blocks from the shop, trying to work using the town's crappy Wi-Fi, and now *this*, I'm about to just… I don't know. Take up day drinking or something."

"It's evening now," I pointed out. "So technically, it's the cocktail hour."

He snorted softly, turning towards Buttermilk Road. "Sun's over the yardarm somewhere."

The drive back to Two Moons was quiet until he pulled over a few doors past the B&B and shut off the engine. "You didn't ask me why Renee Rhodes chose me to be her lawyer."

"I didn't know I needed to."

He smirked. "You're a suspicious person, but not very good at it," he murmured. "Why would she choose little ol' me, a Lester Cove boy who went to a mid-ranked law school and works for a run-of-the-mill firm in Boston, to represent her interests when it comes to contracts?"

I shook my head. "I mean, maybe she just had your card handy? Hometown guy, she wanted to throw some business your way?"

"Renee's hometown is New York. Long Island, if you want to get picky about it."

I threw up my hands. "I don't know. Maybe she drew names out of a hat? Spun a wheel? Coincidence?"

Ben shifted onto his hip to face me, giving me an assessing, curious look. "Did Margie put you up to looking into her death?"

"What? No. I mean," I corrected, "she'd seemed freaked out about it, and she was worried Ms. Rhodes had been killed by someone in town and there might be a murderer lurking around, but she didn't say *Damien, please look into this murder.*" At his expectant look, I hesitantly offered, "In fact, Charlie Arnold seemed more proactive about the whole thing than Margie. He was the one who was trying to get Lieutenant Nichols to look into her death more, and he was the one who had some compelling reasons she might have been killed and it wasn't an accident."

"So, Charlie asked you to do it?"

"No! Not Charlie, not Margie, not Carmel, not Belinda! I mean, I think they're right and this is a murder, but not a single one of them asked me to do it!" The words landed with a thud between us. "I just wanted to help," I admitted. "Because Renee Rhodes thought we had a lot in common, and I think she was just being nice, but I was thinking… I mean, look, I'm not that famous, right? I'm literally like a year away from needing to get a job at the Gap or something to make rent if I don't get some decent jobs soon. Not just some low-tier horror movie jobs that pay scale, but *actual* work. But I'm going to have to take those scale jobs so I can keep my insurance." I was sounding manic, but I couldn't stop myself as I blurted, "I don't want to be dead and forgotten one day. If god forbid, I ever turn up dead under mysterious circumstances, I want someone to at least try to look into it.”

He was quiet again. The rain was falling in earnest now, heavy thumps and whispering sheets racing over the car’s hood and windshield. The thick clouds made it darker than it should have been, plunging six p.m. fully into nighttime rather than a glowing late evening twilight. The entire situation felt entirely more intimate than I was wanting, but it wasn’t entirely awful. Instead, it was… nice, almost. In a weird way.

I really needed to get out more.

Ben sighed and unlocked the doors. “I’m assuming you have some evidence, otherwise you wouldn’t be risking your reputation and possible career.”

“I… have some, yes. But I don’t think I should show it to you.”

“Because I’m a suspect?” he asked, a small smile gracing his lips. “How about if I provide an alibi?”

“How can you have an alibi if I haven’t told you anything about the murder?” I challenged.

“I’m her lawyer,” he repeated. “The state police and Nichols have both given me access to all the records so far. I know her time of death was put between eleven and midnight, just about the time you found her. Which, by the way, makes you an excellent suspect.”

“My shoes are my alibi. No blood.”

“I wonder where they got their crime scene training,” he grumbled. “Not a single person there considered you might have changed clothes? Or the fact you’re an actor and might have been faking being scared?”

“I… Huh.” I sat back, staring out into the rainy evening. “Huh.”

“Didn’t cross your mind either, hm?” When I didn’t answer he continued, “I was with Charlie Arnold. We were at the Sleepy Pelican. He was drinking his feelings, I was having a late-night dinner because I skipped the buffet at the gala. Buffets are disease breeding grounds.”

"I'm guessing you're not a fan of Vegas," I muttered.

"Not especially. Gambling is a tax on people who are bad at statistics."

That made me snort, then laugh. Ben's smile was bigger then, though he did try to hide it by looking out the driver's side window. I saw it, though, and it made me have a warm and fuzzy little feeling low in my tummy. "So, you and Charlie are off my list," I said. "Unless you're lying. Or were working together. That's still a possibility."

"Who else is on your list?"

"Um. You and Charlie," I repeated, ducking my face so he couldn't see my cheeks grow red. "Or a mysterious third party I don't know." *Belinda.* Someone had been in the house before me, unless that was just the way Renee Rhodes kept her living room. I doubted it, though. The furniture was out of place, the address book was just out there on the floor. What had whoever it was (*Belinda?*) been looking for? The rain picked up even more, so heavy now I couldn't see the house beside without squinting. "What time was the silent alarm tripped?"

"Ah, I got the call from the office around half past four, and they'd gotten it a bit before that. The alarm company had rung through to my desk and since I'm off this week, it got rerouted through the answering service."

"So conceivably around four or so?"

He shrugged. "I would say no more than half an hour to forty-five minutes."

"And it took you time to drive over."

"A bit. I was at Bull's. It's my paralegal's birthday next week, and she collects china animals. He's got a new line of hedgehogs painted with state flowers."

"Huh."

"What's going on here?"

I think maybe I need to adjust my suspect list and I really don't want to. "Um, I was just thinking… Would you like to grab dinner with me tomorrow?" And maybe get bumped to the top of my suspect list…

Ben leaned back, brows drawing together. "Dinner?"

"Third meal of the day for most folks? Usually in the evening?"

"Damien, I'm flattered, but—"

"But," I huffed, slipping on a smile, letting the charm ooze to the surface all treacly sweet. "Maybe I just want to grab dinner with someone who's not trying to get my autograph or ask me to do a favor for them."

Ben snorted softly. "Right."

"Okay, maybe I just want to get to know you a bit better. You're interesting. And not hard to look at."

"Damien. I'm going to agree to dinner with you mostly to put you out of your misery. But this is not a date, understood?"

"I'm in town for less than a week. Of course, it's not."

Ben drummed his fingers on the steering wheel before letting out a heavy sigh and shaking his head. "Alright. Tonight then. I have some calls to make and a few things to tie up, but why don't you come by Witte House around seven."

"Witte House. Seven."

He smirked, reaching for his buzzing phone. "Ask one of the Moons. They'll give you directions. I need to take this so…"

I nodded, slipping from the car. Right. I could do this. I'd played a spy once and totally nailed the role, even if it did get cut from the final print.

TEN

I watched as Ben drove off, talking on his hands-free device to someone who was lucky they couldn't get the full force of his glare. Inside the inn, I could hear Sienna calling to Alice B. Toklas and Gertrude Stein and Carmel laughing, so now seemed like the perfect moment to make a call.

Paul Santos answered on the second ring, slightly out of breath. As soon as I introduced myself, he made a funny little gasping sound before clearing his throat. "I'm sorry, I'm trying to be all professional here and I'm sure you get this *all* the time, but I'm such a big fan!"

"Oh, thank you!" Not gonna lie, that ego boost helped me shake off a bit of the funk that'd been creeping in. "I'm always glad to hear someone's enjoyed my work!"

"You're fantastic at the camp-kitsch roles," he gushed, and a tiny bit of that ego boost waffled. "A true natural."

Eeeeeeeeh… "Well, I really appreciate hearing that," I said through gritted teeth. "Listen, I know you're a busy person and this is no doubt an imposition on your time but—"

"Anything for a friend of Max's," he declared. "Well, within reason. I know some of the shenanigans Max has gotten up to!"

I winced inwardly. You streak down Hollywood Boulevard *one time* when you're twenty and no one forgets.

Of course, that might've had something to do with the placement of the birthday hat.

"Nothing so dire," I chuckled, hoping it sounded real. "I'm working on a eulogy for Renee Rhodes' memorial here in Lester Cove, and I was hoping you could help me out with something. I have a few names and numbers from her address book, and I wanted to reach out to her friends and ask if they had anything they wanted to add."

"Why do you need me for that?"

"Well, you're still involved in the scene. I never have been."

He snorted dryly. "What are you really looking for, Damien Murphy?"

"Honestly?"

"Try me."

"I just want to know who I'm dealing with when I talk to these folks."

Paul was quiet for a moment, his joviality fading into a heavy sigh. "Renee Rhodes was definitely something," he murmured. "Really one of the last of the old-school Broadway sorts, you know? Are you sure you want me to dig into these names for you?"

"I'm sure."

"Be careful what you ask for. Well, I can't promise anything, but I'll see what I can do. Send the names and numbers over."

With a promise to get back to me soon as possible, he hung up, and I sent the pictures from Ms. Rhodes' address book his way.

There. One thing off my list. Now just a few more to go before I could collapse in a heap for the evening and pretend this never happened. But first… coffee. I followed my nose downstairs to find Carmel stirring something that smelled amazing when I stuck my head in the kitchen. "Oh my god, that's making my mouth water! I'm sorry I won't be here for dinner tonight."

She tossed the spoon she'd been using into the sink before shooting me a small smile. "Anything to do with you sitting outside with Ben Witte chitchatting in his car for the past ten minutes?"

"No… maybe. Yes?"

"Which is it?" she laughed. "Or is that some new Hollywood slang for *of course it is*?"

I grinned, unable to stop myself under the spell of her infectious laugh. "I *might* be having dinner with him tonight at his place. Just as… well, not as friends, but not a date either."

"Mmmhmm." Carmel folded her arms, barely managing to hide her smile. "Well, just so you know, Witte House is kind of intimidating. The first time I ever went there, I was terrified to touch anything. The place is practically a museum."

"Seriously? Witte *House*? Like… It has a name and everything?"

"Yep. It's that huge old gray semi-Federalist place up the hill near Shore Drive. I don't know if you passed it or not, but if you look out your window upstairs, you can see the octagon room one of the previous Wittes built for one of their daughters. Or maybe it was his wife? Or maybe it was just part of the original house. Well, any way you look at it, the place is a freaking mansion."

I let out a low whistle. "Now I'm second-guessing myself. I don't know if I'm dinner-in-a-mansion material."

She shook her head, reaching out to give my shoulder a friendly push. "Well, you said it wasn't a date, right? So, no pressure to be all *boyfriend me, handsome lawyer man*."

"Oh my god!"

She cackled, turning back to her pot of stew. "What? You think I'm serious all the time? Was it the hippie braids and the hand-sewn skirt that made you think I was a super crunchy, humorless lesbian stereotype?"

"No," I protested, laughing, "I just never expected the teasing!"

"It's just a little friendly ribbin'," she protested, giggling. "It's not often we hear about someone having a thing for Ben Witte."

"It's not like that," I muttered, feeling my cheeks go a bit warm and no doubt pink. "I've just run into him a few times this week. He seems… nice?"

Carmel raised her brows at that. "Nice? Well, I suppose you could call him nice. He's not *mean*, not really. Are you asking because you're interested, then?" she asked, that teasing lilt creeping back into her voice. "He's not hard on the eyes. Even I can see that, and he's very much not my type."

"Oh, I mean, not interested like *that*. Just like… as a person?"

Carmel snorted.

"Besides," I pressed on, "Margie mentioned she had hopes he and Nichols would get back together, so even if I *was* interested like that, I'm not in town long and I definitely am not cool with getting in the way of people I like."

"In like," she chuckled. "Well, Ben's definitely not going to get back together any time soon. It's been, oh lordy, over a decade now since they broke up. He and Heath Nichols were a couple for a bit, low-key like, until Ben got dragged out of the closet. I remember the whole thing when he got outed."

"Oh my god, how awful!" I clutched my arms around my middle, stomach-churning in sympathy. "Who'd do that to him?"

Carmel winced and went back to stirring the pot on the stove, the smell of berries and sugar flooding the kitchen as the steam rose. "A lot of folks think it was accidental, but I'm not sure, even now. It was actually Margie's doing."

"Margie?" I gasped, horrified. "No!" Oh my god, had I become friends with a phobe?

"She had good intentions. The road to hell and all that, you know?" She trailed off, frowning at the jam-in-progress. "Well, as one member of the rainbow mafia to another, you kind of get a feeling for when someone really means well and when they're weaponizing allyship, you know? But not on purpose, just because they think they *have* to be the loudest, most supportive person in someone's life?"

"Oh god, yeah, I know." I sighed. "We've all been through it, I think. For me, it was my Uncle Pat. He was like, weapons-grade supportive. Mom had to threaten him with a restraining order or something when he wouldn't stop giving interviews about how proud the family was of their gay member."

She hummed in agreement. "Well. Margie made a big deal about the school board allowing the kids to start a GSA club on campus. Some of the old farts were against it and had the usual BS reasons why, but Margie made a huge deal about it and, oh god this is making me cringe even now and it's been *years*." She shot me a glance, one that said *brace for incoming*. "Margie staged a one-woman pride parade in front of the school. Rainbow flag, disco music, any stereotype you can think of, she dragged it out. She even hired some dancers from Bangor to come do some routine in short-shorts and a drag queen to come out… I mean, it wasn't awful, but the fact she wore a shirt and held a sign that said *My Step Son Is Gay And I'm Proud!*"

"If I could sink through the floor right now, I would do it," I said solemnly. "That's *awful*."

"Ben skipped school for like a week and when he came back, you can imagine some of the crap he had to deal with. He just sort of crawled into his shell and stayed there. The school board let the GSA happen, but Ben never joined. Ironically, I think it was only straight kids who joined. The rest of us were too embarrassed for Ben to take part, you know? Especially since Margie made herself the parent liaison for the group." She poked at the contents of the bowl thoughtfully, a small frown on her face. "I think that was kind of the final nail in the coffin for him and Heath, too. They'd been really private about their relationship, as much as two teenagers can be." She chuckled. "They used to be in the same after-school clubs and always having 'study groups' at lunch together in the library. After the whole debacle, though, Ben started keeping to himself a lot more. Got real snappish with everyone. Eventually, he stopped going to the clubs and stuff. He just closed himself off."

"Jesus."

Carmel sighed, putting a lid on the pot and wiping her steam-damp hands on her apron. "Margie didn't mean any harm by it, I don't think. Just wanted to show support for her stepson. Sienna thought it was malicious, but Sienna thinks everyone's up to no good once you scratch the surface. No, I think Margie just wanted to support her new stepson but it just sort of cascaded."

I nodded slowly. "Um, this is a weird question but… Did he ever get like violent or anything because of that?"

"Because his stepmom embarrassed him and decided she was the main character? Nah. At least, not that I ever heard. He just sort of scrunched himself up then the second he graduated, he was off back to Boston to go to college and only came back to visit his dad now and then."

Carmel's story made my stomach hurt for Ben, and I wasn't sure if I was okay with that or not. I wanted to not like him, but I also didn't want to pity him.

She winked over her shoulder as she gave the pot another sniff, reaching for the spoon again. "We're full of surprises here in Lester Cove. What time's your not-date?"

"Seven-ish."

"You've got time to freak out, then be good to go before dinner."

"I still need to work on the eulogy."

She made a face at that. "Sorry. Need a hand?"

"I don't suppose you know how to get hold of Charlie Arnold? I tried earlier, but he's not answering his phone."

That made her draw up straight and go very still. "He's not?"

"I thought maybe he's avoiding me or something…"

Carmel shook her head, her expression losing all traces of good humor from just moments before. "He's usually pretty good about answering calls. And you guys have that festival this weekend, so he'd definitely be answering since you're involved in scheduling and stuff."

"Oh. Well. Let me try again. Maybe he was in the bathroom or something?"

Carmel didn't reply. She grabbed a lid for the pot and covered it, shutting off the heat and taking off her apron, already forgetting I was there. "Sienna, I'm going out!" she called.

Muffin emerged from under the table in the silence that followed. He gave me a soft *wuff*, and I shook my head. "I think I just kicked a hornet's nest, doggo."

Muffin followed me upstairs, pointedly ignoring the remaining baggie of treats on the desk and instead heading for the Kong chewy full of stinky treats over by the hearth. "This is a long freaking day," I muttered.

Muffin flopped in commiseration.

I still had a little over two hours before I needed to meet Ben, which meant really closer to one hour since I needed to spruce up and then walk there since this town lacked public transit or any sort of rideshare system. The papers for the eulogy lay across the tiny desk in an accusing way (trust me, it can be a thing—paperwork can totally be accusing!) so I gave in and grabbed my phone, intending to try Charlie again and fail.

When he answered, I nearly dropped my phone in surprise. "Charlie! It's Damien! Do you have a few minutes? I wanted to talk about tomorrow's schedule and, well, Ms. Rhodes' memorial."

Charlie was quiet, had been since he answered. The only sound from his end of the line was heavy breathing.

"Charlie?" I whispered. "Charlie, do you need help? Are you at home?"

"Hm? Oh. I'm at home. Home." He sounded fuzzy, a little loopy maybe because he giggled softly as he repeated the word *home* a few times. "Not where I thought I'd be, though," he murmured. "Not even close."

"Mr. Arnold, would you like me to come over? We can talk, I'll make some coffee."

"Don't got any in the house."

"Then I'll buy some and bring it over." Did Witte's Tea Shop have a secret java stash or maybe the grocery had instant? I doubted Sienna would love the idea of me borrowing their coffee maker and grounds.

His laugh was watery and sloppy. Christ, he was drunk? Ben said he drank his feelings Wednesday night. Was this a regular thing for him?

"Charlie, listen to me, okay? You said you live in the apartments on Oyster Road. What apartment number are you?"

He hummed tunelessly for a moment before replying. "Renee was never happy with enough," he blurted. "She always wanted more. Not money, not always. Just… more life. Bigger."

I winced. There were plenty of people like that in my circles, and they never seemed happy at all, not once you scratched the surface. "Like what?"

"She wanted life to move faster, but only for her. Not," he hastened to add, still fuzzy-voiced, making the words bleed together, "not like she wanted to hurry up to an ending! But her successes, her fame, she didn't want to wait for it to come. She worked for it, but not… not in a good way." He stopped, hiccoughing and coughing. The phone clattered, and he groaned, the sound muffled. He was wretchedly sick on the other end of the line, thankfully muffled, and it was a long few minutes before everything went quiet.

"Charlie? Charlie?" I called, hoping he could hear me even if he wasn't near his phone. "Damn it! Mr. Arnold?"

The phone hummed with the sound of an open line, but there was no response from Charlie Arnold. Hesitantly, I disconnected, then dialed the local police number. It rang out, rolling to voicemail. "Thank god it's not an emergency," I grumbled, hanging up and trying again only to have the same results. With great reluctance, I pulled up my address book and scrolled to Heath Nichols' name, the number he'd put in two days earlier. He answered on the first ring.

"Damien Murphy," he said by way of greeting. "Here I am hoping this is a good call."

"Ah, no. I don't think so. Maybe?"

He huffed. "Of course not. This is my afternoon off and I'm doing laundry, so unless you're calling to tell me you'd like to go to dinner tonight, I need to get back to my rinse cycle."

"Something's wrong with Charlie Arnold. I just got off the phone with him and he sounded drunk. I think he may have passed out."

Nichols was quiet for a long moment, then swore under his breath. "He by himself?"

"I think so. He said he was at home, and I didn't hear anyone else there over the phone, but I can't say for sure."

"And you decided to call me instead of the department to ask for a wellness check?"

"I did," I defended myself. "No one answered. *Twice.*"

"For god's sake, Robbie." He groaned. "He keeps forgetting to take the phone off night mode when he gets back from the can. Fine, I'll get Robbie to go by Charlie's place and make sure he's alright, just sleeping one off."

"Thanks. I'll let you get back to your delicates."

"Hey," he said before I could hang up. "Why were you talking to Charlie Arnold, anyway?"

My voice was sharp when I replied, "The festival's still happening, in case you hadn't noticed. He's the one in charge now."

"If you're stirring up crap about Renee Rhodes' death, I want to know now before it comes back to bite both of us on the ass."

"I thought you were sure it was an accident. What could possibly come back and bite us on our respective asses?"

"Damien—"

"Let me know if he's not okay," I said. "Talk to you later." I hung up on him cursing a blue streak.

ELEVEN

It was surreal, having dinner with Ben Witte. The conversation was light and of the getting-to-know-you variety, though not very deep. Lots of *do you like this band, where have you traveled*, and a few amusing work stories that were low stakes, and the sort that really aren't that funny, but you laugh at anyway. We ate spaghetti and a rather anemic salad ("Sorry, I haven't been to the store in a few days and Margie prefers to eat out over in Malm's Corner or Baskingtown."). He produced a box of fancy cookies for dessert, admitting almost shyly he'd brought them from Boston to snack on during the drive but never got around to it. "They're really good," he assured me. "From a bakery near my apartment. These are ginger-orange- cinnamon."

"Autumn cookies," I remarked and barely managed to hold back a groan at how good they tasted. "Between you and Margie, I'm going to end up on an all-carb diet."

A complicated look flickered behind his eyes before he spoke again. "Margie's a lot of things I don't like, but she does keep the family recipes in rotation pretty heavily and never changes them, so I have to give her at least that."

"Does she own the shop now?" I asked, drawing up my best *guileless and curious* expression, one I'd perfected over an entire season as Special

Guest Damien Murphy as Dominic Blue on *Tell Me Why*, an after-school special sort of thing for CBC.

Spoiler: Dominic Blue was actually the secret pot dealer at Real Kids Don't Act Like This High School and not so guileless as all that.

"Nope, that would be me. When Dad passed, the shop and all associated entities became mine. Which Margie wasn't pleased about, but she got over it. I think her feelings were hurt I didn't quit school and come home to run the shop with her."

I fussed with the crumbs on my plate, deciding whether to admit what Carmel had told me earlier. He must have recognized something in my expression because he sighed and leaned back in his chair, spreading his hands in a *come on then* gesture. "What is it?"

"Um. Okay, don't be mad at her, but Carmel told me the GSA club thing." His face went so red so fast, I was surprised he didn't stroke out. "Sorry," I muttered. "If it helps, when I came out, six teen magazines ran stories about it and for a solid year, I had protesters show up at every set I worked on. And I didn't really 'come out' so much as my agent thought it was the gimmick my image needed to stand out in Hollywood."

Ben leaned back, expression oddly stuffed. "Wait, so you're *not* gay?"

"Oh, I'm gay. Super gay. Like… the gayest. But when I was twelve, I wasn't ready for the world to know and made the mistake of thinking my agent wouldn't use that very personal info for his own gain."

Ben's scowl was fierce to behold. "You know I do contract law, right? I can get you out of whatever you've got with that guy."

Warmth suffused my face and spread down my neck before I could remind myself that wasn't a kindness but an offer of services. "I'll keep that in mind. Right now. I don't know what I'm going to do after I leave here. This was gonna be my reset."

"A festival for one-act plays and the adoration of Renee Rhodes in a tiny coastal town in Maine? Let me tell you, that sounds a little… not like a reset and more like running away from something.”

“To-may-to, to-mah-to.”

Ben shook his head but didn’t pursue the subject. “Well, we’ve got that in common, then. Being booted out of the closet before we were ready and being used for someone else’s gain.”

“I don’t think Margie—”

He shot me a quelling glare. “Margie didn’t help. But no, I meant Heath. Nichols, to you. He rode that train all the way to college, using the entire incident as fodder for admissions essays, even did a little PSA for the state’s anti-bullying initiative about being a gay cop and being outed in high school.” He fussed with his silverware, setting it on his empty plate before shoving his hands through his hair and getting to his feet. “I think I need some tea,” he muttered. “You?” He didn’t give me a chance to answer, heading to the counter to get the electric kettle going and pull down some boxes of tea from the cabinet over the sink. The boxes all had Witte’s Tea Shop logos except for a bag, which was clear plastic and looked like someone had thrown some mulch in there and added a few flowers for color. “Peppermint, Earl Gray, John’s Blend, Ben’s Brew, and this”—he shook the plastic bag—“is Margie’s Blend. Which, to be absolutely honest and not at all because I don’t get along with her, is really awful. Too tannic, but some people like that.”

I made a face. “Ew. I liked the Ben’s Brew I had the other day.”

His smile was a touch sly. “You said I was delicious.”

“Oh my god, stop! I’m trying to be all serious and you’re reminding me of how I shoved my entire foot into my mouth.”

He shook his head, grabbing a bag of the Ben’s Brew and one of the John’s Blend, putting them in cups, then adding water as the electric kettle chimed. “I’m about to kick myself for saying this, but I feel like it has to be said since we’re trying to be serious here. I told you Charlie couldn’t be a suspect because he was with me the entire night after the gala, and it’s unlikely Belinda could have done it since her mom is pretty strict about her curfew, right?”

“That’s what I gathered, yeah.” I reached for the cup nearest me and took a sip before adding a single sugar cube under Ben’s watchful eye. “I like things sweet.”

He looked as if he wanted to say something, but instead pursed his lips and added a squeeze of lemon to his own tea, giving it a desultory stir before sipping. The silence that fell was awkward, nothing like our earlier easiness. After another too-quiet minute, I set my cup down and leaned towards Ben, catching his eye with my earnest stare. “So, why Boston?”

“I’m sorry?”

“I mean, it’s pretty far from Lester Cove. What made you choose Boston?”

“It’s pretty far from Lester Cove,” he echoed dryly. “And that’s where the firm is. And my life.”

“You’re not a fan of this town, huh?”

“Damien—”

“I mean.” I fiddled with the thin, gilded china handle of the teacup before me, breaking our little staring contest with a dose of innocent curiosity courtesy of years of oatmealy television roles where the worst things that happened involved a zit on prom night or breaking Mom’s favorite vase. “You’ve got a lot of ties here. People seem to rely on you, you know? Margie. Charlie. Ms. Rhodes…”

“Christ,” he huffed, pushing away from the table again. “Damien, you’re clever, but you’re not good at it. I think it’s time to wrap this up. I need to work on some briefs, and you need to”—he waved one hand at me as he carried his cup to the sink—“go make some conspiracy theories or something.”

“Ben, listen,” I protested, but he shut me down with a glare. I took my cup after his and followed him to the front door, where he waited as I slipped my shoes back on and grabbed my light sweater from the hook by the door. He seemed to relent a bit, watching me get ready, and some of his icy shell melted under the porch light, but it was an awkward goodnight as I headed out into the dark, brushing off Ben's offer to drive me back.

"Wait," he called as I was halfway down the flagstone walk. "Give me your number. Just in case. Let me know when you make it back since you can't seem to avoid getting hit by cars in this town."

We exchanged numbers quickly, and he watched until I was at the end of the drive and swallowed by the dark night.

No one passed me on my way back to the inn, the soft whir of night bugs and the occasional larger beastie rummaging in the underbrush and hedgerows making me move a little faster as I reached the curve leading to Lester Square.

The inn was quiet when I returned. It wasn't quite ten yet so I doubted the sisters were asleep, but I still made sure to mind my steps on the stairs and not clatter too loudly as I got settled for the evening, my not-date with Ben churning in my thoughts even as I tried to untangle my concerns for Charlie Arnold and… well, everything that had been happening since Wednesday night.

An hour and a half of showering, conditioning, exfoliating, moisturizing, then doing a tweezer patrol for strays (some people's eyebrows are sisters, some are cousins, mine are one long caterpillar unless I strike down like the fist of an angry esthetician god with my Tweezerman Point), and I was finally ready to sit down and poke at the eulogy a bit more. Muffin was snoring the snores of the truly exhausted, and it was like a siren song to my own sleepy brain. *See,* it told me, *that could be you, but better groomed and on an actual bed.*

Just when I thought I would give in to the urge—the eulogy wasn't till Sunday, anyway, I had time, right?—my phone buzzed.

"Swear to god, Max," I muttered, grabbing it before it could wake up Muffin. An unknown number flashed up at me with a local area code.

I let it go to voicemail. Almost immediately, it rang again.

Cautiously, as if it were ready to bite me, I answered. "Hello?"

Margie's voice was paper-thin. "Damien? Did I get the right number? I peeked at Charlie's phone but, oh lord, my hands were shaking so bad I'm worried I misdialed. Is this Damien?"

"Margie, it's me. What's going on? Where are you? Do I need to call Ben to come get you?" I got to my feet, already looking for something clean to put on. "Is Charlie okay?"

"He's… Well, he's going to have a doozy of a hangover in the morning, I think. But, well… Do you have a minute to talk?" she fretted, still whispering.

"Sure. Where are you? Is someone listening or something? Why so quiet?"

"Oh," she breathed, "I'm at home now. It's just…" and there was the sound of china on china. I thought maybe she was drinking tea and could just picture her bundled up in a comfy robe at that fancy kitchen table over at Witte House, Ben somewhere upstairs working, always working, hiding away from the world.

"It's just what?" I asked gently. "What's going on?"

"I saw Charlie earlier," she said in a soft rush. "On my way home from Malm's Corner. See. Tony's had a bit of a skin thing and it got so bad earlier, I thought maybe I needed to take him to the after-hours clinic and I'm so glad I did! He'd scratched himself a little hot spot on his chin and the vet tech said it was an allergic reaction to his treats, but that's just ridiculous. He loves those things and they're *organic!* They can't be bad for him if they're *organic!*"

"Okay, so there's like about ten things wrong with that, but let's set it aside to unpack later."

"Ah, what?"

"What's wrong, Margie?" I asked again. "Something with Charlie?" My head was starting to throb, and I wondered if the Moon sisters had any gummies downstairs because I'd left mine in LA and they were the only thing that worked for migraines like this.

"Oh! Well, now, maybe I'm just being paranoid and talking about Renee's murder"—she whispered the word—"might have me jumping at shadows, but… Charlie said something that got me thinking earlier, and he was acting awfully odd about Renee's death."

"People grieve differently," I allowed. "Maybe he's just not handling it well?"

"You didn't even hear what he said," she shot back primly. "He was all kinds of sauced, but he… he said that maybe Renee deserved it."

I winced, my stomach quivering at that casual cruelty. "Sometimes people get angry at dead loved ones," I reasoned. "If he was drunk, maybe —"

"That's not all," she interrupted. "He said…" She blew out a breath and I could just picture her squaring her shoulders and stiffening her spine for this. "He told me that *he* was the one Renee was afraid of. He'd been bothering her about the divorce, he said, trying to get her to see it had been a bad idea and, well, Renee had signed the papers and never looked back."

Oh, hell. "Where's Charlie now?"

"At home, last I checked. He was complaining that people wouldn't leave him be and how Heath had been by to bother him earlier."

So at least Nichols had checked on him. That was something.

"Do you think I need to send Nichols over again? To make sure he's okay?"

"Oh, dear, no. Charlie's had a problem for ages," she admitted sadly. "He'll sleep this off and be back at it again tomorrow, for sure. But Damien, what he said… I'm worried it *was* him."

"It… Hell, it can't be counted out," I admitted. "Damn it."

"Oh, lord, it's nearly midnight, isn't it? I should let you get some sleep."

As if I could now…

"Come by the shop in the morning? I know you're still holding that workshop tomorrow and announcing the one-act winners, right? That's what was on the schedule?"

"How did you know?"

"Oh, Charlie was on about it when he was more lucid, going on and on about needing to take some projector up to the theater, and lord knows what else." She sighed. "Go on," she urged. "Try to sleep. We'll talk some more in the morning."

I hung up after saying goodbye and shut off the desk lamp. But, as expected, sleep was as elusive as that People's Choice Award nomination.

TWELVE

S ienna was at the helm when I popped into the kitchen Saturday morning. "Coffee," she muttered, gesturing at the pot on the stove.

"Thanks, but I'm heading out early. I'm stopping by the tea shop, then getting my nails done before the workshop."

Sienna made a disinterested sound, pouring herself a cup from the stove before turning back to fix me with a solid, *don't mess with me*, look. "Be careful, hear? You come into the Cove, acting big city—"

"Big city." I laughed. "Seriously?" I didn't think I had… had I? Had I been a snob about things? Mocked something unknowingly? What was it big city people did? I'd missed those notes on my script…

"Acting big city," she reiterated. "And you think we're all some meek and backward folks. There are dangerous people here just like back in Los Angeles," she said, clutching her cup with tight, white-knuckled fingers. "I don't mean murderers, Damien."

"Are you… are you threatening me?" I rasped.

"Warning, more like. Head out on your day, then, but know that some folks here, they're more desperate than you think. It's not some fairy tale little town."

I stared, mouth gaping like a landed fish, but Sienna was done with me, busying herself at the stove with needless scrubbing, just waiting for me to leave.

Sienna's warning weighed heavy on me all the way to the tea shop. Muffin had been unwilling to come along, preferring to loaf in the side yard of the inn, so I left him there with a bowl of water and some of the expensive dry food he seemed to actually like.

The walk to the shop was weirdly quiet, the street emptier than I'd anticipated. It wasn't quite nine yet, but I'd expected some business to be going on, a few tourists maybe. But a heavy gray sky seemed to have driven everyone inside, the lights in the open shops bright against the threatening weather. I honestly missed having Muffin at my side—he was surprisingly good company, and being paired up with a dog the size of a small pony did make me feel a bit safer. By the time I reached the shop and ducked inside past the only customer, a woman in a hurry clutching a large bag of tea and gift cards, I'd convinced myself I was being watched by unseen eyes and quietly judged as an outsider or whatever it was Sienna had implied.

"You look ragged," Margie announced, eyes wide as she took in my appearance.

"Hey now! This is vintage Peter Max," I announced, fingering the bright scarf loosely draped around my neck. "And… okay, the rest is random thrift store finds, but I do make it look good."

She giggled as I preened, motioning for me to sit. "I Just meant you look tired. Though I suppose you're gonna tell me you primped and spruced all morning, so I shouldn't think that!"

"Well, just a bit of CC cream. And some lip gloss. And light mascara. And I did my brows. My mom always said you can face anything so long as your brows are behaving."

She brought two cups of tea over, one for me and one for her, and sat down across from me. "You do look nice," she admitted. "But I can tell you've been fretting." She tapped the side of her nose before reaching for her own cup, something fragrant and floral. "So have I."

"About Charlie," I began, but she shook her head slightly, leaning in close. "Margie…"

"No, let me talk. Because I think… Oh, lord, this is hard." She sniffed, reaching for one of the paper napkins on the table to dab her eyes. "I really think he did it," she whispered raggedly. "And he said… Oh, he said he'd get away with it because no one ever liked her and, and…" She broke off in a soft sob, burying her face in her hands. I scooted around the table to tug her into a one-armed hug, letting her hide against my shoulder as she tried to get herself together.

"Margie, are you *certain*? People say some wild things when they're grieving, and he was drunk to boot. Maybe he was just rambling, you know? Raging against the situation, getting out some old hurt feelings?"

She shook her head, sitting back with a sniff and dabbing her ruined mascara from beneath her eyes. "No. Charlie was… he was different from that. Now, I've known him since we were young, Damien. I've seen him angry. I've seen him hurt, sad, elated, bored—you name it, I've seen Charlie go through it. But this? This was different. He was *enraged.* He… Well, I didn't want to say it out loud because I just couldn't believe it, but he *threatened* me, Damien. Told me he'd *do me like he did her.*" She shook her head, fingers creeping to her lips as her eyes welled up again. "I just didn't want to believe it. But when he started going on about how Renee had hurt him so bad, and she deserved what happened and, well, I suppose it might make more sense if you knew what happened back in New York. See, he and Renee were married for a very short while, and Renee treated him like absolute trash." Her lips tightened, her fingers twisting in the napkin and tearing it to shreds. "Renee was… well, very determined is the nicest way to put it. Once she got a taste of her dream, nothing was going to stop her. Being married to Charlie wasn't the image she wanted." Margie gave a tiny shrug.

"That's…" I trailed off. Nauseating. Upsetting. Disgusting. "And you think he waited all this time?"

"I think he finally snapped," Margie said softly. "Seeing Renee up close after all this time, knowing she didn't care, she'd never changed…" Another tiny shrug. "I think Charlie just had it."

The chime over the door chirped cheerily and, with a tight, small smile my way, Margie got to her feet and bustled behind the counter, the mask of genial shopkeeper firmly in place.

Shit.

I stood hesitantly, but Margie didn't glance my way again as I made my way to the door.

Today was going to be one giant pain in the backside, I could feel it already.

THE *AND NAILS* side of O'Neill's was brightly painted and noisy in the best way, the sharp smell of acetone and the hum of a nail dryer making me feel comfortable at once.

No matter where in the world you go, nail shops always smell the same, and have the same background rattle of sound. I found that kind of nice, really. Whether it was LA or, apparently, rural Maine, some things were always familiar.

A tall, blond man with a truly impressive beard and an intimidating dermal piercing across the bridge of his nose waved at me with a cheery smile. "Be with you in a sec," he called over the music—classic nineties Bikini Kill, which I'd never dare call classic rock in front of someone older than me, but it was totally classic rock. The woman at the counter gathered her purse and turned to leave, stopping short when she saw me.

"Damien Murphy, right?"

"Um, guilty as charged." Fan Friendly Smile Number Two. Honestly, I only had two of those smiles in my repertoire—I didn't exactly have to trot them out often.

"My daughter talks about you a lot," she said, offering me her freshly manicured hand to shake. "Denise Gleaves, Belinda's mom."

"Oh! Hi!" I shook her hand, maybe a bit too enthusiastically, judging by the surprised look on her face. "Belinda's a great kid. She's really doing a lot, taking on this memorial service."

Denise made a moue of confusion. "She said you were in charge of it."

"Ah." *Damn it, Belinda.* "I am. I mean, I'm going over in the morning, to set up the auditorium and, uh, stuff after the last workshop. Charlie Arnold's really the driving force," I rambled. "Belinda's just been very helpful, getting me the eulogy she'd like to contribute."

Denise nodded slowly, a distrusting expression now at home on her face. "Well. I'll be sure to tell her I saw you."

I could only nod and smile in a stiff, very non-cataloged sort of way, stepping aside as she bustled out.

Ron raised his brows at me. "What the hell was that?"

"I'm not entirely sure, but I may have gotten a kid in trouble with their mom."

"Belinda?" He laughed, motioning me to head over to the chair. "She's one of those kids where sometimes her mouth is faster than her brain, you know? Whatever filter other kids have, she's lacking it entirely. Her and Ollie, they're an adorable couple but between you, me, and the fence post, if he's still with her at the end of summer, I'll be shocked."

As he was talking, I selected my polish. Handing him the bottle of Guava Peach Sunrise and another called Golden Daze topper, I asked, "Really? From what Ollie was saying on Thursday, he seems fine with how things are."

Ron shrugged. "I could be wrong. Just saying what I think I see, you know? And I think I see that Belinda's as high-strung as a cat in a rocking chair factory. I've known her since she was in diapers, and Belinda gets real intense about things, you know? Every time something doesn't go her way, it's a *betrayal* and *how dare you*." He chuckled, starting on my left hand with a delicious massage. "Ollie's more levelheaded. Not saying it's a bad thing to dream big like Belinda does, but Ollie, he's more grounded, you know? Last summer, she pitched a walleyed fit on the Fourth of July right in the middle of the town square, between the St Stephen's Church choir's medley of Americana and the first round of fireworks all because Ollie told her running off to New York and just showing up at some producer's office with her plays in hand was a bad idea."

I felt a smidge bad about the burst of startled laughter that slipped out of my chest. "Wow. Just… wow."

"She dreams big." He shrugged. "And hates being told that dreams aren't the same as reality. Now, are we doing tips or just color?"

"Just color. I can never keep up with tips. I try. but I'm so hard on them!"

Ron was funny, chatty, and almost as big of a gossip as Max. By the time he'd gotten my nails all pretty in Guava Peach Sunrise with a sparkly Golden Daze topcoat, I knew all about the shopkeepers up and down Buttermilk Road and was very invested in the saga of the Starlight Drive-In possibly reopening after the new year.

"You have to stay long enough to come to the grand opening," he urged as he led me to the checkout. "Or come back for it, at any rate. It's going to be amazing. Fireworks and everything! It was the first drive-in in this part of Maine," he reminded me. "It's like welcoming the old girl back to life, you know?"

"We'll see," I said.

Ron pursed his lips and gave me a once-over. "See that you do, mister. I'll be bugging you on your socials about it come December! Do you need a ride to the theater? You've got about an hour before the workshop starts, I think. You said eleven, right?"

I nodded. "Eleven. But I should be okay to walk."

He hummed. "If you're sure. But change your mind, call me here at the shop and me or Bitty can pop out and give you a lift. It's not far and won't take but a minute!"

I left feeling surprisingly lighter than I had in days, even though the thought of December was daunting, not because I might be expected to make an appearance back in Lester Cove, but because I had no idea what would happen between now and then.

My future was uncertain, but my nails looked damn good.

IN THE TIME it took me to walk from the salon to the theater, I'd come up with a plan of attack for Charlie.

I'd corner him after the audition workshop—he was going to be running the improv for beginners one right after so there'd be at least five minutes between the two and I could get him in the manager's office, away from prying eyes and ears.

It wasn't a great plan, but it was the best I could come up with without a writers' room and a production budget.

The parking lot was half full—not everyone had decided to come in light of Ms. Rhodes' death, but the numbers hadn't been huge to start with —and a few people milled about on the grass between the parking lot and the theater. I stopped near the Palais Theater sign and snapped a selfie to post to Insta, then shot a quick reel where I talked about Renee Rhodes' legacy for up-and-coming actors in small towns like Lester Cove and how, even though we were in the midst of a tragedy, we'd decided to keep it together in her memory. It took all of thirty seconds for the first comments to pop up.

I sighed and shoved the phone deep into my pocket and headed inside.

Charlie was nowhere to be seen, which wasn't too concerning at first. The audition workshop was rather solemn, all the fun exercises and anecdotes I'd planned seeming inappropriate now. Still, I didn't have any other material to use, so I sallied forth. Most of the attendees seemed fine with it, but a few scowled and one left, muttering about how I was a fame- hungry ghoul.

Keepin' it classy in Lester Cove.

I nearly cheered with relief when the workshop ended, forcing myself not to bolt for the door and instead following the attendees out into the foyer. Charlie was talking with Belinda near the sign-in table. Both looked rattled and pale, Belinda's eyes were red-rimmed and Charlie was unshaven, his hair a mess, and his shirt wrinkled.

Weaving my way through the small clusters of people milling about, I reached Charlie's side before he noticed my approach. "Hey," I murmured.

"How're you both holding up?"

"Fine," Belinda bit out. "Just…" She hesitated, then huffed out a ragged breath. "Margie wanted me to come in after the festival was over for the day, and I feel like she just doesn't get it! She knows this is an important day!"

"The festival is kind of off her radar," I pointed out gently. "Not everyone is as into theater as we are." Belinda muttered something under her breath, dashing at the tears leaking from her eyes. "Margie didn't mean any harm by it, Belinda. Did she say something when you told her you couldn't make it in?"

Belinda shook her head vehemently. "Just… *Oh, okay. See you for your shift Monday then.*"

Charlie and I exchanged a look, and he lifted his eyes heavenward with a sigh. "I'm sure it's all fine, Belinda. If you want, I can talk to her…"

She shook her head again, less sharply this time. "No, it's okay Mr. Murphy. I just…" She sniffed wetly. "I don't understand why she doesn't understand, you know?"

The tears were coming fast and heavy now and Belinda just sort of folded over herself, hunching over crossed arms as she sobbed quietly.

Charlie patted her awkwardly on the shoulder. "Go get a drink, kiddo. Maybe some fresh air. We'll hold off on announcing the one-act winners till you get back."

I nodded. "Promise."

She threw up her hands and growled under her breath in frustration. "She's not the only one, but it's like she's ignoring Renee's death, you know? This is a *sea change* moment! Theater will be *forever altered* and it's like we're the only ones who care!"

Charlie shifted uncomfortably, Belinda's outburst drawing all sorts of attention our way. "Belinda," I urged, "maybe take a breath, okay? Margie's not doing this to disrespect Renee. I bet she just… forgot."

I was a good actor, if I did say so myself, but that was different from outright lying to someone's face. Thankfully, Belinda was too wrapped up in her own performance of grief to notice. "I'm going to quit," she announced, yanking her phone out of her sweater pocket.

"Belinda," I called after her. "Don't—" The door to the manager's office slammed behind her. "Damn it!" I sighed, turning towards Charlie.

Or where he should have been.

He was gone, his would-be improv group waiting at the auditorium doors for a teacher that had just bailed.

I wanted to follow him, but I forced myself to smile and stride forward. "Hey, folks. I'll be filling in for Charlie! Let's head in and get started. Who here knows about *yes and*?"

The workshop went faster than I thought it might, ninety minutes speeding by as the remaining attendees got into the spirit and had fun with some of the exercises I dredged up from my early days of acting classes. Many of them had some real talent at improv after shaking off their nerves, a few asking if I'd be holding more workshops in the area soon or where they could find some classes to keep going. It was heartening, to say the least, and I let that mood boost buoy me into the Auditioning Tips for Beginners workshop after the short break.

The lack of Charlie's presence still wormed at the back of my mind, but I pushed that worry down as I led the less energetic but still enthusiastic group through my little lecture about how to audition and some dos and don'ts based on my own experience in the industry. The group was smaller and included, surprisingly, Ben Witte. He didn't participate so much as observe, his gaze intent as I led the group through my loose lesson plan, though he did laugh at a few of the funny stories I relayed about audition fails and winced at the particularly egregious ones. By the time I wrapped up, I was feeling a mix of relief that the workshops were over for me and a tinge of elation—it had gone well, and I'd felt like I really gave some good advice, or at least positive experiences, to people who were interested in performing. Ben noticed, smiling at me as I reached the door. "You look less wound up than the last time I saw you."

"Maybe that's all part of my evil plan to convince the people of Lester Cove I'm not here to stir trouble," I sassed, heading past him for the snack table Belinda and Ollie had set up that morning. Ollie was at one end, doling out cupcakes and tiny quiches, while, to my surprise, Margie stood at the far end, determinedly operating a bank of tea kettles and portable water coolers.

Ben shook his head, following my line of sight. "She swore she wasn't going to help out today, but apparently, Charlie convinced her to come, said it was the very last thing she could do for Renee."

That… made zero sense. Something on my face must've shown it because he smiled tightly and directed me, by way of his hand on my lower back, towards the little seating area by the doors. "Margie's receptive to guilt trips and the opportunity to be praised."

"That's rather uncharitable of you."

"But true," he said. "It's not a bad thing. We all want praise, don't we?"

I started to protest, but the keen glint in his eye caught me up. "I was going to deny it, but that'd be a big fat lie, considering I'm an actor. It's kind of what we live for."

"And I'm not going to deny enjoying being praised for my work at the firm and getting professional accolades," he shrugged. "Everyone in this room enjoys being told they're good at something or they're valued in some way."

"So, are you going to tell me you came to the workshop so you could get some tips on how to present yourself in front of judges or something? That's a bit like an audition, isn't it?"

He wobbled his hand from side to side. "I suppose, but not really. No, I came because I wanted to know more about you. More than what you told me over dinner. I wanted to see who you were when you weren't being defensive."

I sniffed at that. "I'm not defensive around you."

He tipped his head questioningly.

"Oh, shut up," I grumbled. Over at the snack table, Margie was hurrying from the back room, heading for the tea kettles and urns to start packing up. "Looks like everyone's wrapping up for the day," I murmured.

Ben nodded slowly. "We should continue this conversation over—"

"Tea?" I suggested, and he laughed, a pleasant and warm rumble of sound that I did *not* want to think too hard about.

"I do drink other things, no matter what the name on the shop suggests. I was going to say dinner, take two. There's a really good place over in Malm's Corner that does lobster rolls. I'm guessing you haven't had one since you've been to Maine."

"Not yet, no."

"Speaking as a lawyer, I must advise you that it's illegal to visit this state without trying a lobster roll at least once."

"Well, I don't want to break any laws while I'm here."

Ben stood, and I followed, joining the trickle of people heading toward the parking lot.

Milling about a while longer, I spoke with a few festival attendees, most of whom were already asking about next year, or a "do-over" for this one. Some locals were genuinely upset at Ms. Rhodes' passing, and there were more than a few visitors from out of state—theater fans, Renee Rhodes fans, and other kinds of vultures who'd been hoping for some sort of show or maybe even a peek at her body. But most people were respectful, subdued, and, by the time Margie started running out of coffee again, bored.

Nichols and one of his deputies scattered the paps who'd set up outside finally, and Belinda was helping pack up with a few of the volunteers from the high school theater club, Carmel having given up on her search for whatever was missing and joining in the tear-down. Without discussing it, we headed for Ben's car, parking in the back of the lot under some heavy-limbed locust trees giving shade. We were only a few feet from Ben's car when I drew us up short. Ben walked a few more steps but stopped when he noticed I wasn't with him.

"Ben. Look."

Slumped over the steering wheel, Charlie Arnold wasn't moving. The driver's side window was broken, and the door open just a bit, like someone couldn't be bothered to shut it all the way in their hurry.

Ben walked forward slowly. "Charlie. Charlie, talk to me."

I shook my head. I knew without having to be told it was too late. But Ben persisted.

"Come on, Charlie," he muttered, stopping beside the car and peering inside. The color drained from his face, and he took several steps back. "Damien, go get Nichols. Charlie's dead."

THIRTEEN

The note clutched in Charlie's bloodied hand had been simple. *I never stopped loving her. Let me be.*

The knife on the floor of the car finished the story for him.

The wording felt stiff, formal, but who was I to say what was in Charlie's head when he decided to end things.

Nichols had been stiff, hollow-voiced. It was a shock to everyone, and not even his professional mask could hide his horror at Charlie's sudden end. "Ben," he murmured as he came over to stand with us, "I'm afraid you're going to need to be available for questioning. It's your car, after all. Might go ahead and make time to come down to the department ASAP." Ben only nodded, his jaw set. He was unable to look away from his car. From Charlie.

"Of course," Ben said, barely above a whisper. "I… whatever you need. Of course."

Margie drifted over while Ben spoke with Belinda and Mrs. Gleaves inside the lobby. "This is so bizarre," she muttered, her tone subdued but her hands unable to stop fidgeting, first with the tissues she was tearing to shreds, then with her blouse's cuffs, little nervous plucks at a loose thread, a wiggly button. "Poor Charlie. I can't help but wonder…" She shot me a glance, catching her lower lip between her teeth before she sighed and shook her head. "Well, it's fantastical, really, but do you think he, you know what-ed, because he felt guilty?"

The thought had occurred to me pretty much right off the bat. "Or it's possible he was just so heartbroken, he couldn't see a way forward," I suggested.

Margie nodded thoughtfully. "Do you agree that he… you know?"

My neck crawled with unease as I admitted, "I think he's the most likely suspect of the ones we identified."

Margie made a tiny, disapproving noise, staring at the police gathered around Ben's car. "Charlie, Charlie, Charlie. Why did you do it?" she murmured. "Things could've been fine if you'd let them."

It was some unspoken agreement that led Ben and me to get in Margie's car with her, following Nichols to the department offices once the MCU squad arrived in town for the second time in a week. Ben had remained outside as Margie and I were ushered in, calling his office to sort out possible representation.

Just in case.

Nichols approached, looking exhausted and ready to quit.

"Heath." Margie sighed. "What on earth is happening?"

"We think he chose Ben's car because it was parked so far back. He could see the theater through the windshield, but it'd be hard if not impossible to see him inside the car," Nichols offered. We'd been ushered into the lobby by one of Nichol's men, offered water or yet more coffee as Ben paced just outside, gesturing and scowling as if the person on the other end could see him.

"Why does he think he needs a lawyer?" Nichols mused. "No one's accusing him of anything at this point."

I shrugged. "People metabolize stress in different ways. I shop. He arranges for legal representation."

Nichols gave a soft laugh. "Match made in heaven."

"Ugh, don't," I muttered. "Today's not the day."

Nichols rocked back on his heels, regarding me intently in the silence.

"What? Do I have something on my face?"

"You don't have to be *on* all the time," Nichols said. "No one here expects you to be Damien Murphy: Actor twenty-four-seven."

"I think I'd know better than you what people expect of me," I muttered. "And it's definitely not finding two dead bodies in one week."

"About that." He sighed. "Some guy named Rory Flick's been calling for you all morning. Apparently, you won't pick up your phone, so he's decided to ask for a welfare check. And thanks to the news about Charlie's death hitting the internet in a hot second after you guys found him, this Flick character has changed tactics demanding to speak to his client. He's under the impression you're being detained."

"Oh god," I moaned. "Why?"

"That might be because someone spread that around on social media in the past hour. Cherry's an avid user," he added dryly. "She's been keeping me abreast of the whole shit show."

"Great. Fantastic." I glanced out to see Ben leaning on the low fence along the walkway, his expression grim. And instead of working to get my name cleared in the court of public opinion, knowing Rory, he was letting it ride because *all PR is good PR.*

"Look, I need to make some calls to Charlie's kin, and you're free to go whenever you like. Where'd you stash Muffin by the way?"

"He's at the inn with the sisters."

Nichols nodded, frowning. "I'll give you a ride back to Two Moons. I need to talk to Carmel."

"I'll come too," Margie offered. "I should tell Carmel. We were both friends with Charlie and, well, times like this, sometimes you need that connection, you know?"

"Not really," Nichols muttered. "I've never had two people I know murdered in one week, but sure, let's go."

Ben wasn't too pleased about riding in the back of the squad car his ex-boyfriend was driving, but his car was evidence for the time being. Even though Charlie's death was considered an obvious suicide due to his note and the means of his death obvious, a wicked-sharp chef's knife still held in one hand, the state CSI wanted to 'make sure' and Ben was begrudgingly accepting of the fact. The ride to the inn was quiet, Muffin waiting at the gate to greet us when Nichols pulled to a stop.

Margie was first out, hurrying past Muffin with tiny, nervous steps until she reached the porch, her entire body relaxing once out of reach of Muffin's growling face. She disappeared into the inn, leaving me and Ben with Nichols.

"It goes without saying." He sighed. "That Renee's case is open again."

"Why's that?" I murmured. "Possibly because it's a murder?"

"It's *possibly* a murder."

In the back seat, Ben muttered something under his breath before trying to open the door. "For god's sake, Heath, let me out of here before you try flirting with him."

My face heated. and Nichols rolled his eyes. "Keep your shorts on," he said, getting out of the car and going around to let Ben out. I joined them on the walkway, stepping back as Ben strode up to the house, ignoring both of us.

I crouched to give Muffin some love and Nichols stood beside me, awkwardly quiet. "So, what is it? Were you telling the truth or am I suddenly a suspect?" I demanded when the silence had stretched too long. "Or are you just wanting an autograph and you're too shy to ask?"

He snorted. "Not really an autograph guy," he said.

"So, it's the other?"

"Well, yes and no."

Oh hell. "Okay then. Hit me with it."

Nichols made a growly, tired noise low in his throat as he exhaled, leaning forward so he could keep his voice low. "Look, we both know it was an accident—"

"Do we?"

"Fine, *I* know her death was an accident, but we have to reopen it at the request of the state due to some new evidence that puts that finding in question. At least in their mind."

"What's the evidence?" I leaned forward too, finding myself suddenly *too* close to Nichols but unable to move back without seeming awkwardly rude.

"Ah, can't say."

"Can't or won't?"

"Can't. I was just told the case has to remain open, and we can't close it off as an accident until a further investigation is completed. For now, it remains *pending* in the files."

"Pending," I repeated. "How depressing."

He hummed thoughtfully, glancing down at Muffin between us, staring back at him. "You really gonna find someone to take him off your hands?"

"I can't take him with me when I go. My apartment back home is tiny and no pets allowed. And I don't even have a car right now, so…"

"So, it sounds like you're stuck here for a bit," Nichols smiled, sitting back. "Looks like you're gonna be pet sitting for a while."

"Ugh. Looks like." Muffin laid his head on my knee, daring me to say *ugh* again. "You're still saying it's an accident even though someone has enough pull to keep this open, huh?"

"Mmhm. Because it *was*. Shit happens sometimes, Damien. And sometimes it's horrible. Ms. Rhodes was in the wrong place at the wrong time. There's been zero evidence found to indicate she was murdered, so that's what I have to go with."

Annoyance burst out in a torrent of words that made Nichols recoil. "No evidence? Seriously? You guys didn't even bother to do more than a cursory glance around! If you had, you'd know the theater didn't even *have* a sandbag system anymore and hadn't in years! It was all taken out! And you'd know that Charlie Arnold has credible reason to believe Ms. Rhodes was afraid someone was out to harm her! And you'd know—"

"I'd know," he shot back, "that you really are good suspect material, Damien Murphy. So, if you want to keep pushing it, feel free, but just know that's gonna turn the magnifying glass on you, too. Do you have an alibi for the night she was killed?"

"I was at the gala. Then I was walking back to the B&B and…" I trailed off. "I was nearly hit by another car. So, there's at least one witness for where I was when she was being killed."

"Not really," he smirked cruelly. "Just your word for it. And frankly, that's not worth much in a case like this." He pushed to his feet and gave me a curt nod. "When you decide to stop pretending like this is some show you're on, give me a call."

Muffin huffed at Nichols' retreating back. "Me too," I muttered. "Me too."

* * *

CARMEL'S SOBS were muffled through two floors and several closed doors, but they were heart-wrenching, nonetheless. Margie had lingered for a bit, until Ben chivvied her out, firmly insisting Carmel needed time alone. Margie had agreed, somewhat dejectedly, but insisted on cleaning up from our half-assed lunch first, packing away the uneaten sandwiches and washing up the utensils, promising to come by with some muffins or something in the morning so they didn't have to make breakfast.

Muffin and I retreated to my room, Muffin picking up on the somber mood of the house and sighing himself into a loaf in front of the hearth, head on his crossed paws as he turned sad eyes up to me. "I don't know either, doggo," I muttered. "I wish I did."

Paul Santos chose that moment to call, relieving me of my spiraling for the moment. "Hey," he greeted breathlessly. "It's all over the gossip columns. Are you okay?"

"Okay as can be," I admitted. "How bad is it?"

"Eeeeeeh. Let's just say that your name is trending, and it's about fifty-fifty on whether or not you want to check that out."

I winced. "Let me guess, I did it?"

"Theater fans do love some drama," Paul said diplomatically. "I'd been intending to call you later today with some of the info you'd been wanting, but I saw this pop up in my alerts and couldn't wait. The address book pics you sent really helped me with the research, and I was able to track down two of the people listed. The others have either passed away or are unlisted, but I'm gonna send you these in just a sec. They knew Renee back in the day, when she was just getting started, and I'm just gonna go ahead and say it—you might not want to include what they have to say in your eulogy."

I sat down on the edge of the bed, phone clutched so tightly I was surprised the plastic wasn't creaking. "That bad?"

"Renee's reputation for having a strong personality was really a kindness. Apparently, she was a bit of a monster." Paul huffed out a breath and there was the sound of keys clacking. "Should be in your inbox in a sec. I have to admit, I've been really digging into Renee Rhodes, and it is *wild*. Her reputation is *nothing* compared to some of the stuff I've been finding. I don't know if it's because she had the goods on some people and kept it quiet or if it was a case of the theater world not being as attention-grabby as movies and TV back in the seventies, but there's a *ton* of dirt that I'm just shocked was never made public."

"Maybe," I said slowly, "because the people hurt weren't famous, so no one cared."

Paul was quiet for a moment, his enthusiasm still simmering in the silence. "Maybe," he allowed. "It's a sad fact of the industry, isn't I?"

"Yeah… Yeah, it is. Hey, I hate to throw this on your stack of things to do too, but I was wondering if you'd mind doing a little more digging for me? Some names that came up attached to a play Ms. Rhodes was in. It never really went anywhere but, well," I forced a chuckle, "I'm nosy."

He snorted. "It is *no* problem. This is the most exciting thing to happen in theater in years, if you don't count the shit show that was that superhero musical. I've gotten almost five hundred new subs on the site today alone, and donations to the museum have gone up by sixty percent since last week."

That felt grim and gruesome, but I bit my tongue, knowing full well that my own death would likely earn some gossip rag or niche fan a few bucks one day. "I'm trying to find out more about Peggy Trent and DA James. I couldn't find much, just that they were in this one play with her."

Paul made a thoughtful noise as he typed away on his end. "I'll see what I can find and get back to you ASAP, but it might be a day or so—I'm supposed to be at a fundraiser in like an hour and tomorrow is brunch for Tippy Newell's sixtieth—it's the fifth time she's turned sixty, but I'll never say no to bottomless mimosas."

We had our goodbyes, and I hung up with a heavy weight on my neck and thoughts. Carmel's sobs broke through the vents, and I couldn't take another second in the house, pushing to my feet and snapping for Muffin, who gave me a *who do you think you're talking to* look. "Sorry. Walk?"

He deigned to accompany me, rising to his feet with a heave and a shake, standing still while I hooked his harness to the leash. Grabbing my phone and laptop, I decided to head for the tea shop and maybe talk with Margie a bit about this, if she was up for it.

"C'mon," I said, grabbing one of the remaining bags of treats from the desk. "I'll even get you some of the gross, stinky ones while we're out."

FOURTEEN

"Well, this was a bad idea," I muttered to Muffin. The shop was crowded, almost every table full. And from a quick look down the street, so was the little deli a few doors down and the Italian-Mexican fusion place at the end of the block.

Margie, behind the counter, looked steam-frizzled and tired, her mascara racooned around her eyes. Ben was behind her, scowling. Neither noticed my presence, dealing with the line of people casually pretending not to look for gossip.

A few people glanced my way. More than one scowled, and a few leaned closer together to whisper.

Subtle, these people were not.

Muffin pressed close beside me as we edged along the line to reach the remaining empty seat, realizing belatedly that it was actually occupied. A grizzled older man wearing a t-shirt that had maybe once been a band shirt but was now worn so thin there was no telling, the design on the front faded to a few lines and a smudge of orange against the eggshell fabric. His beard was braided in one long queue to the middle of his chest, and he had a definite Daddy vibe happening but in a swipe-left sort of way, at least for my tastes. A tiny Progress Pride flag pen sat dead center on his bucket hat, pulled low over his eyes.

Welp. At least he was Family, so no worries for my safety there.

"Sorry," I murmured, backing away. "Didn't realize someone was sitting here."

"Damien Murphy, right?" he said—growled, really.

I nodded.

"I knew Charlie for years. Since he first moved here. This is some BS."

"I'm sorry," I said. "This has to be a horrible shock."

"Shock? Hell yeah, it is! The man was murdered!"

Everyone went quiet for a moment and the man stood, shoving his chair back noisily. "Charlie was a lot of things, but suicidal? Hell no."

"Jerome," Margie said, tone quelling. "You're making a scene!"

"And you're not? These folks are all jabbering about Charlie being a murderer! Killing himself over it!" Jerome threw up his hands. "That man's been coming to my bar damn near every night for the past ten years. We've spent holidays together! I *know*—knew… I knew him, Margie. Prob'ly better than you." His mouth worked like he wanted to spit. Instead, he turned to me and swept an acid glare from head to toe over my frozen form. "You gonna tell your little social media followers all about the pathetic old man who killed himself then? Gonna make it a whole thing? Get you some attention online?"

I shook my head, trembling. "No. No, never. I… Charlie's death is terrible. Ms. Rhodes' death was terrible. I'd never use that for views or clout or… or…"

Jerome made a growly, disgusted noise low in his throat and turned away, stomping for the door. The chime screamed in protest as he jerked it shut behind him, not letting the door sigh closed as it usually did.

There was a heartbeat of silence, then the whispers and murmurs began again. Margie shot me a curious, dismayed glance, and I shook my head. *Later*, I mouthed, ignoring Ben's grim glare over her shoulder. I followed Jerome's steps more sedately, Muffin still pressed close and cautious, looking both ways on the sidewalk to make sure I wasn't about to walk straight into a fight with the man and headed for the one place I was sure no one would come find me.

Palais Theater was eerily quiet. The gates to the parking lot were closed, the lights off in the building, and doors shut tight against all comers.

Unless you knew about the side entrance that was never locked. Thank you, Margie Witte.

The interior was dark and expectant. Renee Rhodes' ghost lurked around every corner as I made my way to the manager's office, thinking I'd feel a bit better with a few doors between me and the site of two deaths.

I was wrong, but at least it was quiet.

Muffin settled uneasily under the desk, sniffing the room with an almost frantic attention to the space, his entire demeanor stiff until I settled in front of him in the chair, blocking him from the rest of the room with my legs, slipping him some of the stinky treats he preferred.

Over the years, I'd gotten very good at compartmentalizing. Having a bad day and just want to cry about it? Too bad—your character is a happy- go- lucky elf and always smiles, so you better pack that mess away till your scene is shot and in the can. Feeling sick, running a fever of 101 and can barely stand up? You'd better pop some Tylenol and Visine those red eyes away because you're due on set in ten, and you'd better hit your mark and deliver that sidekick speech in one go or you're stuck out there for another hour and a half wanting to just die a little. It wasn't a healthy skill, but it was there for me to draw on as I opened up my laptop and got a playlist going, some Lo-Fi background music to drown out the voices of the dead as I pulled up messages on my phone.

PAUL SANTOS

CALL ME! GOT YOUR INFO!

Well. Okay then.

He answered on the first ring. "Damien! Yes!" The rustle of paper crinkled loudly, then the sound of a door closing. "Sorry about that, I was just going through some old archival stuff I'm organizing for the Queer Broadway show in December. We're holding a sort of pop-up museum experience at one of the small off-Broadway theaters, ironically."

I laughed with him. "Maybe I'll be able to come see it. Stage work is something I've been wondering about lately."

He made a thoughtful little humming sound. "Max suggested as much. I have some more info for you about Peggy Trent and DA James."

"Your timing is perfect. I'm finally sitting down to work on the eulogy."

He chuckled darkly at that. "You're not going to want to include this, not unless you really didn't like the old gal. Renee Rhodes had a bit of a scandal attached to her name. A few, actually, but one big one in particular. She was doing the slow and steady climb thing, retail clerk by day and actress by night, that sort of thing. But she had a sudden big break around 1976. Well, big as you can get for Broadway in that era."

"What happened?" I settled back in the creaky office chair. "Don't tell me it was a casting couch thing!"

"Not in this case. And keep in mind this is all rumor and hearsay, so take it with a huge serving of salt and maybe a bit of tequila and lime. A few of the old, defunct gossip rags I've got in the archive mention her by name and suggest she was a rather integral part of a big shake-up during a production of *Mondays at the Kremlin*."

"I haven't heard of that one," I admitted. "And what do you mean, a shake-up?"

Paul clicked his tongue, settling into the gossip session. "The play wasn't that good, but it had a lot of promise. One of those that needed some workshopping and finding the right audience. It wouldn't have been a big Broadway production by any means, but it fell apart spectacularly and got all sorts of attention on the people involved when the director, a man named

Stefan Horton, offed himself, and Renee Rhodes was briefly accused of being behind it. Two other cast members had suffered some pretty bad injuries during the initial run."

I sat up, my heart kicking into overdrive and making my hands shake. "Wait, Renee Rhodes was accused of murder? *What?*"

"Never officially. Horton's death is listed as a suicide. He'd been having some issues for years. Nothing more than rumors. Renee was not only nowhere nearby when he died, but they hadn't spoken for months. The play was on hiatus due to the injuries of the other cast members. Just rumors," he stressed.

My breath caught in my throat, an orange-size stone settling in my gut. "Peggy Trent and DA James."

Santos shuffled some papers, humming in agreement. "They never made it big. They didn't even make it small, frankly. Other than a brief mention of the accidents, their names never turn up on any other playbills or gossip columns or, well, anything related to theater in New York that I could find after 1976."

"Do you know what happened to them?" My voice was nearly a whisper, but I couldn't bring myself to speak any louder.

"Not really. Just DA James mentioned as being taken to the hospital during dress rehearsals due to a broken femur from a fall off the stage, and a few months later when the play was gearing up to run again, Peggy Trent, the then leading lady of the show, managed to get pinned under some stage rigging and ended up with a punctured lung, broken jaw, and some other injuries that took her out of the game."

I sat up straight, startling Muffin into a soft wuff of surprise. "Wait. Peggy Trent was the lead, not Renee Rhodes?"

"Nope. Renee was the understudy for Peggy, but after Peggy's accident, Renee got the lead. And even though the play failed in a huge way, her name was splashed all over, at least in the right circles, and it was like a rocket was tied to it, dragging her up the casting chain. Within a year she was getting cast in big shows as the second lead and by 1978, she was the main lead in at least one major production per year for the next twenty years, not counting her one-woman show, her off-Broadway shows, and a few special guest star type spots in some of the gimmicky shows."

I nodded. "I know the ones. Hell, I've been in a few myself."

Santos started to say something else, but a voice came up on his end and he muttered *just a sec* to whoever it was. "Look," he said to me, "I gotta go —I have an appointment with one of the original leads from *Angels in America Part II*, but shoot me an email if you need any more info. Is this all for her memorial service? It sounds like it's going to be a juicy one." He laughed.

I forced a chuckle. "It's gonna be something."

"Hey, real quick though—this might sound obvious, but try YouTube. I've found some really W-T-F videos of old plays on there, stuff people dug up from grandma and grandpa's archives, niche fandom stuff, that sort of thing. I haven't had a chance to do a deep dive yet, but you might have some luck with Renee's older stuff on there. Like I'm talking page six of the search type deep dive, get me?"

"Yeah, I get you," I murmured. "Thanks for all the help. I really do appreciate it."

"Keep in touch—this is juicy stuff, man."

We hung up and a moment later, some files popped up in my emails— scanned images of the old articles Paul had dug up in his archives. I saved them to my laptop and, as an afterthought, saved a copy of everything I had so far to the cloud drive where I saved my scripts and notes, so I could access it elsewhere if I had to.

Was that a good idea, safety-wise? Probably not. But I wanted to make sure all my bases were covered if I had to confront Nichols about things again. Or, judging by how some of the tabs were treating my presence in

Lester Cove, cover my own backside. The dig into YouTube was more tedious than I anticipated, and I realized, after about twenty minutes of trying different keywords and flipping through link after link that seemed to be variations on Ms. Rhodes' appearances on TV specials and specially recorded performances for Broadway in the Classroom back in the nineties, I was going to need help.

Max blinked blearily at me as soon as he opened FaceTime. "I have one more day of shooting left before pick-ups," he grumbled. "Are you dead? Because I won't be mad at you for waking me up if you're dead."

"No, but Charlie Arnold is."

He blinked, scrubbed at his eyes, and sat up, telling the person next to him to go back to sleep as he slipped from bed and, a moment later, turned on the light in what looked to be a sitting room. Shirtless, Max looked like about a dozen magazine covers come to life with his wild dark hair and famous green eyes. Even though those eyes were a little unfocused and glaring at me through a haze of sleep. "Start at the top. Catch me up."

Max slowly came more awake as I ran him through the details, his expression growing more concerned with each new detail. "Dude, I think you need to get the hell out of dodge because this sounds sketchy AF." He opened another tab and, frowning, shared his screen with me. "Look. *Ex Child Actor Close to TWO Murders!*" The headline was terrible, the pictures worse.

"Oh my god, why did they use the one of me with that stupid haircut?"

"Everyone had that haircut," Max said defensively. "It's not stupid."

"I look like I was going for a mohawk but forgot halfway through. And curtain bangs to boot!"

"I think we're drifting from the point here," Max said dryly. "Your name is getting associated with murders!"

"Rory must be thrilled. Did I tell you he tried to get the local cops to do a welfare check because I'm not returning his calls?"

Max made a face, pushing his lips to one side as he avoided my gaze.

"Ugh, don't tell me. You think I should call him back."

"He is your agent, despite everything I've tried to tell you about how shit he is."

"I owe him." I sighed. "He's the only one who'd even try to get me roles at this point."

"You just have his word for that," Max shot back immediately.

It was an old argument, one I hated mostly because I had the tiny little suspicion he might be right. But… "Max," I muttered. "Can we please do this later?"

He set his jaw mutinously, but he melted after a moment and nodded. "Fine. But at least tell me why you've jumped on this investigation like Seven Markham's poodle on my handmade Ferragamos."

"You're never going to let that go, are you?"

"Would you?"

"Fair…"

Max shifted forward, his face filling my screen. I missed him fiercely and wished he was close enough to hug because damn it, I needed one. When he spoke, it was quiet and urgent, tinged with worry. "Look, you're beyond my best friend, you know that, right?" I nodded, and he heaved a small breath. "I mean, queer platonic soulmates five ever, right?"

I chuckled weakly, our old rallying cry that had once been just a silly thing to say having long past become true. "Five ever."

"So, when I say that I think you're so into this investigation because you're afraid *you* will be Renee Rhodes one day, know that I'm not being a jerk, okay? Not on purpose, anyway."

"If I died under mysterious circumstances, I wouldn't want to be treated like some salacious story in the tabs," I murmured. "I'd want someone, anyone, to try to give me some dignity in my death."

"But is that what you're doing?" he pressed. "From everything you told me, the Renee Rhodes who was killed is *not* the Renee Rhodes you went to Lester Cove to meet and work with. That Renee Rhodes, the one you thought you were meeting, is a performance. One of her characters."

"Isn't that all of us, though?" I demanded, though it came out softer than I intended. "Does that mean she's not worth helping?"

"That's not what I meant," he sighed. "Just… think about why you're doing this, okay? If this Charlie Arnold guy is likely your killer, and he's dead… What good is it going to do to keep pushing?"

"And if he's not…"

"If he's not, then that's not your problem, babe. I love you to the ends of the earth and twice around, but I think this is getting dangerous, Damien. For you."

I nodded glumly. "Maybe you're right. Maybe… Maybe I just need to worry about making sure her memorial honors her well, and then just figure out where to go next."

"Maybe," he agreed. "Shit. I have twenty minutes before the car gets here. Call me tonight, okay? Like… by ten your time. I should have a break by then."

"Love you, bestie."

"Mwah."

And I tried to take his advice, I really did.

But maybe has a lot of leeway.

And a video of *Kaleidoscope Coffin* was tucked away between two videos of Renee Rhodes on the Today Show, just waiting… I took it as a sign and clicked play.

FIFTEEN

T he video opened with a title card. ***Kaleidoscope Coffin—1978 soft open.*** It was grainy, funky-colored with age, and obviously made by someone using their phone to record off an old video tape playing on a television. On the screen, a woman—Renee Rhodes, I realized—wearing a stunning black gown and an outrageously big ponytail, threw a martini glass to the ground and called the man on stage with her a bastard. I could barely make out his response, but it involved gesturing to a scrim done up to look like a stained-glass window. The lighting changed and made them even harder to see clearly, but the woman screamed, and something fell.

The lights went out entirely and when they came back up, they were multicolored and wavering slightly, though I couldn't tell if it was from the quality of the video or something the lighting director thought looked good. The man on stage stepped into the spotlight. Renee Rhodes lay on the ground beside a comically oversized sandbag, her body positioned so that the audience could see her face peaceful in mock death, her body stretched out in elegant lines.

When the man spoke, it was a deep, rumbling bass. "Your death is your only reward," he growled. "You deserve nothing more than an eternity without recognition, lost to the ages. Soon, you will be forgotten. I will make sure of it."

The video ended, and an ad for some energy drink popped up as the screen counted down to the next video, someone's upload of a bootleg recording of an all-nude version of *The Music Man.*

Shit.

I played it again. Then a third time just to be sure what I was seeing. *Damn it, Charlie, of all the people I need to talk to about this…*

Wait, though—Margie knew Renee Rhodes back then. I pulled up her number and shot off a text. She might have known Peggy Trent or DA James!

ME

Do you remember seeing this play back in the day? I think I might be on to something here. Did you know the lead, Peggy Trent? Or DA James?

I winced at the time—no wonder I felt so lightheaded! It was almost eight! "Muffin, c'mon, doggo. It's past time for you to have some actual food." My stomach gave a plaintive growl in agreement. "Let's see if that tourist trap is still open on Buttermilk!"

Luck was on my side—Denny's Seafood, Salads, and Milkshakes (oh god, that combination sounded just terrible) was still open for another ten minutes when we arrived, most of the customers being of the high school sort, trying to look cool while sucking down half-melted ice cream or coffee that was more milk than caffeine. I ordered a sandwich and bottled water to go, Muffin sniffing hopefully at my plastic bag when I got back outside and untied his leash from the bike rack. "Sorry, dude. No dogs allowed in there. Not everywhere's as nice as Margie's place, huh?"

Muffin was the perfect companion for a walk. He didn't tell me to stop talking when I rambled, he was agreeable with all of my suggestions, and when I just needed to sit down and think, he laid on my feet and took a nap, making sure I knew I wasn't alone.

I could see why Ms. Rhodes liked him so much.

We'd walked around the small downtown area for about an hour, an odd sense of expectation and tension overlaying the previously cheerful, bustling few blocks. Between Ms. Rhodes' death now being considered a murder by most in town, and Charlie's sudden death just that morning, with Belinda's detainment zipping along the gossip vine, Lester Cove was at a loss.

Or maybe that was just my imagination, projecting what I wanted to see and feel on everyone else.

"What do you think, Muffin?"

He woofed softly, lifting his head and sniffing the air. We were in the Lost Seafarer's Park, less than a mile from his old home, and I think he knew it. "I'm sorry, boyo. She's not coming back."

I gathered Muffin, and we headed back towards the inn, keeping to the well-lit main drag for as long as possible. Something about the night felt off, something holding its breath in the darkening evening and waiting for its chance to pounce.

Now who's the dramatic one? I thought as we followed the curve of Buttermilk towards Lester Road and the inn.

Muffin stiffened, yanking against the leash, trying to pull me up onto the grassy berm where the town planners had stuffed another little pocket park, denoting the break between the business district and the historical, residential area. "Settle down, Muffin," I urged. "You're gonna knock me down."

Muffin seemed to take that as a suggestion, leaping up and throwing his full weight against me. I hit the ground with a solid *oof* of surprise as Muffin broke free, rushing into the dark of the park, snarling and barking. There was the sound of a scuffle, muffled cursing, then Muffin yelped. A dark shape came pelting out of the dark, knocking me back again as they thundered past, towards the dark curve of Lester Road where it disappeared between the thick stands of trees, hiding the theater and older homes from the rest of the town. "Muffin!" I scrambled to my feet, hands abraded but otherwise unharmed. "Muffin, come here boy!"

He whimpered but came limping out of the park with one paw lifted, his breath heavy and fast. "Oh my god, Muffin!" Under the streetlight, I could see his paw was already swelling, and there was dark, wet blood on his flank. He'd been cut! "Oh no no no no no! Hold on, okay?"

I stroked between his ears with one hand, shoving the other in my pocket to grab my phone. There was no 911 for pets. I was already thinking about who to call for a ride. Margie? Ben? The Moon sisters? My fingers found nothing but lint. My phone was gone. For a moment, I thought I'd left it at the inn, but no, I'd been holding it a few moments before. Had I dropped it? Muffin whimpered again. "Damn." I'd have to wait for daylight and hope it was still there.

A few shops were still open on Buttermilk, so I scooped him up, staggering under his weight, and lurched towards the nearest one, Lester's Shirts and Cards and Shells.

Little bit of everything for everyone.

"Help," I called, shoving the door open with my shoulder. "I need to use your phone!"

Sienna answered at the inn, and she was the one to arrive a few minutes later in an older Subaru Forester with a plethora of stickers on the back and a towel laid across the bench seat. "Sit with him in the back," she ordered. "Keep him calm."

"I don't know if the vet's open," I said, panic clear in my voice.

"Not the one in town. Malm's Corner has an emergency clinic, though. Hold tight."

Muffin closed his eyes, sides heaving for the entire drive to the slightly larger town of Malm's Corner. The vet clinic was brightly lit and larger than I expected, made to look like a small-scale hospital with a white exterior and red cross emblems. Sienna helped me get Muffin inside and gingerly sat beside him while I talked to the desk clerk. We were whisked back into an exam room where I was shuffled aside as they started to tend to his injuries. "I don't know anything about his history," I admitted on the third round of questioning. "His person died last week, and I've been sort of pet sitting him."

One of the vet nurses glanced up. "Pet sitting?"

"Fostering," I muttered. "Hanging out?"

"How did this happen again?" the nurse demanded. I felt very on the spot, like I was being accused of something terrible as I repeated for a fourth time the story of how Muffin had been injured.

"Sounds like a mugging gone wrong," one of the techs remarked, smoothing the fur on Muffin's snoot. They'd given him a sedative before they started cleaning and stitching the wound on his flank, rendering the large beastie a puddle of dog fur and drool.

"No one gets mugged in Lester Cove," Sienna said, stoutly defending her little town.

"First time for everything," the nurse retorted. "Did you call the police?"

"I was more worried about the dog. He saved me," I added, a pang of unexpected affection hitting me deep. "Is he going to be okay?"

The vet spoke up. "He should be. He'll need a follow-up with his regular vet, though."

I nodded, and we were shown back to the waiting room so they could x-ray Muffin's paw. Sienna settled into one of the plastic seats, giving a very harassed-looking iguana the side-eye. "No one gets mugged in Lester Cove," she repeated, barely above an accusatory whisper. "Whoever did this was trying to get you, you know."

"I figured. They stole my phone."

She made a face at that. "Who steals a phone? It's not like they can use it without getting caught."

"People do it all the time in LA. There're ways to rig 'em so they can't be traced back to the original owner, so you can use them yourself like new."

"That's deplorable. It's also not likely in Lester Cove, or Malm's Corner, for that matter. We're not exactly the big city. There's nowhere to take your phone and rig it up or whatnot."

I nodded slowly. "That's what I'm thinking. Whoever took it wanted to see what I had on there."

"So, like one of those tabloid vultures from today? Someone trying to see if you wanted to sell the dirty details or something?"

"Something."

My head throbbed with the weight of all the things I needed to do as soon as I was back at the inn: report my phone stolen, contact Max, Paul… Hell, Rory too. Sort out a new phone… I closed my eyes and did some breathing exercises a therapist once taught me. They were supposed to be good for lowering blood pressure and managing stress, but they only made me drowsy.

The wait for Muffin to be brought out was doubly interminable, not just out of worry for his well-being but because each minute that passed was just more time whoever attacked Muffin and tried to attack me had my phone and all the information on it, including my notes about potential suspects. Finally, after an hour or so, one of the techs brought Muffin out. He wobbled slightly with the sedative and grinned up at me with his tongue lolling. "He'll sleep a lot the next day or so," the tech told us. "The x-rays looked good as can be—the wound is long rather than deep, but he still needed some stitches. Make sure he keeps them dry and poor guy's gonna have to keep the super stylish collar here on for a bit." He tapped the plastic cone around Muffin's neck. Muffin tried to lift his head and succeeded in only listing to one side, resting against my leg and nearly tipping me over with his dead weight. "Aw, puppy!" The tech chuckled. "We slipped some treat samples into his bag here to make up for all the trauma. And here are some antibiotic samples for his wound, but be sure to get him to his regular vet tomorrow. Come on up to the desk with me and I'll get you signed out and take payment."

Sienna grunted under her breath. "Hope you've got savings. This is gonna cost ya big."

I winced at the number the tech handed me. Muffin was leaning on my leg again, his heavy body warm and trembling with the effects of the attack and the painkillers combined. I couldn't be mad about it, I decided. "Poor guy's had a crap week." I sighed, pulling my credit card out and handing it over. "C'mon, Muffin. I'll give you those stinky treats back at the hotel, and I won't complain when you breathe in my face, so long as you promise not to chew your stitches, okay?"

He huffed softly. I like to think he agreed with me.

Sienna helped me once more carry Muffin, getting him settled in the back seat and allowing me up front this time. Neither of us spoke as she pointed us back down the coast to Lester Cove. It wasn't until we were almost back at the inn that she remarked, "I don't think Charlie killed himself."

"Sienna, we all saw what happened," I said softly. "It wasn't an accident."

Sienna jerked the car into the turn for Lester Road, taking us the long way past Witte House, past the theater. The house was lit up in every room, from the looks of things. Ben's car wasn't outside, but before I could wonder where he was, I remembered why it was gone.

The theater was dark, a gaping black hole in the trees without even a security lamp turned on as we passed.

Sienna slowed as we neared the inn, turning more carefully up the narrow drive tucked beside the old house and parking in the restored carriage house around back. When she shut off the engine, she shifted to face me, pinning me in place with a hard stare. "I wasn't close with Charlie, but Carmel was. She considered him her best friend, outside of me and the cats. So, I've known Charlie for a while now, and when I say he wasn't the sort to kill himself, I know what I'm talking about."

Without another word, she got out of the car and went around to the back to get Muffin. She helped me get Muffin out of the car and up the stairs to my room for the night, pausing in the doorway as if she wanted to say something, but thinking better of it, settling into her stern demeanor with a sharp nod.

"Don't forget you gotta check out by Wednesday night," she reminded me. "No offense or nothing."

It was Sunday now, the clock showing just past midnight. Which meant I had three days.

Muffin whimpered in his sleep, and I could only agree.

SIXTEEN

I t took longer than I liked to work my way through the maze of a website and shut off my phone. The Find My Phone tracker was showing my phone still on Buttermilk Road, but nothing more specific than that big green circle stretching from the top of the road to the memorial park at the end, and my provider couldn't use GPS to track my stolen phone without a police warrant. Somehow, I doubted that Nichols would be able to rustle up something official for me to hand over at this late hour, or at all really. Super fun times. The best I could do was check my phone's activity. The last call it showed on my account was the last one I'd made.

Which didn't help me one damn bit.

Max was next on my contact list. He answered my email within minutes, still on Stockholm time, as they wrapped up that portion of the shoot. He threatened to order me a replacement phone and have it overnighted if I didn't get it done myself in the morning and told me to call him as soon as I had it done to prove I was alive.

Paul Santos didn't reply, and I hoped what I'd sent him wasn't something that would ruin lives or worse if it got out.

Shit… all of that info is on my phone! Was I still logged into my cloud thingy? Damn it! Whoever has it can see everything!

The police department phones rolled over to voicemail again, and I didn't have Nichols' private number memorized, so I just left a message for someone to call me at my room number at the inn so I could report a mugging. Agitated, I looked at the handwritten notes again, and the files I'd made on the laptop and felt all my pointed reasons drifting away.

Damn. I wished I remembered Ben's number. Bouncing this off Max, even if he wasn't currently long-distance, wouldn't work. He'd insist on calling the police, doing so from Stockholm himself if he thought I hadn't. And going to Carmel or Sienna was out of the question.

"Looks like it's you and me tonight, Muffin," I murmured. "You ever listen to true crime podcasts?"

Muffin slept the sleep of the just as I put on something suitably grim and quiet in the background, unable to sleep without getting everything out on paper.

How had everything gotten so out of hand, I wondered. And could I have done anything to stop it? The papers from Belinda were still out on the desk, and a few handwritten notes of my own, trying to piece things together. I felt guilty for even considering Belinda but also, what I'd missed something? Was there some clue, some bit of proof that meant she really was the killer?

I used the back of Belinda's paperwork to make my notes, laying out everything possible about Charlie Arnold. Reluctantly, I did the same for Belinda. I made a separate chart for Renee Rhodes and included her ties to Peggy Trent and DA James, underlining those, as they were double-verified. The databases I could access only went back twenty years, and anything about their divorce was also sealed tight.

Back to working on *vibes* for some of this, apparently.

Compared to Belinda's list, Charlie's was not only extensive, but damning. Belinda's list was Swiss cheese. Charlie's was an entire sandwich. A case could be made, superficially, for Belinda lashing out at Ms. Rhodes, acting in anger or even jealousy over some imagined slight from her icon, but it would be a hard case to make.

Charlie, though… If I were writing it out as a script, the producer would tell me to tone down the drama, so it'd be more believable. Betrayal, heartbreak, thwarted dreams, manipulation… It was a soap opera without the whimsy.

But even so, the two of them didn't hit every box. I drew a line through Belinda's name, marking her off my suspect list entirely. "Someone who knew Ms. Rhodes, who was familiar with her body of work even back to the earliest days. Who knew about Peggy Trent and DA James, knew their way around stage rigging, was in town for the festival, and was able to get into and out of the theater without being noticed." It was all looking like Charlie, except for the fact that he had an alibi for the night Ms. Rhodes was murdered.

"Though if he set it up in advance? But why wait forty years? And why kill himself afterwards?"

I glanced down at the paper I'd been doodling on to see I'd made another column and drew an X at the top as I turned the evidence over and over in my thoughts.

"Unless it wasn't Charlie at all."

<hr>

SLEEP WAS NOT ONLY ELUSIVE, it was downright absent. After a few hours of tossing and turning, I gave it up for a bad job and got the day started quietly, so as not to wake the Moon sisters. I got Muffin settled with some treats after another careful bathroom trip and set to my to-do list. First, call the local vet's after-hours number. Doc Jones was their outcall vet, and she promised she'd stop by around ten or so to check on his wound, once she got the x-rays and write-up from the emergency vet. Next, I checked my emails. Several from Rory about Charlie's death and my proximity—it was doing numbers on the bird app, apparently—and a handful from Max demanding proof of life before he stopped filming and got on a plane to 'kick your scrawny ass for scaring me, you jerk.'

Plus, I was touched to see, he'd sent a scad of pictures of Renee Rhodes, many of them from personal collections from people who knew people who knew Max.

Thought maybe you could use these for the memorial. I know things are defying the laws of physics and both sucking and blowing concurrently, but I love you, you dork, and you know I'm here for you.

BFF5ever.

I emailed him back a promise to call later and told him I loved him, followed by a selection of goofy, weird memes I kept in a file for just such occasions (our love language, really) before taking a deep breath and emailing Rory, then I made my way down the stairs to get a cup of the coffee I could smell brewing.

His call came less than two minutes after I hit send on the message confirming I was alive (what the hell was happening on my socials for everyone to want proof of life?) and I'd be getting a new phone soon. The best part though, was he called the inn's main line, not my phone.

Carmel was at the bottom of the stairs, holding the hall phone with a mildly confused look on her face. "No one ever calls this line," she said shakily, grief still painting her voice heavily. "It's your agent, I think? He said he was. Do you want me to tell him to go away?"

I closed my eyes and bounced my head gently on the wall over the hall table. Rory had tracked me down to the inn, which wasn't terribly hard to do since he knew where I was heading, and there were only so many places I could be staying. When Nichols didn't give him any information on me, and I still hadn't returned messages and even Max had told him in no uncertain terms which short pier to take a long walk off of, Rory started calling hotels.

And bless Carmel's heart, even in her stunned grief, she was too nice to tell him the very physically impossible thing I suggested he do rather than accept the phone from her.

"No, I have zero doubts it's Rory. Sorry, Carmel."

"It's okay," she said, barely a whisper. "I'll be in the kitchen. I've got coffee when you'd like."

I nodded, taking the receiver from her with a barely pleasant, "Hello, Rory. I sent you my new number, you know."

"Yes, and you keep ignoring me when I call it."

"I lost it. I emailed you last night about that."

In true Rory fashion, once he was on a tear, he was oblivious to anything being said that didn't fit the narrative. "You know I hate email. Text, Damien! Text! Or better yet, answer your phone! You're killing me here, Damien. No pun intended."

"Rory, I'm not interested in whatever interview you've got set up for me. I don't want to talk about any podcasts, talk shows, magazines, true crime shows—"

"It's a role on *Sonny Maxwell, PI*. You'd play yourself. One of those special guest start spots. It's perfect. They're doing this whole retro Cali thing. Show's set in the late sixties. Lots of big hair. Wide collars. Tight pants. Groovy. Far out. Yada yada yada."

I was so very tired. Rory seemed harmless enough from a distance but up close, he was worse than Muffin with a chewy toy when it came to PR. "Then how would I play myself?"

"Huh?"

"I can't play myself as a guest star on a show set in the late sixties. I'm twenty-five, Rory. How would that even work?"

I could hear him snap his fingers. "Great question. I'll ask. Time travel, I bet. It's time travel."

"I'd dearly love to time travel myself back about two hours and avoid this call."

"If you'd replied to messages days ago, we wouldn't be doing this."

"Liar."

"Likely. Now, talk to me about this murder fiasco. I've been watching your socials and your name is all over the place. Trending on Insta *and* Twitter. Your impression is climbing through the roof. It's a perfect time to go for one of those brand deals."

"Rory, I'm not going to monetize Renee Rhodes' death. I'm not using this to boost my status. That's sick."

"That's show business, Damien. She'd expect it! You have to strike while the iron is hot, you know? Jump feet first. Whatever those other sayings are. But you gotta do it, or we're both out of luck."

I opened my mouth to tell him to shove off, but a thought popped into my mind, and before I could stop myself, I asked, "Do you think you could do me a favor?"

Rory gasped theatrically. I was sure he'd be grabbing at his chest and flailing around if we were face to face. Instead, he asked in an awed, hushed tone, "Damien Murphy is asking *me* for a favor? Little ol' me? Rory Flick, just an ordinary agent who's been *begging* his client to use his connections for *years,* is finally asking me for a favor?"

"Rory. I can fire you." In fact, I'd never been closer than at that very moment.

"But you won't because you're too nice. What's the favor?"

"I made some statements on my socials earlier in the week about Ms. Rhodes' death, but after today… I'm going to issue an official statement I want released through our office, not just on my socials. About Renee Rhodes and Charlie Arnold's deaths. Just a simple comment on their passing, how they will be missed, how I'm keeping their loved ones in my thoughts, and how the community of Lester Cove is coming together." Okay, that part was kind of a fib, but it was a polite one. "And in light of Charlie's demise, I'll include something about reaching out for help, maybe one of the national helpline numbers."

He was quiet for a long moment. Then, "Are you freaking serious? This is the best time to change your image, Damien! You've been playing kids for years! We have the perfect opportunity to steer you towards some grittier roles. Change up your public persona, butch it up a bit. Go for something a little Byronic, a little moody. A guy who's seen some stuff and it haunts him."

"A guy who's definitely firing his agent if he doesn't post my statement by tonight. I'm sending it in five, Rory."

I hung up to find Sienna not even bothering to pretend not to eavesdrop from the kitchen door. "Your agent sounds like a piece of work."

"I'm a product," I said, spreading my hands wide, mimicking the tone Rory used whenever he'd lecture me back in the early days of my career. "I'm here to be sold."

"That stinks," she muttered. "What's your statement, then? About all this?" When I hesitated, she smirked slightly and gave me a shrug. "Run it by me. I'm a tough audience. If I buy it, then the slobbering masses will eat it up."

"The death of Renee Rhodes is heartbreaking and a real loss for the theater community. The passing of Charlie Arnold is no less of a tragedy and his service not only to the educational community but his work with the theater in New York and Maine will long be a testimony to his talent and heart. In this time of deep tragedy, it's easy to forget there are real people affected by these astounding losses. I ask that you keep their family, friends, loved ones, and community in your thoughts."

She sniffed. "It's alright."

"So go with it?"

"Thanks." I wasn't entirely sure, but I think Sienna winked as she turned back into the kitchen and left me and Muffin to go upstairs and hurry to get ready.

The memorial was due to start at noon, and I knew it was going to be one of the longest days of the year.

———

THE CLOSER WE got to the theater, the slower Muffin's steps became. "It's okay," I murmured. "She's not really there."

She was still in the morgue in Augusta, waiting for the next steps to get underway, but Muffin didn't need to know that.

The parking lot already had several cars parked down the front, mostly out-of-state plates, and a small cluster of people with cameras and mics lingered outside the door, waiting to talk to anyone going inside. Belinda was already cornered by one particularly ruthless tabloid type who had her crowded against the theater doors. Belinda was openly weeping, shaking her head as I drew closer, ignoring the others who pressed close to ask intrusive questions. "Belinda, come on," I urged, putting myself between her and the reporter. "Let's get inside."

"Damien Murphy," the man with the mic crowed. "Just the man I was hoping to see. You're a hard one to get hold of. Tell me, how does it feel to be a suspect in the death of Renee Rhodes?"

"It feels like you should—" I paused, glanced at the others, and changed my choice of words. "You should back off and let people grieve in peace."

He smirked. "Word is you were seen leaving the theater the night Renee Rhodes was murdered."

"So were a hundred other people," I ground out, trying to get the door open and Belinda through it without turning my back on the vultures.

"Belinda, go inside. *Please.*"

Muffin was the best boy ever. His breakfast caught up with him and, maintaining direct eye contact with the reporter, he proceeded to relieve himself of the burden on the man's knock-off Tom Fords.

"Go, go, go," I muttered at Belinda, who took my advice and bolted inside. It was another hour and a half till the service was due to begin and already a handful or two of people milled around the foyer, all there to set up for the event. Belinda broke away from me and made a beeline for Ollie in his ill-fitting dark suit, his gawky figure halfway between grown and adolescent, but entirely full of righteous fury on his girlfriend's behalf as he swept her into an embrace and huddled her away from prying eyes.

When I caught up to her, Belinda was fussing over a stack of memorial cards with Renee Rhodes' most famous headshot on the front, the one that had been used when she was linked with Marlon Brando on a trip to Tahiti back in the late seventies. The bright orange sarong slung over her shoulder was just visible in the picture, making her look like she was on a tropical vacation and not in a cold studio somewhere, posing for a photographer for an hour or more, looking for a perfect picture to use on call outs.

I wondered now if she had really been in Tahiti or if someone started the rumor, boosting her PR and getting her face out there to a wider audience.

"Hey," Belinda murmured, seeing me lingering nearby. "Um, I meant to tell you earlier, but I got kind of caught up in stuff yesterday and, well, this morning…" She gestured limply at the doors blocking out the paps. "Sorry about my mom. She told me she saw you the other day."

"Ah, yeah, at O'Neill's."

"Mom's… a lot."

"Moms can be like that."

Her smile was just a quick flicker, and then it was gone. "Especially mine. She was *so* glad when Margie said she'd handle the arrangements for everything. I mean, I had a handle on it, you know?"

"I'm sure. But it's a big undertaking, Belinda. I'm glad Margie stepped in to give you a hand." Glad and confused—the last I'd heard from Margie about anything to do with the service, she wasn't coming. "Is she around?"

Ollie pointed her out. "She brought a bunch of pastries and stuff. She and Ben brought in some urns for tea and coffee, too."

Belinda sniffed. "We brought a cooler for water and soda," she muttered. "And pigs in a blanket and hummus and crackers!"

"Wow, sounds like you really planned a big send-off for Ms. Rhodes," I said kindly. Belinda's mulish expression softened, though Ollie still looked more exasperated than not. "Is there anything I can do to help with the rest of the set up? I have some pictures a friend sent me that we can put on the screen if you're still planning on using a projector."

"I don't know how many people are coming but we have some AV stuff from the high school so we can project things on the scrim. I have a whole file of video clips from YouTube and Vimeo that folks have uploaded over the years."

Belinda trailed towards the auditorium doors, and I followed, both of us stopping at the top of the center aisle to stare at the stage. It was lit by every light possible, a pink spot roving slowly back and forth across the white lights. "My friend Mark's messing with the lights," she muttered. "He runs them for the community theater in Vanness, just up the coast."

I nodded like I knew what she was talking about.

"Mr. Murphy," she whispered. "I have to tell you something… I lied Friday."

Here we go. "You went into her house."

She nodded, face starkly pale and eyes squeezed shut. "I went Thursday morning, the day before you saw me there. Ms. Rhodes gave me the code to her alarm last year, when she had to go to the hospital for a few days to get her gallbladder out. She needed someone to check on Muffin." She opened one eye to peek at me. "I went Friday, too, but that really was just to leave flowers! Don't tell my mom, okay?"

Glancing around for any hiding paps—those suckers were wily—I whispered, "Why'd you go in?"

"It sounds dumb when I say it out loud. Ollie said it was weird, but he didn't get it, you know? I just… I just can't believe she's *gone*. I needed to see, you know? Like… if she wasn't sitting in her living room, on the phone with someone in New York or drinking one of those weird copper cup drinks she liked, then she was really gone, and I could believe it."

"Did it help?"

She sniffed hard. "Not really. It's still so weird. I thought she really believed in me, damn it!" Belinda's voice hitched, her volume control slipping before she could gather herself together. "I came here, too. Last night. Someone cleaned the stage," she said in a thick voice. "I had to look, you know? See where it happened." She opened her eyes then and cut me a sideways glance. "There's no blood or anything. I mean, not that I can see. There's sand in the cracks, though. Was she… I mean. Did she get, um…"

"I really shouldn't say," I murmured. "I was just wondering which clips you'll be showing. Are any of them from *Kaleidoscope Coffin*?"

She wrinkled her nose. "Ugh, no. I mean, someone did post a short bit of that one, but it was so bad. Ms. Rhodes was *awesome,* though. Just the play and the set design and the dialogue… It was like a kid wrote it."

The absolute lack of irony in her tone nearly did me in.

"It wasn't one of her more famous roles," she added. "Margie suggested I look for it when I told her what I was planning with the equipment. She said it was a really meaningful role for her. I'd never heard of it." She hesitated before leaning in to whisper, "It looks really bad. I was surprised Ms. Rhodes was in something like that, but I mean, it was like really early in her career. Have you ever seen it?"

"Oh," I fibbed, "my mom's a huge fan of hers and remembered seeing that back in the day when she and my dad first started dating. I thought it'd be… neat… to send her the clip." I sent up a silent apology to my mom for not only aging her up a bit but also lying about her, period. I don't know how she did it, but my mom always knew when I'd been telling stories.

Belinda nodded but didn't look convinced. Thankfully, the clatter of chairs being dropped in the foyer drew her attention away from me and on to the memorial service. "Oh my god, David! We don't need that many!"

I used the opportunity of her distraction to slip away—there wasn't much for me to do there, I reasoned, and I'd be reading my eulogy off note cards. It was time for me to do some people watching.

My saving grace was Ben arriving, looking very Darcy, and parting the small crowd in the foyer with a glance. He swept in beside me and muttered, "Someone's been spreading the word about it being a murder, I see." He cut a glance towards the paps visible whenever the doors swung open.

"Whenever someone even a little bit famous dies, the murder rumors start. Remember that young actress who drowned a few years ago? Total accident, but the internet was wild for like a week with people trying to solve the case, pulling suspects out of thin air, even harassing the cops and her family when the ME declared it a total accident?"

He blinked. "Uh, no, I must've missed that since I don't give a rat's about gossip."

"It's not gossip, it's news," I protested. "And fine, I'm sure it happens with some law clients too, okay? People die and their families can't accept it was a natural death, so murder is the first thing that pops up."

"I really need to know what law firms you're working with because they sound far more exciting than where I am."

Some more people entered, pushing us towards the auditorium doors, which Belinda and Ollie propped open, stepping back to let the crowd flow into the theater proper. Ben followed me as I made my way down the side aisle and towards the steps at stage left. Everything on the stage was in a semi-circle, framing the podium where I'd give the eulogy and others would come to give a few words in front of the scrim. Flower arrangements, some artfully arranged poster-sized pictures on easels, and a scattering of generic theater props dressed the set and gave me the unsettling feeling that this was all just for show, not truly for a grieving community at all.

"Where do you think you're going?" I asked at the bottom of the steps. "Making sure I don't pull a Poirot and start accusing people of the murder from my soapbox?"

"The thought had crossed my mind."

"Nice." I tossed my hair (well, it's the thought that counts) and trotted up the steps. Belinda joined me from the other side, pale and nervous.

"I don't know what I'm doing," she whispered as we reached the podium. "I didn't think it would be this big! I thought it'd be like, a few townspeople and maybe some fans, or some folks from the festival." She cast a shaken glance at the suddenly full auditorium and shook her head. "There's too many people!"

"Belinda, listen to me. You've done an amazing job. Seriously. I'm hella impressed with everything here! I mean, look around you! This is incredible! Ms. Rhodes would be thrilled."

Belinda's tears spilled over, and she pressed her fingers to her lips. "Thank you. I just… you know?"

And I did just, you know. "Come on. Say your piece, I'll say mine, and we can breathe easy."

Belinda was well-spoken and welcoming, her voice shaking only a little. She thanked the drama club at Lester Cove Consolidated, Charlie Arnold, and a list of townspeople who apparently were part of the defunct community theater group of yore. She introduced me and stepped back.

And I lied my ass off. My speech was a bit of Belinda's from her notes, but mostly my own. Some anecdotes about Ms. Rhodes' career, touching on some of the more infamous gossip rag stories, which made people chuckle and sigh, then a closing bit about how the world loved her, and she loved the world, there may be bigger memorials later but this one is all heart, et cetera et cetera.

"Renee Rhodes was, more than anything, a character," I said as I trundled to the end of my speech. "Both in the sense that she was someone larger than life, flamboyant and groundbreaking in her own ways, and also in that the Renee Rhodes we're mourning here today isn't the Renee Rhodes known by those with whom she was closest." A few people shifted uncomfortably, Belinda being one of them, I noted. "The private, *real* Renee Rhodes was a girl from Long Island who lucked out. And kept lucking out. The Renee Rhodes we're mourning here stood on the other Renee Rhodes' shoulders to reach her star. And when we leave here today, I ask that you spare a thought for Renee Rhodes of Long Island, the one who dreamed big, while you remember the Renee Rhodes who made it."

A few flashes went off, and I winced inwardly. Rory would be blowing up my phone—well, if I had one. Maybe he'd be going old-school and hitting up my emails. Stepping back out of the way, I waited as Belinda came forward again to let the guests know the mic was open for anyone who wanted to make a *brief* statement about Ms. Rhodes. Nichols and one of his deputies were waiting at the foot of the stage steps, ready to bounce any pap types who wanted to stir the pot. Lucky for us, no one did. A handful of people came up to ramble about the dearly departed, a few—like Bitty O'Neill—had some rather snarky comments wrapped under layers of politesse.

Bitty was apparently still annoyed about having to install that electric charging station at her shop just for the one damn electric car in a fifty-mile radius. Bull McGreary, who owned the china shop next to Witte's Teas, had a few tart words about Renee Rhodes' shopping habits, mainly that she thought she deserved free things just for existing.

I was regretting my eulogy.

Ben shot me a sympathetic look, lips quirked in a half-smile that conveyed *I get it.*

The memorial broke up soon after the last speaker, people drifting through the lobby, some getting coffee from the huge urns and a few nibbling on the stupendous amount of nibbles Margie, Belinda, and Ollie had provided. Most people lost interest in the spectacle relatively quickly, and the few who lingered were more caught up in their own conversations than interested in sharing memories of Ms. Rhodes. Someone had propped the doors open, the old building lacking AC and getting stuffy fairly quickly between the summer heat and the number of bodies packed into the lobby. The paps that still lingered seized the opportunity to snap pictures of the gathered, some daring to call out questions to everyone still inside. Nichols and a few of his folks were doing a decent enough job of keeping most of the paps back from the door by several yards, but a few kept dodging past the handful of cops to do their thing.

"There'll be more on the street," I muttered when Ben came up beside me. "It's a public thoroughfare, so it's not as much of a pain for them to get pics and soundbites."

"What do they think they're going to get from this? Wailing and gnashing teeth and rending garments? I think the most dramatic thing that's happened so far is when Denny Cross said the f-bomb during his little speech about how Renee bumped his fender with her car last Fourth of July."

"The possibility of her death being murder draws 'em out," I said quietly. "They're vultures. Even if it wasn't a leading headline for some of the trashier tabs, any time someone remotely famous dies, there's a flock of these bastards who try to build their reputation off the corpse."

He assessed me with a curious, thoughtful gaze for a long moment. "It sounds like you're speaking from experience."

"There's been a few people I've worked with over the years who have passed. Most from natural causes or things they couldn't prevent but a few…" I trailed off, thinking of a small handful of actors I'd come up with in the industry, all of us around the same age, who succumbed to bad choices or were taken by violence. "Well. These paps stop seeing people as *people* once they become famous. We're dollar signs."

Ben was quiet, staring at the photographers Nichols was currently heading back from the door as another patrol car—actually the only other patrol car for the town—pulled up to the curb. "It's a trade-off, isn't it? I mean, that's what it seems like." He shot me a sheepish sort of smile and added, "That makes me sound heartless, doesn't it? I just mean, the way things are, people end up having to trade bits of themselves to maintain their status, you know?"

"It doesn't have to be. There's plenty of people who go their entire careers—their entire lives—without being a spectacle for these carrion feeders."

And yes, I may have said that last part a little loudly, hoping the two lingering paps heard me. Nichols definitely did—he glanced back over his shoulder and gave me a small, amused smile before turning back to herding the last two vultures off the theater grounds.

Belinda came up clutching a stack of cards, Ollie trailing after. "Hey, I'm about to leave. David and Jerome are gonna lock the place up once everyone is gone," she said, subdued.

"Do you kids need a ride home?"

"No, my mom's waiting out back. Oh, here." She handed Ben a handful of the memorial cards. "I printed too many."

Ben took the cards, waiting until Belinda had gone before tossing them into the nearest trash can. "What?" he asked when I scoffed. "Why would I need over a dozen memorial cards?"

"Sell 'em on eBay or something?"

"And you were just talking about how celebrities are real people and not commodities."

"Was I?" I asked archly. Ben smiled a little, and by some unspoken agreement, we sauntered towards the open doors. People trickled out around us as we stood, awkwardly quiet. Ben broke the silence as Jerome struggled past with one of the coffee urns.

"Do you want me to take you back to the inn?" Ben asked, hastily adding, "Might be good for Muffin to stay off his injury."

I glanced back to where Muffin had holed up under one of the tables, the same spot he'd been the night of the gala and nodded. "Probably. If you're sure…"

"Oh my goodness!" Margie cannonballed into the lobby from the manager's office. "Oh my goodness! Damien, Ben! Thank god! I was just in the back lot and…" She gasped, bending over to grab her knees and try to breathe. Ben looked alarmed, hurrying to her side.

"Margie, what's going on?"

"Belinda! They're arresting Belinda!"

SEVENTEEN

The back parking area was a hive of activity, all centered around a sobbing, red-faced Belinda and her irate mother.

"She is not a murderer!" Denise Gleaves shouted. "Get your hands off her!"

"Ma'am, we're not arresting her. We're asking you to bring her in for questioning!"

"Who on earth thinks my daughter killed Renee Rhodes?"

Every eye in the group, except Belinda's, turned to me. "Um, to be fair," I muttered, "I pretty much dismissed Belinda as a suspect."

"Pretty much?" Denise growled. "*Pretty much*? She should never have been one to start with!"

And a flash of movement near the theater drew my eye, and I groaned. Two of the paps had made their way back and were getting as much footage as possible before Nichols' people got them gone.

I was sure I'd be seeing the pics and prurient headlines popping up in my socials before the end of the day.

"Ma'am, step back, please." The trooper's glare doubled in intensity, making me shrink back. "We're not going on any suggestion from him regarding your daughter's role in the Rhodes case. We had a credible call this morning, laying out some pretty suggestive points against her. We're taking her in for questioning, not arresting her."

Margie shrugged at Ben's annoyed glare.

"No one is being arrested yet. This is *just* for questioning."

Ben stepped forward. "Does she have a lawyer?"

"Don't you do contract law?" I asked.

Yikes, if a man could die from a dirty look, I'd be the third body the state was dealing with.

"I do. But Mario Keene, one of the attorneys I work with, specializes in criminal law. He's in Boston but can be in Augusta in a few hours," he told Belinda's mother.

"Thank you," she muttered. "I'd appreciate it."

It was another few minutes of chaos before everyone got sorted and Belinda, with her mother following in a very proper SUV, was heading towards Augusta, Ollie riding along with her.

Nichols and his people got the paps shoved off, and Margie fluttered after them, making confused, sad noises about Belinda.

"I'm pretty sure she'd have ridden along if they'd let her," I murmured. "She seems really fond of Belinda."

"Margie does like her projects," Ben said. "You're looking awful."

"You do know how to flatter a boy," I muttered. "It's been a very long, stressful twenty-four hours."

"Is that why you didn't reply to my texts last night?"

"You texted me?" I asked, wincing at the uptick in my tone. "And I didn't text back because someone stole my phone."

"What?"

Ben's expression grew thunderous as I relayed the previous evening's shenanigans. "I'm going to sue the police department," he growled. "How can no one answer the phone?"

"What could they have done?" I countered. "Tell me too bad, so sad, replace my phone?"

"And it's still in Lester Cove?"

"That's what the pin said on the map when I double-checked this morning. It just doesn't give me anything more specific than that."

"Come on. We're dropping Muffin off at the inn, then getting you a new phone."

"What?"

He grabbed my hand and started tugging me along the sidewalk. "There's a store in Malm's Corner. Might not have the latest smartphones, but it's not going to be an out-of-date brick. It'll get you by until you're able to go to Augusta or wherever you're heading after this."

"And how are we getting there? Your car…"

He grimaced. "Yeah. Well. I'm driving my dad's car. I've paid one of the Samson kids to take it out for a spin once a week or so since I haven't been able to come home as often, so it's still working." We drew to a stop beside an old VW Super Beetle, lemon-yellow and polished within an inch of its life. "My dad like the classics. I helped him restore it, before he got sick. Even a bit after…" He trailed off, face going cloudy with remembered grief. "Well. Up until he went into the hospital for the last time. We were pretty much done with the work by then, but we kept fussing over it," he murmured. "Just because."

Because you knew it was goodbye. I bit my tongue at that statement and instead ran my hand over the sleek yellow fender with an appreciative murmur that got him to unlock the doors.

"Holy cats, this is awesome," I praised, climbing into the front seat. "I haven't ever ridden in one of the old ones."

Ben seemed pleased by this and spent the entire drive to Malm's Corner talking about the car, trips he took with his dad in it, and how he learned to drive and nearly killed the transmission the first time he took it out on his own and tried to impress a date.

By the time we pulled up to a snazzy little phone store that looked like it had once been one of those old Foto-Mats, I was laughing so hard my stomach hurt and just for a few minutes, it was like all the bad parts of the past week hadn't happened.

Until I saw a flier for Charlie's memorial someone had managed to bring this far from Lester Cove, plastered to the front of the phone store.

Ben followed the direction of my gaze and sighed. "Margie… This has her metaphorical fingerprint all over it."

I nodded. "Carmel told me this morning. She was pretty upset about Margie kind of steamrolling over her."

"It's Margie's M.O. Come on, let's get you sorted, and we can get out of here so you can check on Muffin."

The man behind the counter seemed thrilled to have customers. Ben busied himself fiddling with his own phone while I looked at some of the newer smartphones. They had one not too much older than the one I'd been using, so the guy got it down from the display for me and started gushing about the features as I nodded politely. "And how can I transfer my number over?" I asked when he took a breath.

"Oh, that's easy!" And he was off and running again. It took the better part of an hour to get set up, and I ended up being a soft touch and let him up-sell me on accessories. Ben had wandered out of the store and was pacing the sidewalk in a call by the time I finished, leaving with a new phone, phone case, extra car charger (if only I had a car to go around it), some nifty little charms that lit up when the phone rang, and a sticker of a crab that said *I Got Crabs in Maine* to go with the shirt I wore to the gala.

Ben wrapped up his call and headed back to join me in front of the store, just a few doors down from the emergency vet's office. "We good?"

"We good. Work?"

"Mario Keene. He's going to meet Belinda and her mom there and see what he can see.

We'd walked past his car and were now in front of the vet's office, on the regular office side rather than the veterinary ER. A few people entered with cat carriers, all smiles as someone inside called a greeting.

I turned to face him but came up short. In the window of the vet's office was a display of pet food and treats arranged in baskets, tipped over to look like they were spilling out from an abundant harvest. "Damn it, do you think we could swing by a store on the way home? I'm almost out of treats for Muffin, and he refuses to eat the ones they gave him at the emergency vet visit."

"That is the pickiest damn dog," he muttered, though it lacked real heat. "Sure, we can stop by one of the big box places in Fish Head."

"Fish Head."

He stopped just a few steps away from me and shot me a curious look. "Yeah. Fish Head. It's right up the coast a few miles. They have a Walmart and a Petsmart. I think the Target is opening this winter."

"Fish. Head." I repeated. "They named the town Fish Head."

He narrowed his eyes, jingling his car keys at me. "If you're going to make fun, you can walk."

"Alright, alright," I chuckled. "I'll save my Dr. Demento sing-along for when we get back to the inn."

He made a face at me but let me into the car, anyway. We kept up a light chatter as I fiddled with my phone, trying to get my old settings back. "Huh," I muttered during a lull. "Paul Santos texted me last night too."

Ben sighed gustily and pulled into a layby. "Go on. Call him back."

I shot him a glance. "It can wait."

"It's about your investigation?"

I nodded reluctantly. "Just some people who used to know Renee Rhodes. Um, it's not exactly complimentary, apparently. Chris Aames and

Gwen Markham. They worked with Ms. Rhodes in some shows and, ah, well, Paul seems to have gotten them to agree to talk with me about their experiences.

Paul's text was fairly blunt.

Ben set his flashers going. "Go on. Call 'em."

"Ben…"

He pulled out his own phone and wiggled it at me. "I'll check on Mario and see if he's caught up with Belinda yet."

I nodded reluctantly and pulled up the first number in Paul's text.

Chris Aames was cautious when I introduced myself and explained I was calling because I was trying to put together a picture of the "unknown Renee Rhodes, not just the Broadway star and pop culture icon."

"Yeah, fine, but why talk to *me* specifically? No one knows who the hell I am because of her."

"And that's why I want to talk to you."

He grunted, sounding like he was settling into a comfy chair wherever he was. He muffled the phone and told someone to *go on, I'll be there in a minute* before coming back to me. "Sorry, grandkids are over, and I promised them we'd have a bonfire out back tonight. Kinda worried about how into fire they are, but so long as it's supervised, I suppose it's fine."

"Er, sounds like it. I'll make this quick then. What did Renee Rhodes do?"

"Gotta narrow it down." He laughed bitterly. "To me? To the people she called friends? To people she thought were slighting her? Be specific, kid."

"Start with you."

"Renee fancied herself the center of the universe and made sure anyone who thought differently was put in their place. She and I screwed around a bit back in the late seventies. I didn't know she was married at the time and when I found out, I called things off."

"To Charlie Arnold?"

"No, some guy… Damien? No, that's you… James. Something James."

"DA James?" My heart gave a funny little lurch and decided to pause inconveniently.

"That's the one! He was a good one, had no idea what he saw in her." He snorted softly. "Even after she left him, he followed her like a lost puppy. I think she loved it, to be honest. And she hated that I could walk away from her so easily, so she made sure to tell every casting director she knew—and trust me, she knew a *lot*—that I was bad news. Drugs, orgies, you name it, she accused me of it. And if that didn't work, she turned on the waterworks and claimed she felt unsafe being around me because I'd forced myself on her."

"Holy…"

"She didn't go to the cops, just started the rumor around the theater companies and with a few of the directors. Spread like wildfire. The more I denied it, the worse I looked. Ruined any chance I had at making a name for myself. Years later, hell, back in eighty-five or early eighty-six, she issued a statement through some publicist saying she'd heard our names had been tied in a scandal and yada yada yada, hoped I was doing well. It was too late by then and she knew it." He sniffed, more angry than sad, before continuing. "I read the gossip columns and see those stories on Twitter and shit. These actors out there now, assaulting fans and their own girlfriends, and all that happens is the internet calls them misunderstood cinnamon rolls or emo bad boys. Back then, unless you had top billing or a ton of money, there was no getting out from under rumors like that, no matter how fake they were."

Jesus… "Mr. Aames." I gently redirected, not comfortable with how true his words were. "Why did Renee Rhodes have you sign an NDA?"

"Because," he ground out, "she was smart. And she had me by the short ones, If I signed the NDA and kept my mouth shut about everything I knew about her, then she wouldn't tell her stories to the police. That would've been worse than just idle gossip—my rep would've been ruined, not just in the theater world but anywhere I went. She'd have made sure the rumors followed me. Hell, she'd have put it on a billboard in Times Square if it meant keeping me quiet."

"And, ah, what did you know?"

He sucked on his teeth a moment before he answered, the sound grating my nerves and making me want to throw the phone. "Well, I knew some things I wasn't supposed to. Like the fact she was illegitimate. Not a big deal now, but back then? It would've blacklisted her with a ton of producers. And the fact she was the one to drop those sandbags on Peggy and James."

I sat up straight at that. "Mr. Aames, are you sure she did that, that it wasn't just a story she made up to scare you or something?"

"Hell no! I know she did it. I know because I was there. I saw her do it to DA James. Dragged that sandbag up the catwalk, used a strap and some rope because the pulley system was broken. When she did it to Peggy, same thing. Rigged it up with an old purse strap and some rope and waited till Peggy came looking for her for rehearsal, then BAM." He smacked his hand against something on the other end of the line. "Saw the whole damn thing twice." He sucked those teeth again and sounded like he was struggling to stand up. "I'm not sorry she's dead. And I hope it was painful."

He hung up on me then and I could only stare at the dark screen of my phone. "Hell," I breathed. "Hell."

I dialed Gwen's number with slightly shaky fingers.

Gwen Markham was very excited to talk to me. She said she told Paul Santos everything earlier, but she was still happy to share the story again. Gwen was Renee's understudy for a musical off-Broadway in 1976. Gwen was also cozy with the director of the musical, and Renee expressed concern about favoritism to anyone who would listen. When that didn't get anything done for Renee, she started a rumor that Gwen was pregnant. Out of wedlock pregnancies weren't uncommon back then, but they were still a deal breaker for an up-and-coming actress. She confronted Renee about the rumors and a day or two later, she narrowly missed being hit by a piece of scenery that could've done a lot of damage.

"I bet you're wondering why I didn't report her," she remarked when I just sat in quiet horror after her story.

"An NDA?"

"Ha. No. Because I was scared to death of that crazy bitch. She spent a year stalking me after I left the production, showing up at my house, and at the community college when I started classes. She threatened my boyfriend when he tried to chase her off one night. We ended up moving to New Jersey just to get away from her!" There was a pause as she took a drink of something with a lot of ice in it. "She's dead, huh? I hope it was agonizing."

"That seems to be a popular sentiment," I muttered faintly. "Thank you for speaking with me. I'm sorry to dredge up old—"

She hung up before I even finished the sentence.

"Jesus," I breathed.

Ben raised a brow at me as I tucked my phone away. "I couldn't help but hear…"

I nodded.

"The thing is," he said after a brief pause, "I know for a fact she's only been married once."

"I was kind of afraid of that."

After several moments of silence, Ben put the car into gear and turned off his flashers. We drove the rest of the way back to Lester Cove in silence. "I think maybe," I said as he turned onto Shore Drive, "I'd like it if you dropped me at the tea shop."

"Damien—"

"I want to ask Margie about these two. Maybe she knew them and can shed some light on everything."

"Even if she had met them once upon a time, what good would that do now? They didn't kill Renee or Charlie."

"But maybe it wasn't Charlie after all, not if Ms. Rhodes was out there making enemies for the past four decades!"

Ben ground his jaw but turned towards Buttermilk Lane, not saying a word as he stopped in front of the tea shop, and I got out. When I tried to thank him for the ride, he drove away.

EIGHTEEN

The lights in the shop were still on but Margie was nowhere to be seen when I stepped inside. The entire place had an air of being closed but the open sign still shone brightly in the window. "Margie?"

"Back here," she called, sticking her head out from the kitchen door. "Damien! Hello! Oh, I'm so glad you're here. I could use a hand! Come on back. Mind turning off the light and flipping the lock while you're there?"

I did as asked and headed back toward the kitchen area. Margie had several trays of scones and a few of hand pies in the works, the mix of sweet and savory smells reminding me I'd skipped lunch and it was well towards dinner time now. "What's all this? Getting a head start on tomorrow's bakes?"

"Oh, well, Jerome over at the Sleepy Pelican—you know," she made a gesture to indicate a beard while making a scowly face that made me giggle. "Well, the folks over here want to have a little memorial for Charlie and asked if I could make some things. Jerome said to bake for fifty, and I figured I'd aim for at least seventy-five because you know how these things go," she said, bustling over to pull a large tray of the savory pies from the oven. "These are chicken rosemary pot pies," she announced. "You can try one if you like."

"Oh, I don't want to throw your count off!"

"Let you in on a secret, I always make extra because I do love to sample while I bake." She laughed, patting her soft tummy before fading into a sigh. "I can't believe Charlie is really gone. I keep expecting to see him pop through the door or call me or…" She trailed off. "Keeping busy keeps me from crying," she admitted airily.

"I understand. What can I do?"

She set me to work flouring trays, which went horribly—more flour on me and the floor than in the tray. "Well. How about you just keep me company, then?" She laughed when the next task, working the giant dough mixer, managed to cause more problems than solve them.

"I can do that. I'm a great talker."

"Was that Ben dropping you off? I thought I caught a peek of Johnny's old car while I was grabbing the pearling sugar from the storeroom!"

"Ah, yeah, he drove me into Malm's Corner to replace my phone."

"Your phone? What happened?"

One more time, I relayed the events of the night before, Margie making a horrified squeak when I got to the part about Muffin's injury. "That poor baby! First, his human is gone, and now this! Oh, is he going to be okay? I couldn't live with myself knowing he wasn't!"

"Doc Jones came by this morning for an emergency outcall and said he should be okay so long as he takes it easy. He needs to go in tomorrow or Tuesday for a check though to make sure the stitches are alright."

Margie breathed a sigh of relief. "Thank goodness! I know you keep saying you can't keep him with you, but I do wish you'd consider finding a way. I'd volunteer, but my Tony would just *die* of fright!"

She went on then for a bit about her Tony, how he'd been such a comfort after Johnathan's death. We were startled by a shrill beep. "Oh! The lobster rolls!"

Margie hurried to pull them from the oven and get them on the cooling rack, frowning all the while. "These are looking a little… meh. I think I need to spruce this up a bit! Be right back!" She headed for the big walk-in fridge at the back of the kitchen, muttering about cheese.

I chuckled to myself, deciding to check messages again before she came back. And work up my courage to ask her about Chris Aames and Gwen Markham, to boot.

A message from Ben was waiting:

MR. DARCY

Mario got Belinda released. It was all BS, fell apart on examination. She's on her way back to town with her mom now.

Making a mental note to email him later, I thumbed back to Max's last text, the one with all the pictures.

"It's hard to believe she's gone," Margie said from over my shoulder, startling me. She held a huge bag of shredded cheese under her arm and was smiling faintly at the picture on my phone, one of Renee Rhodes as a very young woman, wearing a wig that looked like it belonged in *Pippi Longstocking*. "Where'd you get that one? I don't think I've ever seen her looking so happy."

"Ah, a friend of mine sent me some pictures to use at the memorial. I never got the chance to add them to the reel. I'm thinking of maybe adding them to my socials later as a sort of online memorial for her."

Margie made a vague sound of interest at that, heading back for the still-hot lobster pies. "I keep trying to get into using those apps, but I'm horrible at it. I forget to check half the time and people keep sending me dirty messages!"

"Good ol' bots." I laughed. "After a while, you get good at blocking them or just outright ignoring them."

"Renee had a few accounts, if I recall correctly. I never bothered to keep up with her online, but I seem to remember her mentioning a Twitter or something."

I nodded. "She had a few. I don't know who'll run them now that she's gone or if they'll get archived or what."

Margie snorted darkly. "Wouldn't that just get her goat? Disappearing like she was never here. What other pictures do you have?"

"Oh, uh, here." I turned my phone to show her. There were some old publicity stills from plays that never got big and a few that looked like they were from friendly outings or after parties. Margie smiled faintly at a few, her expression going grim at some others. "What?"

"Hm? Oh. Just… just thinking of how short life really is, I suppose. Johnathan was on track to recover, so the doctors said, but the next day he took a turn and died before they could even start the new therapy they said would do wonders." She set to adding the cheese to the pies, frowning at them as if they'd personally wronged her. "Charlie was fine, until he wasn't. And Renee…"

I glanced down at my phone, looking at the picture that had set Margie to frowning. ***Me, Chuckie, Peggy, and Renee at Bongo's 1975*** the handwritten caption across the bottom of the picture declared. Renee Rhodes was front and center wearing a tinsel crown that looked like a cheap imitation of the famous Heddy Lamar headpiece. Several people crowded around her, some wearing party hats. I had the feeling it was a New Year's get-together based on how festive everyone looked. The man next to Ms. Rhodes gave me pause. If I squinted, and added a few years, took away the mutton chops and the absolute beast of a mustache, I could recognize a young Charlie Arnold with his arm around her shoulders. Beside him, her smile not reaching her eyes, was a young woman with dark hair wrapped in a complicated, braided bun atop her head, a wreath of silver and gold sparkles dangling over one ear.

Margie.

Margie, short for Margaret. Which could also be shortened to Peggy.

Margie, who had gone very quiet across the kitchen.

“Oh.” She sighed. “Hell.”

NINETEEN

"I hated that damn play. I only auditioned because it was supposed to be a stepping stone to the big time. The director's brother-in-law was a producer. Big shows, you know? Life changing roles. But Renee took that from me. Just like that," she snapped, the sound loud in the quiet kitchen.

I took a half step back, just settling my weight on my other foot. Just getting ready to bolt. It was late enough that many of the shops on the road were closed but, if I strained my ears, I thought I could hear movement next door at Bull's China.

Or I was having a stroke. Either-or.

"I thought maybe someone would get blamed for it," Margie whispered, her focus pulled entirely inward. "No one ever noticed me around her. That's why it was so easy for her to steal everything that was mine."

She smiled sadly, something far off in her eyes as she swayed side to side just a little, buffeted by something in her memory. "That would've been Chris who told you, hm? She screwed him over good, too. But he never did get over things when it came to her. *MrReneeRhodesFan*, hm?" Her gaze sharpened, and I nodded. "Figured. Even when she ruins our lives, we can't let go of her."

I took another half step back, and she shook her head. "You can run off if you'd like. You can even go tell Lieutenant Nichols what you suspect, but do you think he'll believe you any more this time than he did the last two times you've tried to convince him?" She slipped her hand into the pocket of her apron to pull out a wickedly sharp little paring knife. She smiled when my eyes widened, and the blood drained from my face. "It's not mine," she assured me. "I don't have much use for something like this running the tea shop. But the Moon girls do. Carmel, she's big on her locally sourced this and organic that." She tapped the knife against the side of the counter smiling serenely at the sound it made. "She has so many knives in her kitchen. I wonder if she dreamed of being a chef before she got stuck at the inn. She didn't know I'd taken this when I left last Tuesday after popping in for tea with her and Charlie. She left it on the table after she used it to peel the apples we had with cheese."

"That looks expensive," I murmured, afraid if I spoke too loudly, it might cause the fragile tension to rupture and Margie's calm to snap. "I'm sure she'll miss it."

"She will. But she'll find it later. Bless her heart, she does get distracted when they have large groups coming in. Last year, I took that lovely curved filet knife she keeps in the block near the stove. I wanted to see if she'd notice." Margie's smile was proud now, self-satisfied as she tested the weight of the blade. "It took her over a week. Turned up on the porch, of all places. She thought she'd gotten forgetful somehow, left it outside for some reason. Things like this, they're very dear. Costly. People don't like to use them too often. Carmel has so many knives in that kitchen. It'll be so hard on Sienna when this one turns up lodged in your neck."

When I didn't move, her smile fell. Her eyes narrowed. And she looked just the tiniest bit miffed, the pique slipping through her stony calm I. "Sorry," I said after a heartbeat. "I wasn't sure if you were done. It's so annoying when the audience can't follow the beats, you know? If I started clapping too soon, it'd throw you off your rhythm, ruin the performance. That was a great monologue, very chilling. But I do have a few notes—"

Margie still didn't take criticism well. She lunged for me, the knife held underhand and secure as she slashed out, the keen edge slicing along my jacket, splitting open the tweed sleeve but missing my skin. I ducked under her arm, driving my shoulder into her ribs like the stunt coordinator on *Legal Beagle* had taught me. Margie gasped, staggering back, but it wasn't enough to knock her down.

What else had Sven shown me? Think, think… Oh! I spun to face her as she swung around, closer than I realized. Margie snarled soundlessly, tasteful mauve lipstick smeared on her teeth, chignon still firmly in place though. Sven had been a big proponent of sweeping the leg, something he said looked cool on camera but was also effective in real life.

I swept out with my right leg, but it just made Margie tumble against me, the knife caught between us with the flat side of the blade pressed against my sternum.

Sven was going to be getting a call if I didn't die.

"Now, Damien," Margie chided, panting roughly, "please don't make this harder than it needs to be."

"Who are you going to blame for the murders, Margie?" I ground out, pushing against her to get some breathing room. She was stronger than I expected, planting her feet to keep me from budging her. Her hand shifted on the knife handle, trying to get a better grip, trying to work it free and use it against me. "What story will you spin to pin the blame on Carmel, huh? You're running out of people."

She cried out, shoving against me hard enough to bang my head against the open trunk. For a moment, everything was black, and pain exploded through my skull. Margie gave me another shove, and I went down on my knees. The trunk slammed shut and, as my vision cleared, she yanked me to my feet. "Inside," she hissed. "Or I'll do it here and tell everyone you tried to rob me. *Down on his luck actor, last shot at any sort of fame gone… Such a shame he turned to crime. But he was desperate,*" she continued, pushing me along towards the open shop door. *Damn it, why weren't any of these shops open late? Doesn't anyone need to buy pet food at half-past six? Or china? Surely someone out there needs a new tea set...* Margie monologued our way into the seating area of the shop. The charming striped shades were firmly pulled down, the lights off and the door locked thanks to me.

Damn it.

She shoved me down into one of the chairs, her confidence of a moment before wavering. "If you try to run," she said, breathless, "I'll shoot you."

"You don't have a gun," I reminded her. "Just a knife."

"Then I'll stab you!" she snapped, making a slashing motion at me, missing me by a few inches. "I'll get Johnathan's gun from the safe once I've cut you. I'll tell them we fought. You were desperate. Another ruined child star. You were leaving town, begged me for money, and when I said no, you tried to take it by force, and demanded I open the safe. We struggled and—"

"And this has some third-act problems," I noted, my heart beating so hard it hurt. "How about this? You put the knife down. I walk away. Later, you meet me at the police department, and we talk to Lieutenant Nichols together."

"And what? You'll tell him it was an accident? You were wrong? All that evidence was a mistake? Or do you think Nichols is so gaga about you that you can just ask him prettily to pretend this never happened and we all go on with our lives?"

I remembered one of the consultants on set while we were filming *Hostile Intentions 3: Hostage of the Heart* talking about how to deal with kidnappers by always using their names when you talk to them and using the victims' names. It personalized them and made it harder to feel they or their victims were disposable. *Might as well give it a shot,* I thought. *At this point, what can it hurt?* "Margie," I murmured, "you know that's not how it'll happen. I won't lie to you, okay? You're my friend, Margie. I won't lie to a friend."

Margie's face went slack, all emotion draining away in a heartbeat. But in the next, it was back, rage and sorrow and frustration and decades of thwarted hopes, illuminating her from the inside out. She leaned against the table, pinning me in place when I would have tried to move back. "Chris doesn't know jack about what Renee did. He was so in love with her, he'd have looked the other way if she killed me on stage in front of a packed house. They all would have!"

My throat was too dry to swallow. I made myself hold still instead of ducking away as I so desperately wanted to do. When I spoke, my voice was a raspy whisper. "She cost you everything. Your job, your dream, your friendship, your lover… Renee Rhodes used you as her stepstool to get on stage finally, didn't she?"

Margie's keening cry was worse than her threats. The knife clattered to the table as she sank her fingers into her hair, tugging at the strands hard enough to make me wince just seeing her. "Renee used me," she spat. "She used everyone! It was *my* role, she was my understudy but—" She broke off in a shuddering, hitching sob. "She was my sister. My bastard sister! My father moved all the way from England when he found out some slut he knocked up was in New York. Moved his wife and baby across an ocean when he found out that whore was raising *his baby girl* all on her own. His *baby girl* didn't need him," she shouted. "I did! Renee was already six years old when he found out about her! I wasn't even talking yet, and she replaced me!" Her scream was feral, decades of anger and pain erupting in a geyser of sound that faded into a hitching, gasping sob.

"Margie, I'm going to stand up now, okay?"

Margie hesitated, then nodded.

Slowly, I stood. She didn't stop me when I reached for the knife and moved it out of the way. "Margie, I know about the play she stole from you.

I know about Chris. And Charlie. I know what Renee Rhodes did to Peggy Trent."

Margie's face twisted in distaste. "Peggy Trent was weak. She *let* Renee hurt her. I killed Peggy Trent the day Renee literally walked over her broken body and left her bleeding on the stage."

"That's why you picked that play, *The Kaleidoscope Coffin*, isn't it? I saw how you arranged her body. I saw the playbill."

"I know you did." She smiled, serenely. "I know you put it together. I saw your searches on the phone. I know you went into her house. God, I was so glad you decided to get your damn nails done that day! I was sure I had time to get rid of those damn playbills. Where did you find them?" she wondered. "I looked until Belinda showed up, wailing like a freakin' banshee at the front door!"

"Inside her coffee table. I picked the lock."

"More than just a pretty face, aren't you?"

"I try."

She laughed softly. "I'm sure you do. But the thing is, you don't *understand*. No one does. Not anymore. Charlie did, for a bit. He knew how she stole Daddy from me. How he gave her everything—every advantage, every compliment, every possibility he denied me… Have you ever been to the beach, Damien?"

"Well, I live in SoCal so… yeah." I inched back a tiny bit, my head throbbing with every breath, every slight change in position.

"When I was a girl, my mother took us to visit family in Florida. We went to the shore quite a bit during that visit, always being warned off touching anything that wasn't a shell or a bit of driftwood." Her smile was far off, soft, but something in my gut told me not to chance it. She was in a reverie, but any sudden movement would snap her out of it. And I wasn't sure I could outrun her with my head throbbing as it was. "One day we saw the most *beautiful* blue shapes on the water. They looked like little jewels. I wanted to touch one so badly, but Mom told me no, they'd hurt me."

"Jellyfish."

"Man o'wars," she murmured. "I learned later they're not true jellyfish but at the time I just thought they were beautiful, and I wanted that so badly. Mom was distracted by one of my cousins, so I decided now was the time. At first, I felt nothing. Well, not nothing. Only happiness at being so close to these beautiful blue jewels. Then the pain started. Their reach is quite long, and for a small child, it seemed infinite. One, maybe two, I'm not sure to this day, you know? Well, some tentacles wrapped me up. The pain was…" She shook her head, gaze sharpening as she found me again, slipping out of her reminiscence. "The pain was immense. And it felt like it went on forever. My mom, my aunt and uncle, a few bystanders, they all got hurt, too. One little creature caused so much pain. One beautiful, innocent-looking little thing had these venomous tentacles dragging along, out of sight."

"And that's what Renee Rhodes was like."

She snorted softly. "It's what I'm like, too."

She was faster than I expected, or maybe I'd just slowed down a lot lately. I saw her moving but couldn't make my legs work to get out of the way in time. She leaped across the narrow table and bore me down to the ground, snarling as I clawed at her and kicked, bucking to throw her off. "She took everything. Don't you understand? *Everything*! She took my *life*. Whenever I tried to rebuild, to reclaim, she came back and took *more*! My father, my career, my lovers! My own damn husband thought she was wonderful, a true friend! But he never knew what hit him," she cackled. "Not like Renee!"

I found leverage and pushed, shoving her off me and scooting away, scrambling to my feet before she got to hers. "And killing her brought it all back? Margie, you murdered at least two people. How did that fix things?"

Her lip was split, and her hair was a halo of fuzzy curls and snarls as she advanced on me, looking every inch the nightmare she really was. "It certainly didn't hurt. Well, not *me*."

The knife was *right there*. I had a brief, very movie, vision of grabbing it and swinging it at her, using it to drive her back, but between the two of us she was the one who had actually wielded a knife to hurt someone—kill them—and I was the one who still used my teeth to open plastic packaging because I was afraid of cutting myself. So, I threw it.

Because that made absolute sense at the time.

It clattered behind the counter, out of reach. Margie's lips quirked in a smile that was familiar and sweet, but now that I knew better, I recognized the lie it was. "You tried to take everything from me, too," she said, voice low and quiet. "I tried to steer you in the right direction, but you insisted on going your own way. If you'd just *let it the hell go*, you'd be on your way out of town right now. Charlie and Renee would be rotting in their graves, and I would be *happy* again! I just couldn't get away from them." She stalked forward, grabbing her purse from the table as she moved. I skittered to the side, aiming for the end of the counter with the thought of at least putting something between us, giving me the chance to dial 911 or *anything* else. "I had just a few years here without them *looming*. New York was impossible—Renee was everywhere! If it wasn't some gaudy poster, it was gossip, or *memories*. Do you know what the last thing Father said to me before he died?"

"I'm going to guess it was begging you not to kill him," I challenged.

She drew back, startled. "He didn't know it was me. He thought I was *her*. Praised me up and down, and told me how proud he was of me. I thought." She paused, staring at something in the distant past, her eyes unfocused. "I thought maybe it was time, maybe we'd be able to patch things up before he passed. But he called me Renee. *I'm so proud of you, Renee. I've been so happy to be your father, Renee. Forgive me for not knowing sooner, Renee.*" She snapped her gaze back to me. "It was easy, for him. A tiny overdose of his morphine. Oops." Her smile grew more edged as she added, "And it was even easier the second time. Johnny never even woke up when I came into the room."

A quick flick of her wrist and the strap to her purse was off, the bag thumping and spilling across the floor as she wrapped the strap around her hands, leaving a length between. "I had nothing," she seethed. "She took it all away, and Charlie protected her. When I tried to show the world what Renee Rhodes really was, Charlie interfered. When I finally got out from under their stupid, smirking presence, they ended up here. I can't have *anything* without Renee Rhodes tainting it!" She lurched forward, bringing up that makeshift garrote.

Crap.

I bolted, turning to run for the back door of the shop only to get yanked back, the leather strap tight around my neck as she twisted it, pulling me to the table. I fought against the hold, turning away as the plastic bag she dragged from the counter came towards my face and settled over my mouth and nose.

"Margie!"

She froze but didn't remove the plastic or the garotte.

"Margie, let him go."

I had never been happier to hear Ben's voice.

"Oh, for god's sake!" Margie hissed. "I'd hoped to get rid of you when I got rid of him!"

Ben edged closer, reaching out towards me with one hand while keeping Margie in his sights. "I got to thinking, after I texted you, that I owed you an apology," he said to me, still watching Margie. "I came back, hoping you were still here and hadn't headed back to the inn yet."

"You don't think I mind getting rid of you both?" Margie snapped. "It'll be a lover's quarrel. A murder-suicide. Tragic, sad Damien Murphy and angry, volatile Ben Witte. No one will bat an eye.”

“Heath Nichols will. I called the police when I got here. I heard everything, Margie,” Ben snarled. “My father…”

A heavy pounding started on the front door, and Ben seemed to unwind just a fraction.

“That’s Nichols. Let him in.”

I nodded. I’d been right—this had been the longest damn day ever.

TWENTY

C harlie Arnold's memorial was awkward, to say the least.

All the food Margie had made was technically evidence—no one was sure if she'd decided to become a poisoner or not—so the MCU had taken it all in heavy plastic baggies, labeled with bright orange tape as evidence. Margie's arrest had blazed through Lester Cove in minutes, it seemed, that small town communication chain working triple time. By the time the state troopers had arrived with the MCU, the street was full of people who suddenly needed to do something very urgent on the sidewalk or in front of the shops.

I'd never seen so many windows being polished at night in my life.

Jerome didn't want to cancel Charlie's memorial, though. Ben had asked him, since he'd shown up and made no bones about the fact he was there to see Margie 'dragged off in chains.'

"Nope. We're not gonna put off celebrating Charlie for that bitch."

Which is how I found myself standing in front of a crowded bar at half past ten on a Monday morning, my neck sore and bearing a necklace of bruises from Margie's attempt on my life. The room was quiet, partly with prurient interest to see an almost-murdered man in front of them and partly —I hoped mostly—for Charlie.

Jerome gave me an encouraging nod, and I began. "I really shouldn't be up here. I didn't know Charlie Arnold as well as most of you, and I can't help but feel like I'm in some way responsible for what happened to him." A ripple of unease moved through the crowd. I pressed on. "But that's survivor's guilt talking, I think. And I don't want to make this about me. I want to talk about Charlie. How he was a devoted friend. How he loved his students. Loved theater. How he… how he kept the faith for years, even when he knew it was a lost cause. But Charlie played a part in our lives— even mine, for a short time. And so did Renee."

That caused a bigger murmur, some loud comments that told me exactly how well-liked—or rather not liked—she had been in town. "We all play parts in one another's lives, don't we, though? We're all someone's good guy, or evil villain, or chorus member. Some of us think we're the main character all the time, but others, like Charlie, never realize that it's them, at least for some people. That they're more than just an unnamed extra."

I glanced up and caught Jerome's eye. He gave me a small nod again, which I returned. "Like I said, I didn't know him as well as some of you, and I want to make space for his friends to talk, but I want to say that I will miss him, and I'll miss the fact we never got to know one another well. Maybe, in another life, we'll get that chance."

The memorial had more speeches, some ribald and some teary, the best a mix of both. Someone brought huge boxes of pizza and lobster rolls from Fish Head, which made Ben give me a look and made it hard not to laugh. After a bit, I took myself outside with my lobster roll and a bottle of beer, taking a break from the noise and crowd inside.

Belinda found me there, sitting at one of the empty outdoor tables, and took a seat across from me in the grungy plastic chair. "Hey," she murmured, subdued.

"Are you doing okay?" I asked. "Ben told me yesterday the questioning fell apart, and they let you go pretty quick."

She gave a birdlike nod. "It was dumb. Someone—we think it was Margie now—called the cops to say they'd seen me with some jewelry that belonged to Renee and that they could find my prints in her house. I was able to show them some pictures from my Facebook of me and Renee together and me wearing the necklace, her post about how she'd given it to me…" She sniffed, fidgeting with her dress's sleeve. "I guess she was using me for attention too, huh? That whole main character thing you talked about. And Margie…" Her voice wobbled, then shattered into a reedy sob.

I found a clean napkin in the stack beneath my roll and handed it to her. She dabbed at her eyes, smearing the bright green shadow around heedlessly. "Sometimes people aren't what we think, or who they say they are. And that's not our fault."

"I feel so used," she admitted. "Just some dumb kid they manipulated."

"No, Belinda, it wasn't because you're a kid or a pushover! They did it to so many people, over and over again. And that doesn't make you—or any of us—bad people or less-than for believing they were who they pretended to be."

"I still feel ridiculous," she mourned. "Mom says I should go to therapy about it."

"That might not be a bad idea," I allowed. At her sharp glare, I held up my hands. "It's helpful for a lot of people, even folks who haven't had horrible things happen. Maybe listen to your mom on this one, okay? You've been through some really awful things just this week alone. It can't hurt for a professional to talk you through some of what you're feeling."

"Belinda?"

Denise Gleaves strode around the corner, her expression a complicated one. I knew she'd heard us then, and she was torn between chewing me out and agreeing with me. "I gotta go," Belinda murmured. "I just wanted to come say goodbye to Charlie. Mr. Witte said he's gonna be cremated and some old friends are gonna sprinkle his ashes at some place back in New York."

I nodded. "I heard that, too." But it wouldn't be till after the murder investigation was over. His, not Renee's.

"Guess I'll see you around, Mr. Murphy."

I waved, Denise Gleaves ushering Belinda away and leaving me in the quiet of the bar's back patio, the ruckus inside showing no signs of abating.

"Up for company?" Nichols asked, peering around the corner from where Belinda and Denise had just disappeared. "I wanted to give you a minute with Belinda, but her mom is kind of hell on wheels."

"It's her daughter's well-being." I shrugged. "I don't blame her." I'd seen enough kids neglected by their parents, treated like little adults, to know a parent who gave a damn about their kid was beyond rubies. "What can I do for you, then?"

"Just checking up on you, really," he admitted, taking the seat Belinda had vacated. His cheeks were pink, and his gaze darted between my eyes and my mouth.

Aw, hell.

"Nichols—"

"Heath," he corrected. "Your neck okay?"

I gingerly touched the necklace of bruises slowly taking on a dark hue there. "I'm just glad I packed some scarves."

Nichols nodded slowly, seeming to weigh options in his head before deciding on which one to present. "Looks like Margie might be on the hook for a murder or two in New York about twenty years ago, before she moved to Lester Cove."

I bolted upright at that, a fresh pulse of adrenaline and, yes, prurient interest jolting me out of my slide towards an anxiety attack. "Seriously? Who?"

Heath narrowed his eyes at me. "Nosy thing, aren't you?"

"Hey, that woman tried to stab me with a kitchen knife, then choke me with a designer knock-off bag strap! Consider it recompense from the local law enforcement for not listening to me sooner."

"I don't think that's how it works."

I batted my lashes at him. "Pretty please?"

"That might work on Ben Witte, but it definitely doesn't do a thing for me."

I jerked back. "Say what now?"

A cluster of people clattered out onto the patio, heading for one of the long tables near the railing. "Heath," one of them called. "I brought you that dark stout shit you like! C'mon! We're gonna get a game going!"

Heath gave me a sideways, curious look before joining the others at the table. The memorial seemed to be heading definitely into a party sort of mood, so I took that as my cue to leave. No one looked up as I made my way down to the far end of the patio, heading around the bar and onto Shore Drive to walk back to the inn on my own.

MUFFIN WAS a glad recipient of some belly rubs when we got back to the inn. . "All those times you were growling, it was at her and not her little dog or Belinda or any of that, huh?" I murmured, giving him some deep neck scritches. "You must've remembered her smell from the theater."

"Dogs are smarter than you think," Sienna remarked, snapping beans like it was just a regular day and my entire world hadn't turned topsy-turvy in one morning. "Especially that one."

"Why especially him?"

She glanced up, a small smirk tugging at the corners of her lips before she answered. "Well, he was the first one of all of us to put the blame on Margie, wasn't he?"

Muffin thumped his tail against the floor in agreement.

"He was probably the only witness to Ms. Rhodes' murder, other than Margie."

"Probably the only witness to a lot of Ms. Rhodes' shenanigans as well," Sienna muttered, pointedly avoiding my gaze.

I sighed and sank down onto the kitchen chair across from her. How had this place come to be so comfortable for me after just three—wait, no, five—days? Two Moons, even Lester Cove itself, was welcoming in ways LA wasn't. And maybe a big part of that was how different it was, how removed from the stress and failures and near-misses of Hollywood this small town was, but there was something else about it that made me feel like maybe not going back wasn't such a bad idea.

"Hey," Sienna said suddenly, "I know Ms. Rhodes was your friend and all, but—"

"I know." I sighed. "I know. She wasn't my friend. And she wasn't the person I thought she was. All of that was smoke and mirrors. Acting."

"Are you, um… Are you gonna be okay?"

"Probably."

Sienna nodded, snapping those beans with more intensity now that she'd done her duty.

Carmel, red-eyed and more pale than usual, stuck her head around the kitchen door, giving me a soft smile when she spotted me. "Damien, you've got a visitor."

I followed her out to the foyer and was surprised to see Ben Witte fidgeting under the faux gas lamp chandelier. Out of all the people I'd been braced to confront—Rory, my parents, hell, even Max, Ben hadn't been on the list.

"I wasn't expecting you" I said as I reached the foot of the stairs.

Ben's lips tightened, that tiny, oddly placed dimple just by his upper lip dipping inwards for a moment before his expression smoothed out into his usual Resting Bored Face. "Would you rather it be Heath, maybe? He seemed really… chatty with you before."

I shook my head, feeling my nose wrinkle before I could stop myself. "Why would I want to talk to the cops if I didn't have to? Besides, I already talked to him at Charlie's memorial earlier. He wanted to know how I was doing since…"

"Since Margie tried to kill you?" He threw up his hands at that, his carefully neutral expression cracking just a hair.

"But she didn't succeed," I said. "I'm still here."

Ben's gaze was assessing as he swept it over me, then around the foyer. "So you are. Until Wednesday, if I recall?"

"So Sienna likes to remind me." I hesitated, the words burning on my tongue as I said, "Ben… about your dad…"

He shook his head. "I know. But I just… I can't right now. I can't." I nodded slowly. "Okay."

He was quiet for several long moments, then motioned for me to follow him as he turned away. "Come with me."

"Excuse me?"

"Bring the dog," he said, as if I hadn't said a thing.

I threw up my hands but went and got Muffin from the kitchen, where he was skulking under the table in the hopes Sienna would accidentally drop the pot roast for him to clean up. "I'm going out with Ben Witte," I announced.

Sienna raised one of her eyebrows. "Are you now?"

"Not like that!"

"Hmm."

Carmel looked up from where she was dicing vegetables. "Damien, I know you're supposed to check out soon but—"

"It's okay," I said, cutting her off. "I'll figure something out. You've got that big group coming and need the room."

She nodded, lips thin. "Sorry."

Ben was waiting by the front door, frowning at his phone. "This has to be quick. There's an issue at work I need to get to this evening."

"Seriously? It can't wait till business hours?"

"The fast-paced world of contract law," he muttered, opening the door and gesturing me out, giving Muffin a wary frown in passing.

We took his dad's car down Lester Road, turning at the end of the square and going right on Shore Drive, back up the slight rise away from the shore. "This is the back way," he admitted after a moment. "I'd usually go up the other way but…"

"It passes by the theater," I murmured. He nodded once, curtly, and we were quiet for the rest of the short drive. He pulled up to the open gate of Witte House. It was surely my imagination, but it looked brighter somehow, despite the heavy clouds overhead blocking out the sunlight.

"What's that look?" Ben asked, glancing between me and the house. "Would you rather not go in?"

"Just thinking it seems happier somehow," I admitted. "Less gloomy."

Ben's lips parted as if he wanted to say something, but instead, he settled for a wordless *huh* and continued up the drive.

"This is going to sound strange, but hear me out," he said as soon as he'd shut off the engine. "I know you're not sure if you're gonna stay or go yet."

"I need to find someone to take Muffin," I put in. "I can't take him with me." It was a weak excuse, and we both knew it. "Besides," I added a little more honestly, "I really haven't had a chance to see the town yet. What with the whole… murder thing going on."

He nodded. "Right. Well. I know you can't stay at the inn much longer."

"Big party coming in for a wedding," I murmured, repeating what Sienna and Carmel had been saying for the past few days, always sounding just a bit apologetic but more frazzled. "My room's already spoken for by the maid of honor, apparently."

"There aren't a lot of hotel options around Lester Cove, and I'm heading back to Boston this evening. This house is going to be sitting empty —Margie isn't welcome back into my family home, even if this has all somehow been some bizarre mistake and she isn't a murderer. The thing with my dad is just… God, I don't know what to think! " He hesitated, fingers tapping against his thigh as he glared at something inward, something that made his scowl deepen for a moment "I can't help but think that if it was so easy for her to do this to two people she'd known for most of her life, would it have been as simple to…" He pressed his lips into a thin line and shook his head, refocusing his attention on me. "My offer, Damien. Do you accept it?"

I swallowed down the bubbling words in my throat, the moment passing swiftly. There would be another one soon. There had to be. "Are you… Are you asking me to stay in your house?"

"It's a proposition."

"Excuse me?"

Ben's face was so red it nearly glowed in the heavy shadows from the overhanging tree. "A *business* proposition. Of a sort. I need a house sitter. Muffin needs a pet sitter. And… well. So does Tony."

"Margie said Tony was terrified of Muffin." He shot me a look that made me wince. "Okay, yeah, she's not exactly a barometer for honesty, is she?"

Ben motioned for me to follow him, getting out of the car and jogging up the shallow steps to the front door. I followed far more reluctantly, Muffin tiptoeing behind me as we trailed up the steps. Ben unlocked the door and Tony, apricot ball of fluff and high-strung nerves that he was, launched himself at Muffin.

Muffin was in heaven, the pair of them play-lunging, barking, and basically having a little doggy rave on the front porch. Ben's lips quirked into an actual smile at the sight of them before he caught me looking and schooled his features into something more stoic.

"You can't fool me," I muttered, following him into the house, leaving the door open behind me for the dogs to come and go as they liked. "I saw that smile. You love dogs."

"I plead the fifth," he replied tartly. "Now, the cops have already come and gone, so that's out of the way. They took some things from Margie's room and the kitchen, her laptop, your phone… Well, everything they think they'll need. I can't guarantee they won't be back, but for now, they said they're done. The feds and the locals. They seem to think they have all the evidence about her, ah, previous incidents, too."

"Who was it? Back in New York. Who did she kill?"

"Ah. They weren't entirely forthcoming about details, since the surviving family members haven't been updated on the possibility Margie was the one who did it. But from what I can gather, a young man who worked with her once upon a time, and possibly a stagehand during *Kaleidoscope Coffin*." I held off mentioning her father's death, and the possibility of Ben's dad being one of her victims, too. As much as I wanted to say something, I didn't know the truth and, until Margie actually confessed, telling Ben his father's death might have been sped along by an angry Margie didn't feel good.

"Ah." Chances were good I'd never know the reason behind their deaths, at least according to Margie. No matter what it was, though, they were dead because she decided she had control over their existence. Maybe she'd felt slighted in some way. Or maybe they'd succeeded in something where she failed.

Maybe it was all practice for Ms. Rhodes. For the person she felt had ruined her life, ruined her chance to be a star.

Ben cleared his throat and made a vague gesture towards the kitchen. "Come on. I'll make some tea."

"Who'll be taking care of the shop now? You're going back to Boston, and, well, I know nothing about retail."

He snorted softly, pulling a kettle out and filling it with water as he said, "Don't worry. I'm not about to propose that particular task for you, even though you are at a loose end job-wise at the moment."

"Thank you, Captain Obvious."

"That's Admiral Obvious. I've been promoted."

"Was that a joke?" I gasped and clutched at my heart. "Ben Witte, did you just joke with me?"

"Don't get used to it," he muttered, setting steaming mugs of brewing tea on the table, one in front of me and one across. They were redolent of cinnamon and oranges, making me think of autumn just around the corner. "No, I'm hiring some hands for the shop. I still own it, thanks to the conditions of my father's will, and I won't be selling it. It's been in the family for generations."

"And me staying here, house sitting…"

"And pet sitting." He smirked. "I know how much you love that."

"You're not funny anymore." I blew on my tea, taking a sip that was a bit too hot and wincing. He wordlessly passed me the small wooden tray with the creamer and sugar arranged in the middle.

"I don't like the house sitting empty," he finally said. "And, so long as you're staying in town and need a place to stay, I thought, *why not*."

"Why not," I murmured.

"I can't have pets in my place in Boston and, well, Tony's Margie's dog, but he doesn't deserve that. You haven't found a home for Muffin yet, and this place has a ridiculous backyard. Those two are nuts about one another so…" He shrugged, taking a sip of his own tea, obviously inured to the Satan's bathwater temperature of it.

"Alright. Alright, I'm in. Walk me through the details and, I don't know, draw up a contract or something to cover our rear ends on this one."

"Way ahead of you." He pulled out his phone and tapped away for a moment. My phone beeped in response. "Just emailed you a copy of the contract I drew up. Take your time, it's pretty standard. Basically, you're responsible for any damages that aren't acts of God or due to the age of the house. You're also responsible for the welfare of the animals—specifically Tony. I'll provide a bursary for their care and one for house maintenance. You just make sure anything that needs doing gets done. I'm to be notified if there are any urgent repairs or maintenance needed, or health issues for the dog. If, at any time, you decide to leave, you're to give me seventy-two hours' notice so I can make arrangements."

"Huh."

"Huh?"

I looked up from my phone to find him looking slightly concerned, fussing with his teacup as he tried his best to maintain a stern facade. "Just that it seems like you've already put a lot of thought into this. I mean, how long have you been thinking of asking me to stay here? Margie just got arrested yesterday."

"About twenty-three hours," he muttered. "I drew that up over lunch. One of my colleagues at the firm double-checked it. If you're good with the terms, I can direct you to a notary here in town and we can get this signed and dealt with this week. In the interim, you're welcome to stay here, but I ask that you have the paperwork completed and returned so I can file it before the end of next week."

I shook my head, setting my phone aside, unable to hide my smile. "You're ridiculous and it's kind of great."

He drew up, an offended feline crimp to his brow. "How am I ridiculous? This just makes good sense. I'm covering my ass legally, making sure you're covered if anything goes wrong, and—"

"And," I shushed him, "I never said ridiculous was a bad thing. There are a few concerns I have. Mostly the fact I'm very sure the media will figure out where I am, thanks to my agent. I'll do my best to make sure they don't track me down to this address specifically, but they'll likely get some pictures of me around town. I need to know if this is a problem for you, being associated with someone in the tabloids."

Ben's upper lip curled in distaste. "If it cannot be avoided."

"Once Rory gets his mind set on something being great PR, it's hard to shake." Setting my tea aside, I stood and spread my hands, giving him a real smile, not one of my cataloged magazine shoot numbers. "Now, show me around. I just know the sitting room, kitchen, and half bath. What's off limits? What's open?"

Ben gave me a thorough tour of the house, including a freaking adorable turret room that I immediately claimed for my own.

"You're welcome to any of the larger rooms," he pointed out. "If you want the main one, let me know and I'll have Margie's things sent to storage."

"I've always wanted to live in a tower," I protested. "Oh my god, look at that stained glass!" I rushed to the window positioned to catch the morning sun and sighed. "This is amazing."

Ben was giving me a funny look when I turned back.

"What?"

"Nothing. Just glad to see you're not going to run screaming into the night after everything that's happened." He cleared his throat and motioned for me to follow him. "Let me show you the garage."

He led me through the locations of the fuse boxes, the master power switch for the entire property, and where the water main was located just past the side of the old carriage house turned garage. We walked back through, past the old VW that Ben had to touch lightly in passing.

"Hey," I said, teasing only a little. "Do I get to drive this while you're gone?"

"Sure. It's under the clause labeled *Over My Dead Body.*" At my startled laugh, he glanced back over his shoulder, halfway into the house. "So, do you still think I'm a stick in the mud?"

"I think you're exactly what I expected," I corrected him. "Very Mr. Darcy. And very much trouble."

Ben's ears pinked, and he looked away, into the mudroom through the open garage door. "Maybe… trouble isn't always a bad thing."

"It definitely isn't."

———

THE HOUSE WAS huge and quiet and a little spooky. I'd never lived in a space larger than a shoe box on my own. All the quiet was a little unnerving. I turned on some lights, the living room TV and then the TV in the bedroom just to feel like I wasn't on my own before settling in to make some food and text my parents. They were less than thrilled that I'd waited too long to talk to them and made vague threats about coming for a visit,

> DAD
>
> Mom's not too happy. Had to turn the hose on some paps.
>
> They trampled her peonies.
>
> Also, clear your calendar for the second week of October.
> We're coming to you or you're coming to us.

I made a mental note to send Mom a flat of peonies and find out which paps it was who smooshed her garden so I could bill them for it.

And also figure out where I'd be in October.

The evening spooled out in a nascent domestic scene: dinner, a shower, take the dogs out back, hose off the dogs because oh my god what did they roll in, take another shower, then find something to read on my e-reader.

That took me up to nine, and then I had no idea what to do next. Max, ever the mind reader, chose that moment to text.

He didn't answer, but I knew he wouldn't jerk my chain like that. "Well, guys, looks like I'm here for at least a month," I murmured. The dogs didn't seem to mind.

It was late enough for me to talk myself into going to bed. The guest room Ben had shown me was just off the stairs, overlooking the expansive back garden and a small pond some ancestor of his had put in ages ago. I left the TV on for noise—I might complain about how loud my apartment complex back home was, but the fact remained I hated silence—and found myself curled up on a huge, soft mattress with two sleepy dogs vying for space at my feet.

Tomorrow I'd argue with insurance about Bonnie's remains. I'd find that notary Ben gave me the number for. I'd stop by and say hi to the Moon sisters while I walked the beasties.

And I'd start thinking about what I should do next.

WHERE TO FIND ME...

My Linktree: www.linktr.ee/meredithspies

Subscribe to my newsletter and find my entire back list, ARC opportunities, social media and more!

Also find me online at www.booksbymeredith.com

ALSO BY MEREDITH SPIES

Damien Murphy Pet Sitting and Murder Mysteries *Tea and Antipathy (Book 1) Arsenic and Old Ladies (Book 2) (Coming 2024)* ***

In the Pines

Fetch (book 1) (2024) Witch's Bone (book 2) (2024) ***

Medium at Large (M/M Paranormal Romance) *Bump in the Night Ghoul Friend*

Old Ghosts

In the Spirit

After Life

Ghost of a Chance (Coming 2023) Ghost Stories (Anthology) (Coming 2023) ***

Science of Magic

Data Sets

Fuzzy Logic

Discrete

Scientific Method (Coming 2023) ***

Bedeviled

The Devil May Care The Devil You Know The Devil's in the Details ***

Marked

Nearly Human

Howl at the Moon Book Three TBA (Coming 2024) ***

Stand-Alones and Shared Worlds *Leo (Single Dads of Gaynor Beach) Ring My Bell (Ever After) Between the Lines (standalone) The Calms (End of Days)* ***

Keep up to date on new releases and upcoming projects by subscribing to my newsletter or following me on social media! There's tons more to come!